Theresa,

Best Wishes

Nigel James

D1740434

DEEP SECRET

Nigel James

Bright Pen

A Bright Pen Book

Text Copyright © Nigel James 2011

Cover design by Jamie Day ©

British Library Cataloguing Publication Data.
A catalogue record for this book is available from the British Library

ISBN 978-0-7552-1378-8

Authors OnLine Ltd
19 The Cinques
Gamlingay, Sandy
Bedfordshire SG19 3NU
England

This book is also available in e-book format, details of which are available at www.authorsonline.co.uk

DEEP SECRET

Alec Hammond is the country's leading jump jockey, popular amongst his peers and adored by the betting public. He has won the jockeys' championship several times and every big race in the racing calendar...with one exception, the Cheltenham Gold Cup, the blue riband of steeplechasing and the highlight of the Cheltenham Festival in March. After several near misses, Alec finally has a horse capable of filling the gap in his glittering CV.

Nicola James ran away from home at the age of sixteen after systematic abuse by her stepfather. Homeless, penniless and lacking in self esteem, she uses the only asset that she believes will lead her to a better life...her body. She drifts into glamour modelling and eventually into the world of adult movies, where, under the name Susie Stone, she becomes one of world's biggest stars.

Frank Morris is a crooked bookmaker who established his business by bribing jockeys to ensure that their mounts did not win. Secure in the knowledge that those horses would not win, Morris offered longer odds on them than his rivals so as to attract more money. Morris had stopped bribing jockeys some years previously but could not resist taking big risks so as to maximise his profits. His gambling failed, and to keep afloat he borrowed huge sums from the sort of people who do not resort to courts to get their money back. Desperate to pay back his debts, he threatens and bribes one of his former team of jockeys to 'throw' selected races. Pat Duggan has become a leading jockey since his early days working for Morris but terrified as to what Morris might do if he refuses, he reluctantly agrees.

Nicola is persuaded by her agent to accompany him to a day of corporate entertainment at Sandown racecourse, posing as his PA. There, she meets Alec and although she initially rejects his advances, she eventually agrees to a date. Soon, she falls madly in love with Alec but is desperate to keep her background from him. Ashamed of her past, she gives up her 'acting' career and is happy for the first time in her life.

Meanwhile, Morris realises that he cannot repay his debts on the basis of Duggan throwing the occasional race and and hatches a plot to ensure that Alec's mount, Deep Secret, does not win the Gold Cup. Murder, blackmail and kidnap ensue, leading to a dramatic climax on Gold Cup day.

About the Author

Nigel James was educated at Felsted School and Cambridge University. After obtaining a law degree, he was called to the Bar, since which time he has practiced as a barrister in London. More used to writing legal opinions, this is his first novel. His main interests are sport and travel. He has homes in Hertfordshire, London and Spain.

1

The glamorous young woman paced up and down the hotel suite, an anxious expression on her face, her stiletto heels leaving depressions in the lush velvet carpet. Every now and again she looked at her diamond encrusted gold watch.

She was dressed in a simple but elegantly tailored short black evening dress. Low cut, it revealed a generous view of her ample and tanned cleavage. Exquisitely made up and with her long blond hair tumbling over her bare shoulders, she exuded wealth, class and sex appeal. Perhaps the only incongruous feature of her appearance was the small tattoo of a bird in flight on the back of her left shoulder.

When the telephone on the low coffee table rang, the woman grabbed it before it had completed its first ring.

'Yes,' she said in a breathless tone. Then after a brief pause, 'Send them up'.

She then went and stood by the door, rubbing her hands together in a gesture of anxiety.

After a couple of minutes there was a firm knock on the door. She answered it immediately and two tall well built men of about thirty entered. The woman was dwarfed beside them. They were both dressed in expensive suits but looked somewhat awkward in them. One had long dark hair tied back in a ponytail and the other short cropped fair hair. They seemed out of place in such a luxurious suite.

'Well, what happened?' The woman asked.

'No worries. The job's done,' the fair-haired man replied, sitting down on the sofa and putting his feet on the coffee table. His cockney accent was in complete contrast to the woman's upper class tone.

'You mean...'

'Yeah. He's dead. He won't be bothering you again'.

The other man walked over to the cocktail cabinet and poured three large whiskies. He handed one to the woman and then took the other two drinks over to the sofa, gave one to his colleague and sat down beside him. The woman sat down in an armchair opposite them.

'How did it go?' she said, 'I want to hear all about it.'

'It went just as we planned,' the dark haired man replied. 'He spent two hours in his girlfriend's flat with his car and driver waiting outside. As soon as he stepped out of the building we shot him several times. We'd disappeared before the chauffeur realized what had happened. We dumped our coats and hats in trash cans well away from the scene and the guns in the river as you suggested, left the car in a long stay car park and came here by tube.'

By this stage, both men were quite openly ogling the woman sitting opposite but she seemed not to notice and crossed her legs revealing an even greater expanse of thigh to the extent that one of her stocking tops became visible.

'It will look like a political assassination,' the man continued, 'all you've got to do is act the dutiful wife and look sufficiently upset for a time.'

'That's going to difficult. Most people know I hated his guts!'

The woman then leant forward, picked up the phone and dialled a number.

'Is that room service? This is the Countess Malinsky in the Grand Suite. I want a magnum of champagne and three glasses.'

She replaced the phone and looked at the two men.

'I think this calls for more than whisky, gentlemen. We have something to celebrate.'

'Is that wise?' the fair haired man asked. 'Ordering champagne when your husband was killed half an hour ago!'

'Do you expect me to mourn him?'

'It's not that. Eventually the police will discover that you were staying here at the time of his death and the hotel records will show when you ordered the champagne. The receptionist may remember when we arrived!'

'What's the problem? I'm not to know he's dead. I'm simply entertaining two men I met at Francos last night. Don't you read the tabloids? My love life is notorious!'

At that moment, there was a knock on the door. After the woman had told him to come in, a young waiter unlocked the door and wheeled in a trolley with the champagne and glasses.

'Shall I pour it, madam?' he said, seemingly addressing his words at the woman's cleavage rather than her face.

'Why not?' the woman said with a pout and uncrossed her legs in a manner which appeared to cause the waiter more embarrassment.

After the waiter had gone, the dark haired man leant across and said with a leer, 'We're well aware of your reputation. I take it that's why your husband was going to divorce you.'

The woman took a sip of her champagne. 'If you're aware of my reputation then perhaps I had better not disappoint you,' she said with a smile.

She put her glass down and stood up. She then removed the strap from each of her shoulders and let her dress fall to the ground. She had no underwear on and stood there for a moment wearing nothing but her high heels and stockings. She then plonked one of her stilettoed feet on to the coffee table and stepped over it. She then turned round and sat down between the two men.

Fifteen minutes later, Jean-Paul, the director, brought things to a close.

'OK folks. That'll do. Well done everyone. That was a great scene. Great performance as ever, Susie,' he said to the woman, 'if I wasn't gay I'd be asking you for a private performance later!'

Someone tossed Susie a towel and she headed straight for the bathroom. As she did so she smiled at Jean-Paul. 'That was one of the worst scripts yet,' she said.

'Who cares about the script? What do you think this is, Shakespeare?' he laughed.

Ten minutes later, Susie Stone had showered and dressed in her sweatshirt and jeans. When she left the bathroom, the others were still packing up. Her 'co-stars' were still sitting on the sofa wrapped in towels drinking beer from cans. She barely glanced at them as she crossed the room and left.

2

At about the time that Susie Stone was performing back in London, Alec Hammond was also experiencing a surge of power between his thighs but of a slightly different kind. Having joined the leaders at the second last on the bridle, a spectacular leap had taken him to the front. The slightest squeeze then brought an instantaneous response as his mount surged forward and in a matter of moments drew several lengths clear of the horses toiling behind. Alec then popped him over the last and they coasted home a dozen lengths clear of the field.

Despite all his years in the saddle, Alec could not remember feeling so excited about a horse. After a moderate career over hurdles yielding only three victories, Deep Secret had taken to fences like the proverbial duck to water. After five consecutive victories, he had gone to the Cheltenham Festival in March to contest the championship race for novice steeplechasers over three miles. The favourite had been an Irish challenger, Dungannon, and his fanatical Irish supporters had backed him down to evens. Defeat was unthinkable. Even the British press had expected Dungannon to win on the grounds that his form appeared to be better as Deep Secret had not beaten much of note despite winning all his races comfortably.

However, leading up to the race Deep Secret had been working sensationally at home and everyone connected with the Saunders stable had been confident of an upset. They had put their money where their mouth was and backed him down to 3 to 1 second favourite, no mean feat when you consider the strength of the Cheltenham Festival betting market.

The race had turned out to be a two horse race as the market had expected with both horses drawing clear round the final bend. They were neck and neck at the last but Deep Secret had made light of the famous Cheltenham hill. Alec had even had time to look round at the struggling favourite as Deep Secret won by a comfortable five lengths.

Following the race, Martin Saunders, Deep Secret's trainer, had persuaded the horse's enthusiastic owner that it would be better to by-pass the season's last major meeting at Aintree and put the horse away until the following season when he would be trained specifically for the Gold Cup.

The Cheltenham Gold Cup is the most prestigious race in the jumping calendar, the championship race for long distance steeplechasers run over three miles and two furlongs and the highlight of the Cheltenham Festival. Although the Grand National has far more public appeal, is arguably the most famous race in the world and provides a thrilling spectacle over the unique Aintree fences, it does not carry the same prestige with the professionals. Whereas the Grand National is a handicap, the Gold Cup is a true championship with each runner carrying the same weight.

At thirty one years of age, there was very little that Alec Hammond had not achieved as a jockey. With three jockeys championships behind him, he was still the most sought after rider in the country. However, there was one notable gap in his CV which he was desperate to fill before he retired – the Cheltenham Gold Cup. He had won every other big race in the calendar including two Grand Nationals, three Champion Hurdles and three King Georges but despite near misses, the Gold Cup had always eluded him.

In the six months since Deep Secret's victory at the Festival, Alec had wondered on countless occasions how the horse would fare when he moved up from novice class and took on experienced and established chasers. However, he had had false dawns before. Success at the novice stage was no guarantee that a horse would make it to the top. The novice events at the Festival are notorious for producing winners who find it difficult to win another race let alone return the following year as a leading contender in a championship race. The Triumph Hurdle for juvenile hurdlers is the obvious example but the record of the winners of Deep Secret's race is not much better.

Now, Alec had his answer. Although Deep Secret had been working well at home, only his performance on the racecourse would show whether he was a live contender for the Gold Cup. This race at Wincanton had been the perfect start. The first decent conditions event of the new season had attracted a reasonable field with one or two runners who had had Gold Cup ambitions of their own. Nevertheless, Alec knew that this was a race which not only had to be won but won well. In the event, Deep Secret could not have won more easily.

As Alec patted his steaming mount's neck and thought about the season ahead, he heard a familiar Irish voice.

'I suppose you think you're finally going to win the Gold Cup now!'

Alec looked up and saw Jimmy O'Brien grinning at him from one of the other horses. Jimmy was Alec's closest friend in racing. They had started their careers together as apprentices in the same stable and had been friends ever since. Jimmy had never been champion jockey but had consistently been in the top six and, as he never stopped reminding Alec, had won a Gold Cup a few years previously on a rank outsider when Alec had been riding the favourite.

'Maybe. But there's a long way to go,' Alec replied.

'I'll tell you what. I'll take over if you want to ride something else!'

'In your dreams, Jimmy.'

At that moment, Deep Secret's beaming stable lass arrived and led the horse back towards the winners enclosure. Alec acknowledged the applause of the better than average mid week crowd and when they reached the enclosure touched his cap in the traditional way before dismounting.

Martin Saunders gave Alec a brief pat as he started to remove his saddle. Mary Pickering, the excited owner, was a little more effusive and insisted on giving Alec a hug and a kiss, leaving him with lipstick on his face.

'How did it go?' Martin asked.

'Brilliant. I really think we've got a star here,' Alec replied.

Alec knew how important this was to Martin as well. Martin too had never won the Gold Cup despite having been a leading trainer for over twenty years.

Alec slipped off the saddle and walked towards the weighing room. As he approached the building, a television presenter shoved a microphone towards him and asked him to comment on Deep Secret's performance. Alec was popular with the media and well aware of the benefits of good relations with them. He already had a weekly column in a national newspaper and quite fancied a job in television when he stopped riding. He stopped and looked at the attractive female presenter, the daughter of a retired trainer.

'Just what we were hoping for. We never got out of second gear,' he said with the trademark Hammond smile.

'Where will he go next? The Hennessy?'

'We'll have to see. That's for Martin and Mrs. Pickering to decide. But wherever he goes, he'll take a lot of beating, believe me. I'd better go and weigh in but we can continue this conversation over dinner if you like!' Alec replied as he stepped away from the microphone.

A couple of paces from the door, he turned round and grinned at her.

'Do you always come on to people on live television?' she asked testily, having switched the microphone off.

'Only if they've got legs like you!'

With that Alec pushed his way through the door, smiling to himself. He knew that Charlotte had not really been annoyed and wondered whether to firm up the invitation to dinner.

Alec was right. Charlotte Kingston had not been annoyed on two counts. Although she had been a little taken aback when Alec had made his comment, her director had been delighted and had made some comment in her ear about Alec always giving good value. Charlotte was intelligent enough to know that her recent appointment as the junior member of the channel's racing team was not wholly unconnected with her looks and the fact that her father had been a leading trainer on the flat.

Thus, anything that pleased the director was fine as far as she was concerned. However, she also had to admit that she was rather intrigued by Alec. Although she had been brought up in a racing stable, her experience of jump racing was fairly limited but she was well aware of Alec's reputation as the 'golden boy' of the sport and as a notorious womanizer.

At the relatively few jump meetings she had covered she had seen how popular he was with both the punters and the professionals. There was certainly a charisma about him and she had heard her father bemoaning the fact that none of the flat jockeys could compare with him for public appeal.

In the jockey's changing room, there was the usual good natured banter and as was normally the case, Alec and Jimmy were at the centre of things. However, one man stood apart from the rest with his usual sour expression. Pat Duggan was one of the few people in racing who disliked Alec. In truth, Duggan did not seem to like many people but he particularly loathed Alec. Duggan was the reigning champion jockey and was favourite to retain his title that season but bitterly resented the fact that he never achieved the recognition afforded to Alec let alone his popularity and success with women.

Indeed, everyone recognized that if Alec wanted to, he could regain the title. However, after winning the title three times in a four year period in his mid-twenties Alec had made the conscious decision that he was not going to chase the title again and was going to concentrate on quality rather than quantity.

The jockey's title is decided simply on the number of winners ridden in a season as opposed to the trainer's title which is based on prize money won. Thus, any jockey contesting the championship would usually have to commit himself to an arduous schedule often travelling huge distances to far flung course for perhaps one ride. Alec had had enough of that. His days of going to places like Hexham in the hope of winning the 'seller', the lowest grade of race on the card, were over.

Thus, for a number of years, Alec had concentrated on riding for three or four trainers and on picking up plum rides for other trainers in the bigger races. The latter sometimes involved other jockeys bring replaced or 'jocked off'. This could cause resentment but was normally accepted as one of those things that had always happened in racing. Alec almost certainly ranked as one of the all time great jump jockeys and owners could hardly be blamed for wanting to use him if he was available.

Although Duggan himself had not been 'jocked off' by Alec, he hated the fact that if there was a juicy spare ride going, Alec would nearly always be asked before him.

'So what did you think of Deep Secret?' Jimmy O'Brien asked Duggan. Jimmy did not particularly like his fellow Irishman but was simply trying to be sociable and bring him into the conversation.

'That proves nothing,' Duggan sneered, 'he'll never hack it in a proper race.'

'Jesus, Duggan. You really are a miserable bastard, aren't you?' Jimmy replied.

'I'd rather be miserable than a tosser like you,' Duggan responded.

Jimmy's temper flared and he took a couple of steps towards Duggan but Alec stepped between them.

'Leave it, Jimmy. It's not worth it. If Pat wants to be a misery, that's up to him.'

Jimmy stared at Duggan for a moment and then turned and made his way out to the parade ring for his mount in the next race.

Half an hour later, Alec and Jimmy left the weighing room with their bags and made their way towards the jockeys' car park. Neither of them had a ride in the last, a race reserved for conditional jockeys, and they had decided to leave early and avoid the crowds.

They looked an odd couple despite being the same age, doing the same job and riding at similar weights. Alec was tall even for a jump jockey at five feet ten inches, slim and stylishly dressed. Despite his outdoor life he could have passed for a man five years younger. In contrast, Jimmy was several inches shorter, stockily built and had a weathered face which made him look ten years older. He also dressed in a casual manner which had often attracted disapproving looks from stewards.

Their backgrounds were also completely different. When they had first arrived at Colonel Haworth's yard all those years ago, Jimmy had come from a farming community in the west of

Ireland whereas Alec had come straight from an English public school. To begin with, Alec had acted on occasions as interpreter for Jimmy, so thick was his Irish accent in those early days.

Working for Colonel Haworth had been hard work but fun. He had also provided them with their first rides in public although at that time Jimmy was hoping for a career on the flat so they had not been in competition. They had shared digs together and Jimmy had joked that his family back home would never have believed that he was living with a posh Englishman.

In fact, Alec had not come from a particularly posh or wealthy family. His father had been in the army and Alec's school fees had been heavily subsidized while his father was serving overseas.

Alec's parents had assumed that he would go on to university and then perhaps to Sandhurst.

However, Alec had had other ideas. In the shorter school holidays, instead of flying halfway across the world to wherever his father was stationed, he had often gone to stay on his uncle's farm where he was introduced to riding.

Then, one Christmas, he went with his uncle's family to Kempton Park for the Boxing Day meeting. It was the first time he had been to a race meeting and what he saw there changed his life for ever. Any thoughts of following in his father's footsteps went out of the window from that moment.

The feature race as always on Boxing Day had been the King George VI chase, the only other championship race for three mile chasers apart from the Cheltenham Gold Cup. Of course, at that time, Alec did not know a huge amount about racing and had not appreciated the significance of the race but he could sense the excitement of the crowd. In the parade ring before the race, Alec was impressed by an imposing looking grey horse and told his uncle that he wanted to put two pounds of the money he had been given for Christmas on the horse. His uncle had tried to dissuade him saying that the horse was little more than a novice and would not stay three miles. His stablemate was a better bet and had the stable jockey on board. Alec had been adamant. His uncle had then suggested an each way bet but Alec wanted his money on the nose at 16 to 1.

The grey had set off in front and had set a blazing pace. 'Don't get too excited,' his uncle had warned, 'he won't keep this up.'

But he did. It was the most majestic thing that Alec had ever seen. The grey was never challenged and jumped with a freedom and arrogance which even Alec's inexperienced eye recognized as something special. The horse went on to become one of racing's legends. As for Alec, his mind was made up then as to what he wanted to do.

His parents were not very happy about Alec's plans and when he had started to ride in point to points they were hoping that he would get it out of his system without sustaining a serious injury. Instead, Alec, who rode a number of winners, managed to get himself the job with Colonel Haworth and started with Jimmy at the bottom of the pile.

Alec proved to be a natural and his parents admitted that they were proud to read about his successes in the papers. When his father retired, his parents would often attend meetings where he was riding. Unfortunately, they had both been killed in a car accident several years previously but not before they had seen him win his first championship and Grand National.

'I don't know why owners and trainers put up with Duggan,' Jimmy commented as they walked together towards the car park. 'Not only is he a surly bastard but I wouldn't trust him.'

Alec realized that Jimmy was still annoyed by his earlier altercation with Duggan. If truth be known, Alec was also surprised that Duggan had achieved what he had. Granted, he was a good jockey and he was not the first jockey by any means to make it to the top without a sparkling personality, but in his early years of riding there had been strong rumours that Duggan was not averse to taking a backhander. He had served a couple of suspensions under the non-triers rule and there had been an unproven allegation that he was betting himself, a cardinal sin for jockeys which would have resulted in him being warned off if true.

'I don't like him either,' Alec said 'but he works hard and he's a good jockey. Just ignore him.'

'You may not like him but he hates you, Alec. He knows he'll never be as good as you however many titles he wins.'

At that moment Jimmy's attention was diverted to the television crew packing their equipment away.

'Now there's a rear to die for,' he commented.

Alec looked over and saw immediately what had displaced Duggan in Jimmy's thoughts. Charlotte Kingston was bending over the boot of a car trying to make room for some more stuff on the ground beside her. She had changed out of the clothes she had had on earlier and was wearing a very tight pair of jeans and high heeled boots.

'I see what you mean!'

Charlotte stood up at that moment and they both saw that she was wearing an equally tight top.

'What about dinner then?' Alec called over to her.

Unaware of Alec's conversation with Charlotte earlier, Jimmy was stunned.

'You've got a cheek!' he said to Alec. 'I'm supposed to be the one with the blarney!'

'You're a married man.'

'Separated for over a year!'

'You're also a Catholic.'

'When has that stopped me? Why do you think my wife kicked me out?'

Meanwhile Charlotte had turned to face them and put her hands on her hips.

'Why should I want to go out to dinner with a man who embarrasses me on live television?' she retorted.

'Who was the director?' Alec replied.

'Ian Wilson.'

'So no problem then. I bet Ian just laughed. Where are you going now?'

'I'm staying with my parents tonight. Not that it's anything to do with you.'

Alec knew that Charlotte's parents still lived in the main house at the yard where Charlotte's brother had taken over the training licence. It was about ten miles outside Lambourn, the small racing dominated town where Alec lived.

'We'll never have a better opportunity then,' Alec said.'

'To do what?'

'Have dinner of course. There's a great little place on the way back where we can have a drink and then an early dinner. You can follow me there.'

'You've got it all worked out haven't you?'

Alec could see her hesitating.

'Come on. What have you got to lose? You should get to know the main players in the field if you're serious about your new job.'

That seemed to do the trick.

'Well, I suppose there's that…'

'Right. That's settled. I'll wait for you at the main entrance. I'll be in a silver Porsche.'

'Now why doesn't that surprise me?'

3

Alec watched in his mirror as Charlotte pulled up behind him and flashed her lights. Given her comment about his car he was amused to see that she was driving a convertible Mercedes SLK. Presumably a present from Daddy as he doubted it was a company car.

As they had carried on towards their cars, Alec had told Jimmy about his earlier 'on air' invitation to Charlotte but it had done little to reduce the Irishman's jealousy and they had parted company in good spirits with Jimmy muttering about 'the luck of the English'.

Alec did not want to lose Charlotte and they proceeded at a steady pace until Alec turned into the car park of the Coach and Horses about ten miles south of Lambourn.

They were still too early to eat so they took a table in the bar and Alec fetched two sparkling waters.

'So, what made you decide to accept?' Alec said.

Charlotte looked at Alec. Fair haired and with smiling blue eyes, he seemed the sort of man who did not take life seriously and that was certainly his public image. Nevertheless she knew from having been brought up in a racing yard, that however good you were, you did not succeed in the racing game without a lot of hard work and determination and she had heard that Alec was no exception despite his image. Alec may have had a bit of a playboy image with the general public but no one in the racing industry doubted his dedication.

'As you said, I should get to know the main players and no one can deny you're one of those. That is certainly what I'll tell my father if he gets to hear I've been consorting with you!'

'Hang on there,' Alec replied in mock protest, 'we haven't even had dinner yet. The 'consorting' comes later!'

Charlotte felt that she should have been offended but could not help smiling.

'Anyway,' Alec continued, 'why would your father object to us consorting?'

'He thinks you feature too regularly in the gossip columns, he thinks you're too outspoken in your column in the Herald and he thinks some of your antics when you win a race are unprofessional.'

'But apart from that he quite likes me?'

'Actually, I think he probably does have a sneaking admiration for you. By the way, what is all that business when you win?'

Charlotte was referring to the fact that Alec sometimes teased his fellow jockeys at the end of a race. In fact, it only happened very rarely in circumstances where Alec knew he could get away with it. Unlike flat races which are shorter, quicker and more likely to have closer finishes, jump races can result in the fields becoming very stretched and produce winners by a wide margin. On occasions, Alec had been known when riding such a winner to emphasize his horse's superiority by ostentatiously standing up in his saddle and looking backwards between his legs to see where the other runners had gone or waving at the jockeys behind him. Alternatively, he had on occasions kept his horse on a tight bridle on the run in looking sideways at the jockey alongside driving his mount for all he was worth before Alec let out an inch of rein and passed the winning post a mere half length ahead when it could have been a dozen lengths if he had ridden the horse out fully. Traditionalists hated such behaviour and even disapproved of jockeys waving their sticks in triumph when they passed the post first in a big race.

'We're in the entertainment business,' Alec replied. 'The days when jockeys touched their forelocks to their betters have gone. I'm only trying to give the crowd a bit if fun. Anyway, it doesn't happen often. Unfortunately, when it does, the incident tends to be replayed on countless occasions!'

They continued talking for about half an hour before moving into the restaurant section of the pub. Alec found Charlotte to be lively as well as attractive company. She had long dark hair and big hazel eyes. He guessed she was in her early twenties but refrained from asking.

As they were looking at the menus, Alec's mobile phone rang. He answered it quickly and recognized Martin Saunders' voice.

'Where are you?' Martin asked, 'I expected you back by now!'

'I stopped off on the way for a bite to eat with a friend,' Alec replied.

'Ok. But I've been thinking about where we should go next with Deep Secret and I wanted to get your view,' Martin said.

'What did you have in mind?'

'Well, the obvious target would be the Hennessy but I'm not so sure whether that's a good idea. He's only a seven year old and barely out of the novice stage. It might not be a good idea to run him in a race like that at this stage in his career.'

Alec had been thinking along the same lines in the car. The Hennessy was one of the season's top handicaps run at the end of November at Newbury. It was a worthwhile target in its own right and gave the best horses a month to recover before the King George. However, it was a tough race with a big field and Deep Secret would have to give a lot of weight to more seasoned campaigners. An experience like that could be detrimental to his progress but on the other hand if he was a serious Gold Cup contender he should really take a race like that in his stride.

'I'm inclined to agree with you,' Alec said, 'but what else is there?'

'Nothing much. I'm thinking we should go straight to the King George. We can always give him a racecourse gallop if need be.'

Alec considered this.

'OK. I'll go along with that.'

'Good. I'll ring the owner and tell her you agree. She's bound to want your view as well.'

'Fine. I won't call in at the yard tonight so I'll see you at breakfast.' Alec usually turned up at Martin's yard for breakfast even if he was not riding out.

'There you are then,' Alec said to Charlotte as he put his phone away. 'It was worth you coming. You are the first representative of the media to be told that Deep Secret will go straight to the King George.'

'Some will say you're ducking the Hennessy.'

'Well they'd be right but hopefully there'll be other years for that.'

'You can't keep him in cotton wool.'

'We won't. If things go according to plan in the King George, we'll run him in a handicap in his prep race for the Gold Cup.'

At that moment the waitress arrived to take their order. Charlotte was surprised that Alec ordered a steak with all the trimmings but when it came, he only had three or four mouthfuls of meat and then left the rest. She then felt rather awkward tucking into her meal when he had eaten so little.

'Weight problem?' she said.

'No. I always get nervous on a first date.'

'No seriously. Do you always eat like that?'

'Am I talking to Charlotte the journalist?'

'Don't worry. I'm not about to spill the beans about your weight problems!'

'The truth is I'm finding it more difficult to ride under ten and a half stone nowadays. That's not normally a problem unless I'm riding a horse near the bottom of the handicap and I've got to do ten five on Saturday.'

'Anything interesting?'

Alec looked closely at Charlotte.

'Maybe.'

'Come on them. Out with it!'

'I can't go disclosing stable secrets to the media!'

'I'm hardly the 'media'. I'm a junior TV presenter occasionally allowed to talk to cheeky winning jockeys on their way to weigh in! I promise I won't tell anyone what you tell me. For heaven's sake, I was brought up in a racing stable and know how to keep my mouth shut!'

'OK. Point taken. Robin North is running a horse in the big handicap hurdle at Sandown which has been specially laid out for the race. Robin thinks it's a certainty and he and the owner have already backed it down from 16s to 10 to 1.'

'How many 'certainties' win though?'

Alec shrugged.

'All I know is that there is a fortune already riding on the horse and the price is bound to fall further.'

'So I should get my money on now?'

'What money would that be?'

'Well. If you say it's a good bet I might have a modest bet - say a hundred. So what's the horse called?'

'House of Cards.'

'What an unfortunate name for a jumper!'

'Why's that?'

'Don't be stupid. What always happens to a house of cards? It falls down!'

'This one won't.'

'OK. I'll take your word for it.'

At the end of the meal, Alec paid the bill and suggested that as it was still early Charlotte might care to call in at his place for coffee on the way back as it was en route.

Charlotte was openly amused at this.

'Is that the best you can do? I would have expected something less corny from you! You cannot seriously expect me to agree to that. What do you think I am – one of those little slappers I'm sure you entertain all the time?'

Alec looked hurt.

'No. Of course not. It was a genuine offer. I wouldn't dream of making a move on someone like you after one dinner,' he lied.

Alec looked so genuine that Charlotte felt guilty at her accusation. After all, he had been perfectly charming throughout the evening. Also, she could not help feeling a twinge of disappointment when he had said that he no intention of making a move on her. She wouldn't have minded a kiss. There was no harm in that was there?

'OK. Providing you remain on your best behaviour I suppose there's no harm in a quick coffee,' she found herself saying.

It was only a ten minute journey to Alec's house, a large modern house just outside Lambourn with a stable block and small paddock at the rear. Charlotte asked whether there were any horses in the stables and Alec explained that he let them out to people who needed stabling for horses or ponies. It meant there were always people around during the day which was good for security given that he was away from the property for long periods.

'Do you want to train when you stop riding?' she asked.

'No way,' he said, 'I'm aiming for a job on television as a racing pundit. Who knows, I may be your boss one day!'

As soon as they got in the house, Charlotte began to regret accepting Alec's invitation back to his place. She realized that she had been naïve. Men like Alec simply did not invite girls back for coffee only.

There was nothing in Alec's behaviour which changed. He continued to crack jokes as he pottered around in the kitchen and then led the way into a spacious living room. However, there was definitely what could only be described as a tense or charged atmosphere. Or at least there was so far as Charlotte was concerned. She wondered if Alec felt the same. He certainly wasn't showing it but why should he? This was his home. Charlotte presumed that he'd been in this situation loads of times before. She felt overcome with nerves. She had difficulty keeping the conversation going. What was she going to do if he did make a move on her? A kiss now seemed a bad idea. Kisses often led to something else and a kiss in a man's home was a completely different ballgame from a goodnight kiss in a car or as they went their separate ways from a pub car park. On the other hand, part of her was asking how she would feel if he didn't make a move. After all, he'd made no secret outside the weighing room that he fancied her and she had to accept that she felt the same way. There was only one thing for it. She would have to leave now. She heard Alex saying something about the picture over the fireplace. It was a painting of one of his Grand National winners. She saw her opportunity. She would get up and look at the picture and then move out into hall the saying that she'd had a lovely evening but she had to go, her parents were waiting up for her etc.etc

Unfortunately, this was a fatal error on Charlotte's part because Alec too had seen his opportunity. As she was looking at the picture, he came up behind her, put his arms around her waist and pressed his face gently against her head breathing in the scent of her hair.

Charlotte thought she was going to die. She felt a sensation in her stomach as if he'd put his hand right inside her. He gently turned her round and kissed her on the lips. She did not resist. The kiss became more and more passionate. His hands were all over her. She could feel him fumbling with her jeans. This seemed to go on for ever until she realized that he was trying to find a zip. She nearly broke free of the kiss and laughed out loud. The infamous Alec Hammond was struggling to get over the first hurdle because he hadn't realized that her jeans had buttons, not a zip!

She did break free of the kiss and then gently removed Alec's arms from around her. She stepped back and shook her head. Then she smiled.

'Is this what you are trying to do?' she said.

Alec looked down towards her crotch. He watched as she unbuttoned her jeans, then put her thumbs in her waistband and pushed both the jeans and her knickers down to the floor.

4

While Alec was entertaining Charlotte, Nicola James, aka Susie Stone, adult movie star, was taking a long hard look at herself in the mirror. She had arrived home at her empty flat in Kensington after the afternoon's shoot with the prospect of another lonely evening watching television. She could have gone out drinking with some of the crew or the other performers but lately she preferred to get away from the narrow confines of the porno industry.

Stripped of her make-up she was still a very attractive woman but she thought that she was beginning to look older than her twenty-five years. She was well aware of the fact that the industry aged its performers prematurely and if she did not get out soon she would end up as one of those tired old has beens getting paid peanuts for appearing in downmarket productions.

The question that she was asking herself was how she could get out and what else she could do.

She had long ago lost hope of any normal life or relationship and reflected how her fans worldwide would be surprised to know how lonely she was.

Her world was a fairly incestuous one with most people forming relationships with other people in the industry. She had had a few short term relationships with male performers but they had not lasted long. Male porno stars were not known for their cerebral qualities and after a day's work 'what did you do today, darling?' was not the best way to start an evening.

Relationships with men outside the industry were even less likely to last. Granted, there were millions of men who might imagine that they would be happy to put up with their partner's job but the reality was somewhat different. Nicola had never met one yet who could cope with her job and did not expect to.

Most girls drifted into the industry desperate for a better and what they saw as a more glamorous way of life but once they were in it there was no going back. It was if a line had been crossed.

Nicola however had had a start in life that most of the girls could only have dreamed of. She had been brought up in a middle class family in the south of England. An only child, she had gone to private school and everything had been fine until her father died when she was only ten years of age.

Just as she and her mother were beginning to get over his death, her mother had met the man who within six months became Nicola's stepfather. At first, he had seemed ok but at the age of twelve Nicola found out for the first time something that was going to shape and ultimately ruin her life, namely that apart from natural good looks she had that indefinable quality which acted as a magnet to men, usually of the wrong type.

Not long after her birthday, her stepfather had started visiting her room at night. To begin with, he was content simply to put his hand down inside her bed while telling her how much he loved her. However it was not long before he was taking every opportunity to abuse her and within a matter of months he was demanding full sex.

Nicola had often wondered what might have happened if she had told her mother from the start what was going on but as time went on she found it more and more difficult. Apart from the fact that her mother seemed totally dependent on her husband, Nicola had begun to believe her stepfather that it was all her fault for putting temptation in his way and that her mother would never believe her anyway.

Her stepfather had certainly been right about the latter. Matters had come to a head when Nicola was fifteen. One day, her stepfather had insisted on taking her out saying that they were going shopping. Instead, he had taken her to the address of one of his friends where there were two men waiting. It soon became obvious what was expected of her. When one of them had tried to take hold of her, she had kicked him and made a dash for the door. She managed to escape and then ran all the way home.

Her mother had asked what the matter was and she had blurted everything out. To her horror, far from believing her, her mother had called her a filthy and malicious liar and had said that her father would have been ashamed of her. That was the final straw for Nicola.

She had run upstairs and packed a bag. She had then pushed her way past her still screaming mother and left the house never to return.

A couple of hours later, she had arrived at Victoria Station in London in the same position as thousands of other runaways, penniless, vulnerable and sure that she would never be able to return home.

As it turned out, things could have been worse. Such were her lack of self esteem and desperation that if she had been picked up by the wrong man she would almost certainly have ended up in prostitution or as a drug addict, quite possibly both. Instead, she had met Goran, a young illegal immigrant living in a squat in Pimlico, not far from the station. She had moved into the squat with him and for a time she had begun to enjoy life away from her stepfather. Goran was fun and they had survived for a time on the odd cash in hand jobs that he managed to find.

However, money was tight and after a time, Goran had said

that he had a friend who was a photographer and that maybe Nicola could make some money as a model.

And so, Nicola's 'career' had begun.

She had been an instant hit in the world of 'glamour' modelling and had had no difficulty passing herself off as eighteen years of age. Money had started to come in and before long she had left Goran and the squat for a place of her own. She started appearing regularly in the top shelf magazines and downmarket newspapers not as Nicola James, the runway from Sussex, but as Susie Stone. She had found herself being taken out in flashy cars and attending glamorous nightspots and parties, meeting pop stars, footballers and other celebrities.

To begin with, she had posed topless or in sexy lingerie but tempted by the higher fees, she had then started posing nude in increasingly explicit poses for the soft porn industry. She had promised herself that she would only do this for a while. Her plan was to achieve a degree of financial independence and then maybe get in contact with her mother in the hope that their relationship could be re-established. Of course, her mother would never have approved of what she was doing but by then, she would have stopped and found more acceptable employment.

With that in mind, she had telephoned an old friend to see whether the friend had any news about her mother. The friend had seemed awkward on the phone but Nicola had put this down to having had no contact for about two years. The friend had then said that everyone had been trying to trace Nicola and had then given Nicola the shattering news that her mother had committed suicide six months earlier. Her stepfather had sold the house and moved away. No one had known why it had happened.

Nicola had dropped the phone. She knew or at least thought she knew why it had happened. It was her fault. She had run away never to be heard of again. Her mother had eventually not been able to cope. Perhaps someone had pushed her mother over the edge by showing her pictures of her sixteen year old daughter posing as Susie Stone? It never occurred to her that maybe her mother had found out what her husband was really like.

The news of her mother's death and her feelings of guilt had ruined any chance of Nicola retaining any degree of self respect. It was as if she no longer cared what happened to her.

She soon started posing for pictures with men and other women in simulated sex scenes and before long she was offered a leading role in a hardcore movie. Why not, she had thought. I have nothing else to lose. So she had done it and her life had changed once more for ever.

Work flowed in and she soon became one of the world's top porn stars earning considerable sums and frequently travelling to exotic locations for shoots. However, while she was feted as a star in the narrow confines of the blue movie industry and by the dirty mac brigade, she found herself increasingly rejected by her former acquaintances. No longer was she invited out to the sort of social occasion she had enjoyed previously. She had crossed the line irrevocably. While many men were prepared, indeed pleased, to be seen with a 'glamour model' on their arm, there were not that many who wanted to be seen with a 'porn queen'.

Her thoughts were disturbed by the telephone.

'Hello, Nicola. It's Sol.'

Sol Miller ran an agency out of a poky little office in Soho. He had scores of girls on his books ranging from straight actresses to glamour models and beyond. Of course, he did not advertise the fact that he also dealt with Nicola's end of the market but a lot of her work had come through him. Over the years he had become a friend and he was the only person to whom she had confided everything about her past. He was also one of the few men she had met since she had run away to London all those years ago who had not tried it on with her. She had commented on that one day and he had replied with a smile that it was not as if he had not been tempted but as a short, fat, balding fifty year old he could not compete with the studs she was used to. Nevertheless, he occasionally asked her to accompany him to a function when she would be introduced as Nicola James, his secretary, rather than as her alter ego. As he had said, she was better known abroad than in England where blue films were more difficult to get hold of and anyway, he joked, who would recognise her with her clothes on?

'Hi, Sol. What can I do for you?'

'Don't tempt me! What are you doing on Saturday?'

'Nothing much but I don't want too late a night as I'm flying to the South of France early on Sunday.'

'Lucky you….'

'It's work.'

'Oh. Are you still thinking of quitting the business?'

'Definitely. When I can work out what to do.'

'Come and be my secretary for real then.'

'Apart from the fact I can't type or do shorthand, I want a clean break. I don't want to be involved in arranging the same work for other sad cows! But thanks for the offer.'

'Ok. But let me know if you change your mind. The offer will always be open! Anyway about Saturday. You won't be back late. It's an afternoon do. I'd like you to come with me to Sandown races. A business acquaintance has got a runner in one of the races and is hiring a box. He seems to think that his horse can't be beaten. He's invited me along but I'd rather not go alone as I won't know anyone else and it'll be mostly couples.'

'Won't he mind if I turn up as well?'

'Who would mind *you* turning up? Anyway I've already asked him and he was happy for me to bring someone.'

'OK,' Nicola said, 'I'll come.' She knew a bit about horseracing or rather betting as her stepfather had run a couple of betting shops in Brighton.

'Great. There's a lunch laid on before the races so I'll pick you up at half eleven.'

'Fine. I'll see you then.'

5

On Saturday morning, Charlotte and the rest of the television crew arrived at Sandown early for the morning chat show beamed live from the course.

Any fears that Alec had had about letting Charlotte in on the gamble on House of Cards had been completely unfounded as the following morning's racing press had already picked up on the story given the amount of money wagered on the horse which had brought the odds tumbling down. By the time Charlotte had got to a betting shop the horse's price had already dropped again and to her annoyance, the best she could get for her hundred pounds was 8 to 1. The gamble had continued over the next couple of days and by Saturday morning the odds had halved again to 4 to 1.

The huge gamble was to be one of the main talking points on the morning show and Ronnie Forsyth, the show's betting expert, was predicting that by the time of the race, House of Cards was likely to start as favourite. What had started out as a betting coup by the connections had turned into a massive public gamble as the ordinary punters had rushed to get in on the action. Charlotte had eventually left Alec's house about three hours later than she had intended. She had told him that she had never done anything like that before and although he had appeared to believe her, she imagined that he had heard similar from numerous other women. In her case, it happened to be true. She had sworn Alec to secrecy about their liaison as she did not want to be the talk of the weighing room.

Charlotte was under no illusions as to where she stood with Alec and had told herself not to expect any sort of long term relationship. However, he had phoned her the following day as he had promised. There had been no televised meetings since Wincanton and she had to admit to herself that she was looking forward to seeing him on Saturday. Her excitement was increased by the prospect of her winning eight hundred pounds if Alec won on House of Cards. Charlotte rarely bet and her usual stake was about ten pounds. She had never previously bet anything like a hundred pounds. One date with Alec Hammond and she had been lead astray in more ways than one!

Robin North drove to the course in his Jaguar accompanied by his wife. There was little conversation as Robin had a lot on his mind. Months of preparation had gone into setting House of Cards up for the ABC Bookmakers Handicap Hurdle and the day had finally arrived.

Robin ran a yard of about sixty jumpers but although he had been fairly successful over the years he had never been able to make anything like his counterparts on the flat. Consequently, like a number of trainers, he sometimes tried to supplement his income by having a tilt at the betting market with a horse specially 'prepared' for the race. House of Cards was by far his most ambitious project to date and he really needed the horse to win. In fact, it had to win!

He had been through an expensive divorce about two years previously and his new wife Caroline had proved equally expensive to keep.

Some of the bitchier people in the racing world viewed

Caroline as 'mutton dressed up as lamb' but to Robin she was a delight compared to the battleaxe to whom he had been married for over twenty years. Nevertheless, she had come at a price as Robin had struggled to finance the divorce without selling the yard. Now, he had to finance Caroline and her extravagant ways.

Caroline was nearly fifty years old but her expensively died blond hair and make up made her look younger. She sat next to Robin wearing designer sunglasses and a Chanel suit which showed more of her tanned legs than would normally be expected of a woman of her age. Rumours had circulated about her taste for younger men but none of them had reached Robin's ears.

Robin had bet ten thousand pounds each way on House of Cards and stood to make two hundred thousand pounds if he won. That sort of money would enable Robin to finance his yard and his wife for some time but Robin certainly could not afford to lose twenty thousand pounds.

Further, there was another reason why Robin could not contemplate losing. He had persuaded the horse's owner, Vic Shaw, to allow him to set up the coup. This had involved the horse missing other winning opportunities in the last few months and although Shaw had willingly agreed, he was not a man to take failure lightly. With six other horses in the yard, Shaw was Robin's biggest individual owner and the last thing he wanted was for Shaw to remove all his horses. Shaw had not had much success recently with his horses and defeat for House of Cards could be the last straw.

Robin had realized in the previous season that House of Cards was crying out to be raced over a distance greater than two miles. Nevertheless, he had run him twice more over the minimum distance that season knowing that he would finish down the field. He had then given him a rest before running him on ground which he had known to be too firm for the horse when the horse was not fully fit. A month later, he had again left him deliberately short of a couple of gallops for a race at Market Rasen, a course which happened to be too tight for House of Cards' style of racing. He had told the stable's conditional jockey not to 'knock the horse about' which was as near as he dared get to telling him to finish down the field again. The boy was no fool and knew what he had to do if he wanted more rides.

Consequently, House of Cards had acquired a string of 'duck eggs' or zeros against his name as his recent form figures and Robin was sure that the horse had got into this valuable handicap set to carry at least a stone less than he should have been allocated.

The distance, the going and the course were all perfect for the horse and Robin was confident he had the horse in peak condition. So what could go wrong? Well, in truth, quite a lot. The horse could fall, be badly hampered or simply be unlucky in running even with Alec Hammond on board. Maybe one of the other runners had been similarly prepared. Robin did not have a monopoly on trickery.

So it was that Robin had a lot to worry about and took little comfort that he had done everything in his power to facilitate the horse's victory.

Victor Shaw drove himself to Sandown in his Bentley. A tall, powerfully built man in his mid forties, Victor did not suffer fools gladly. He was a businessman who expected to succeed in everything he did and that included horseracing. Although Robin North had trained a number of winners for him in the past, things had not been going so well recently. He was not prepared to tolerate this for much longer despite the fact that he quite liked Robin and was even screwing his wife. He did not consider this a betrayal of his trainer because as far as he was concerned Caroline was a middle aged bimbo who was taking Robin for a ride even if the stupid old fool could not see what was going on.

Victor had backed House of Cards to win a million pounds. He had put just enough on each way to recover his stake if the horse was placed but second place was no good to Victor. He had put most of the money on to win. Unlike Robin, Victor did not really need the money and his stake was neither here nor there. What mattered to Victor was the winning itself. He rather liked the image that he had acquired recently as a big player in the gambling world and did not relish the prospect of losing, particularly as he had hired a box and invited a number of friends and business contacts to share in his triumph.

If the horse lost, he would probably feel obliged to sack Robin just to save a bit of face.

Alec and Jimmy drove to the course together in Alec's car. On the day after Alec's date with Charlotte, Jimmy had been dying to know what had happened and had pressed him on the subject as they were changing into their kit at Stratford races. Alec had initially replied 'no comment' but that had not been enough for Jimmy. Eventually Alec had said that he had been sworn to secrecy. That was good enough for Jimmy as he therefore knew that there was something that had to be kept secret and it did not take a genius to work out what that was.

During the journey to Sandown they discussed each other's rides although House of Cards was the horse that most concerned Alec even though he had also a plum ride for Martin Saunders in the two mile novice chase.

'Robin's really wound up about House of Cards,' he remarked, 'he's rung me nearly every evening this week to tell me how to ride him. I think he's got a lot at stake.'

'You mean a huge bet?'

'Almost certainly. But I think it's more than that.'

'Maybe he's got financial problems and needs a big win to save himself. Or maybe he's promised Vic Shaw a big win and needs to deliver. If you do win, you could be in line for a big present. Shaw was very generous to me when I rode a winner for him last year and I doubt he had anything like as much on then as he has today.'

'Let's hope so!'

As Pat Duggan drove to the course, he was also thinking about the ABC Bookmakers Handicap Hurdle. He was riding the horse which had been ante-post favourite for the race since the weights had been published. It now looked as though his mount, Radford Lad, would be displaced as favourite on the very day of the race. It made no difference to Duggan whether his horse was favourite or not. In fact, it would suit him better if his mount was not the favourite.

Duggan was determined that the huge gamble on House of Cards would fail for two reasons.

First, he was aware that over the last few days there had been huge public support for the horse. Thus many ordinary racegoers and punters would lose out if the horse was beaten. In that situation, disappointed punters often pointed the figure of blame at the jockey and anything that dented Alec Hammond's popularity was fine by Duggan.

Second, Duggan had been surprised to have been contacted by a bookmaker with whom he had had dealings in the past. The bookmaker had offered him £5000 providing House of Cards lost the race. Duggan would collect his bonus as long as House of Cards did not win whether or not his own horse won and whether or not Duggan actually had to do anything to hamper House of Cards' chances of winning.

Duggan had found this an extraordinary proposition. He had been offered money in the past by this bookmaker to stop his own horse winning but this was the first time he had been offered money to stop someone else's horse winning. Further, the bookie had not seemed concerned about Radford Lad winning. Even if Radford Lad did not start favourite, he was still well fancied and it was usually a bad result for the bookies if either the first or second favourite won.

Anyway, it was just as well that he had not been asked to stop Radford Lad. He might have done that sort of thing in the past but having reached the top Duggan was not prepared to 'pull' fancied horses in big races any longer.

As it was, he had the perfect scenario and although he might not have to do anything to stop House of Cards winning it would give him a degree of personal satisfaction if he did have to earn his bonus.

'So who is this guy who's invited you to go and watch his horse win?' Nicola asked Sol when she had got in his car.

After inviting Nicola to join him, Sol had phoned back the following day to tell her about the gamble on House of Cards. He had been phoned by Victor Shaw and advised to get his money on as soon as possible as the way things were going, there was no point in waiting until the day of the race. Sol was not a big gambler but he knew that Shaw did not mess about and it was clear from the press that Shaw himself must have already piled a fortune on the horse. Sol had therefore taken a thousand pounds from his office safe and gone round the corner to the nearest betting shop where he had backed House of Cards at 7 to 1.

When he had phoned Nicola, he had agreed that she could have a hundred pounds of the bet and she had handed over the money when he had called to collect her.

'Victor Shaw,' Sol replied. 'A very wealthy and successful businessman.'

'So how do you know him?'

'Victor and I go back a long way. In fact I used to employ him!'

'What? At the agency?'

'No, no. Long before then. Believe it or not I started out as a second hand car dealer in the east end. It had been my father's business. He died at the age of fifty and I took it over. I hadn't intended to go into the business but my elder brother had his own business to run and my mother was dependent on me to keep the business going. Anyway I employed this young lad to help me, not that I was much older than him. It was clear then that Victor was going places. He could sell anything to anyone. It was only a matter of time before he started up on his own and before long he bought me out! As it happened it couldn't have come at a better time. I wanted to get out anyway and he gave me a fair price. It was enough for me to set up my mother and eventually I started up the agency.'

'And presumably you've kept in touch?'

'Yes. Victor soon got out of the second hand business and ended up with a swanky showroom in Mayfair selling upmarket cars. Whenever he was entertaining at the showroom I would provide him with the glamour girls who would drape themselves over the motors.'

'I used to do a bit of that sort of work'

'Yes. Well maybe you should have stuck to it.'

'I wish I had but I was too mixed up then. Now it's too late.'

'Not necessarily. You could start again. You're an intelligent woman unlike most of the plastic dolls in your industry. Christ! Some of them think they're serious artists!'

'I intend to get out soon but I'm sure the past will always haunt me. For a start I could never have a family.'

'Why not?'

'Even if I could find a partner who could live with my background, I could never tell my kids and the chances are some schoolmate would dig up an old film of mine and show it to them. I couldn't live with that.'

'Given what happened to you, people would understand.'

'What, children? I could tell them that I did what I did because I'd been having sex with my stepfather since the age of twelve and by the way I also drove my mother to suicide?'

'You don't know that.' But Sol could see that she had a point. 'You could change your appearance...'

Nicola decided to change the subject.

'So what does Shaw do now?'

'Anything that makes a profit! He's not in the motor trade now so far as I know but he's a major investor in numerous businesses.'

'And now he's into racing. Is he fixing races?'

'No. Victor may be ruthless but he wouldn't do anything like that. He may sail close to the wind but he's not crooked.'

'So how does he know this horse is going to win?'

'He doesn't. All he does know is that the horse has been specially prepared or 'laid out' for this race. There's a fine line in racing between blatant cheating and keeping your cards close to your chest so the bookies give you generous odds, or as I'm lead to believe in this case very generous odds. But there is no such thing as a certainty in racing. This is a major handicap and the horse will still start at odds against. That means that even with all the money on House of Cards the bookies still rate him as more likely to lose than win. The advantage for Victor is that he probably got his money on at around 20 to 1 when the true odds should have been a fraction of that.'

The subject of all this speculation had set out early from Robin North's Lambourn yard in a horsebox accompanied by the stable's runner in another race at the meeting. House of Cards was a big six year old bay gelding who had been racing since he had started his career on the flat as a two year old. Oblivious to all the speculation, he was undoubtedly the most relaxed of the leading players in the drama which was unfolding.

Had he been capable of rational thought, he might have been hoping that the course to which he was being taken was more suitable for him than the tight turns of Market Rasen. He might also have been hoping for a different jockey from that stupid boy who, while jumping up and down on his back in an apparent effort to impress, was also tugging on his reins preventing him from running on into a place.

As it was, he just stood there patiently listening to the drone of the engine, blissfully unaware that the destination of millions of pounds as well as his trainer's financial solvency would depend on his efforts later that day.

6

When Alec and Jimmy arrived at the course in time for the first race they were immediately aware of an additional buzz about the place. As they approached the weighing room, Charlotte came running up to them. Jimmy decided to leave them to it and walked on.

Alec could see that Charlotte was excited. He gave her a peck on the cheek.

'Hi, Charlotte. What's up?'

'How do you know that I'm not just pleased to see you?'

'Because you look as if you're bursting to tell me something.'

'Everyone is talking about the gamble on House of Cards. He's down to 2 to 1 favourite on the early exchanges. It's rumoured that if he wins, he'll take millions out of the ring!'

'Thanks for piling the pressure on me! I hope you got on at a decent price!'

'I managed to get 8s. The rest of the crew are really jealous and asking whether I had inside information.'

Alec laughed.

'Did you tell them how you got it?'

She gave him a playful punch.

'What for services rendered?'

'I can give you more tips for more of the same if you like!'

Don't tempt me, she thought, but replied, 'The main reason I wanted to speak to you is that my director has told me that if you win I must grab you for a few words on your way to weigh in. Will that be OK?'

'Sure. No problem. I'll see you then.'

'So you reckon you're going to win then?'

'So everyone seems to think!'

Up in his box, Victor Shaw had laid on a sumptuous spread for his guests. He knew that most if not all would have had a bet and probably quite a large one on House of Cards and he did not want them to be disappointed. The race was the main topic of conversation in the private box. Robin had assured him that everything had gone to plan but Victor knew as well as Robin that 'blots' on the handicap often got beaten and he could see the tension in the trainer's face. The whole situation seemed to be spinning out of control. They had never envisaged that the press and public would latch on to the gamble in such a big way. He had even wondered whether they should have engaged a jockey with a lesser profile than Alec Hammond because him being on board such a steamer in the betting market had only fuelled the fire. Alec was not just the housewife's choice but everyone's. Then again Alec was the best around and rode most of Victor's runners.

At that moment Victor's thoughts were interrupted by the arrival of Sol. He barely looked at Sol as he was amazed to see that he had the most gorgeous creature on his arm.

Although only five feet four, by the time her high heels were added, Nicola appeared much taller than Sol and they looked a very unlikely couple. Nicola was dressed in a well cut pink suit with matching shoes and lipstick. Under the suit jacket, she was wearing a simple white blouse, low cut but not excessively so. Her skirt was only two or three inches above her knees and from what he could see Victor assumed that the nylons she was wearing were stockings of the very highest quality.

Victor was suddenly conscious that conversation in the box had ceased for a moment as everyone stared at Nicola.

At least she's diverted their attention from House of Cards for a while, he thought.

He stepped forward.

'Sol. Good to see you,' he said, shaking Sol's hand. 'And who is your delightful guest?' switching his attention to Nicola.

'Victor, may I introduce Nicola James, my personal assistant?'

Sol had taken the view in that moment that to introduce Nicola as his secretary would sound absurd so he had made the snap decision to upgrade her to personal assistant. As soon as he said it he regretted it as it occurred to him that 'personal assistant' could have other connotations. He could not help but notice that Victor's eyebrows arched slightly as he said it.

Victor took Nicola's hand. With her other hand, she removed her designer sunglasses and after giving her hair a slight shake, placed them in her hair.

'I'm delighted to meet you,' Victor said as he towered over her. 'You've certainly brought a touch of glamour to our little gathering.'

Behind him, Caroline North had looked a little disconcerted when Nicola had walked into the box. After that remark, she glared at Nicola with outright hostility. Victor had said it to annoy her as much as to flatter Nicola. Caroline looked like an old tart beside Nicola and Victor had begun to wonder why he had ever got involved with her.

'I'm delighted to meet you too, Victor,' Nicola said in the low polished tone that she had acquired during her private education. 'Sol's told me a lot about you.'

'Let me introduce you to my trainer, Robin North, and his wife Caroline,' Victor said, waving Robin and Caroline forward.

Robin was charming to Nicola but she could sense the hostility from Caroline. God, she thought, this woman's at least twenty years older than me and she's trying to compete. The sad thing is, I could look like her in five years time if I'm not careful.

Sol and Nicola were given champagne and then Victor started introducing them to the other guests. None of the other women were over friendly towards Nicola but she was used to that and at least they were not overtly hostile like Caroline.

'I hear your horse has a good chance today. Sol and I have already had a bet,' Nicola said to Victor.

Victor winced inwardly. Nicola's arrival had taken his mind off the race.

'Well you never know in racing but I'm hopeful.'

'That's not what you said earlier in the week,' another man said. 'You said it couldn't lose! On that basis I've put a bundle on it!'

'We all know there are no certainties in racing,' Nicola came to Victor's rescue.

Sol was amused as he watched Nicola charm all the men and annoy the women because of the attention she attracted. These people were all seriously rich, and successful in their various fields, yet she was quite at home. Her stepfather had a lot to answer for given the depths to which he had caused her to sink. What could she have achieved but for him, Sol thought to himself.

7

Alec's mounts in the first two races on the card both finished unplaced. The ABC Bookmakers Handicap Hurdle was the third race of the day and when Alec walked out to the paddock, he was immediately aware of the change in atmosphere.

As he and the other jockeys walked through the crowd towards the gate leading to the paddock where they would meet up with their respective trainers and owners before being given a leg up on to their mounts, there were more than the usual shouts of encouragement from racegoers and most of them were directed at Alec.

Amongst the shouts of 'Good luck, Alec', he also heard animated shouts of 'Go, Alec, Go!' and 'Show the bookies who's boss!'

As he paused briefly to sign a couple of autographs he tried to put out of his mind the fact that his horse was now the hot favourite for what should have been one of the most open betting races of the season. Although Alec was not aware of it at that moment, the bookies were marking House of Cards down to 7 to 4 and by the off, the horse would be down to 6 to 4, a quite ridiculous price for any horse in a twenty four runner handicap, let alone one with House of Cards' recent form book entries.

On entering the paddock, Alec soon spotted the small group comprising Robin and Caroline North and Victor Shaw, but as he approached he realized that any hope he had of putting the gamble out of his mind was a forlorn one.

He had expected Robin to be edgy but he and Victor had the air of men about to go to the gallows rather than watch a horse race. Their faces were drawn and neither of them could stop fidgeting about. Completely gone was Victor's usual ebullience before a race and instead of his normal beaming face as he shook hands with Alec, he could barely muster a smile. Caroline too was not her normal flirtatious self although she did at least favour Alec with a smile and attempt to lighten the atmosphere by referring to House of Cards looking a picture.

Alec looked at the horse and smiled. He did indeed look very fit but apart from that he seemed completely unaware of what was going on around him. Indeed, as he was being led around the paddock by his stable lass, he had his head down and looked half asleep. Thank goodness for that, Alec thought. The last thing he needed was the horse getting lathered up in the paddock and wasting his nervous energy. Alec knew enough about the horse to know that he was not the type to be on his toes at this stage and had always been a genuine sort when he got out on to the racecourse.

'The distance and the uphill finish will suit him,' Robin was saying, 'there should be a good pace throughout in a race like this but if you're not happy with the pace, you should go on from two furlongs out…..'

Alec nodded dutifully as Robin repeated the instructions that he had already given him numerous times over the phone and was relieved when the time came for him to get mounted and leave the paddock. Robin gave Alec a leg up and all three of them wished him luck.

The stable lass, Penny, led Alec and the horse to the gate and as she handed over control to Alec she looked up at him and said, 'You won't need luck, you'll murder them.' For some reason, her confidence was a welcome contrast to the nervousness of Robin and Victor.

Alec then cantered the horse down to the start and in the usual manner gave him a look at the first hurdle. Alec felt much better now that he was out on the course even if those watching elsewhere did not. After a few minutes, the starter called the runners into line and the tape was stretched across the course. There were no hitches and no need for the horses to take a turn and line up again so the starter shouted and let the tape go. They were off.

8

Robin had been right. There was a fast pace right from the start as a couple of front runners went off together and the main field followed about two to three lengths behind. For the first part of the race, Alec was content to sit in mid-division, allowing his horse to relax and concentrating on meeting the hurdles right. As the runners went past the stands for the first time, Alec was conscious of the cheering from the crowd but thought no more of it as the runners turned to the right and went out into the country again.

At the first hurdle in the back straight, one of the runners in front took a crashing fall, bringing down another horse and impeding a couple of others. Fortunately, Alec was on the inside of the fallen horses and was not inconvenienced. He decided to maintain his position on the inside confident that at that pace, a number of the horses in front would back peddle and that there was little chance of being boxed in.

By the time the leaders were approaching the final bend, the field was well stretched out. Alec felt that he was travelling very easily and he had not asked his mount to quicken even though there were still half a dozen horses in front. Of those, about half were still going well, including Pat Duggan's mount, Radford Lad, but the rest were being ridden along to maintain their places.

As they were coming out of the bend into the straight, Alec

saw his chance to slip through on the inside in a matter of strides before he set sail for home.

However, just as Alec was quickening into the gap, Pat Duggan, who had been keeping a careful eye on Alec's mount, suddenly pulled his horse to the right 'shutting the door' on Alec and causing Alec to stop riding and to stand up in his irons so as not to collide with the running rail.

House of Cards was almost brought to a standstill as Radford Lad and the other runners ahead gained lengths on him and pulled clear.

Back in the stands, there was a collective gasp from the crowd.

Up in Victor Shaw's box there was also a gasp. Robin and Victor were both gripping their binoculars with such force that the whites of their knuckles were showing. Unlike the other guests, neither made a sound as they saw disaster looming.

'Is that allowed?' Nicola asked Sol. She had borrowed a pair of binoculars from another guest who had preferred to watch the race on the television.

'Debatable,' Sol replied while continuing to look through his own binoculars. 'Hammond will say that he was entitled to go through and Duggan will say that his was an entirely legitimate manoeuvre even if it did look reckless from here. Anyway, I think we've all done our money now!'

In his office in West London, Frank Morris had been watching the race as keenly as anyone. When he saw Duggan cut Alec's mount off, he jumped out of his chair and punched the air in the manner of a football fan watching his team score.

Alec was far too experienced to panic but realized that his chance had almost certainly gone. However, after he had gathered House of Cards together, he found to his astonishment that far from being out of the race House of Cards still had plenty of petrol in the tank. He soon caught and overhauled all the other runners with the exception of Radford Lad who still had three lengths on him. But as they approached the final flight of hurdles, Alec could see that Duggan was flat to the boards while Alec had barely come off the bridle. The run in at Sandown is a long one and many a horse jumping the last a long way in front has been overhauled.

What happened next was pure theatre and if Charlotte's father was watching, as he surely was, he would have been apoplectic.

Knowing that he could pick up Duggan any time he liked, relieved that he was going to win and furious at Duggan's manoeuvre, Alec could not resist playing the showman.

He allowed House of Cards to range up alongside Radford Lad halfway up the run in but instead of going on, Alec brought him back on the bridle and almost stood up as he looked down at Duggan beside him riding for all his worth and waving his stick about. For a few strides Alec held the pose before showing everyone what he thought of Duggan by lifting one of his hands with his fingers and thumb making a circle as he shook his wrist a few times. He then let out an inch of rein and cruised to the front passing the winning post easing down about two lengths in front.

The crowd went absolutely berserk. The roar was deafening and Alec saw hats being thrown in the air. Alec had only ever seen this type of reaction from the crowds at the Cheltenham Festival or after the Grand National. Caught up in the moment, Alec stood up again in his irons and put his right forefinger in the air. The noise increased. Alec Hammond had won. He was still number one!

9

The scenes of pandemonium in the crowd below were being replicated in Victor's box as he and his guests, including Sol and Nicola, cheered and hugged each other. Robin had experienced the despair of defeat turning into the elation of victory in a matter of seconds and he and Victor hurried down the stairs so that they could meet House of Cards and Alec at the winners enclosure. At the bottom, they found themselves part of a huge crowd who had the same idea all surging forward to welcome the triumphant duo.

Back in West London, Frank Morris sat with his head in his hands staring at the scenes unfolding on the television, knowing that it would take a miracle to save him now.

After milking the crowd, Alec sat back in his saddle and leant forward to pat House of Cards' neck. A number of the other jockeys called out words of congratulation as they passed him.

'You'll be even more of a bloody hero now!' Alec heard Jimmy shout.

Only Pat Duggan looked over at Alec with a malicious scowl muttering something about cheating and that the stewards should look into the race.

Alec walked House of Cards over to the gate leading off the

course where they were met by the horse's stable lass, Penny. She looked up to say something to Alec but instead of words all she could manage were tears of joy – little wonder given that she, like most of the other stable staff, had had a months wages on House of Cards.

She then led Alec and the horse down the path towards the winners enclosure while the crowd cheered them every inch of the way. Alec acknowledged the cheers and leant down to touch some of the outstretched hands offered up towards him.

When they finally reached the gate to the winners enclosure and passed through it, a massive roar erupted. Alec saluted the crowd and waved his whip at them in triumph. Even House of Cards himself seemed perky and interested in what was going on around him instead of adopting his usual unconcerned demeanour. He had never had a welcome like this before. After all, his previous visits to the winners enclosure had been much more modest low key affairs.

As Alec dismounted, the cheering continued. It seemed as if everyone at the racecourse had had a bet on House of Cards although Alec realized that that was not quite the case as he caught a glance of the more restrained mood of the connections of Radford Lad in the runners up spot and the still glowering face of Pat Duggan.

'Well done, Alec,' Victor shouted above the noise putting his arm around Alec's shoulders as Alec started to remove his saddle. 'Bloody marvellous!'

'Yes, well done,' Robin repeated. 'And thank you!'

By this time the press were beginning to close in on them. Alec looked at Robin and he seemed to be completely drained. Maybe Robin had had more riding on this than Alec had imagined.

'To be honest it was easy, even after Duggan's attempt to cut me off!' Alec replied. 'You certainly had him spot on!'

Caroline North then grabbed Alec and gave him a big kiss,

whispering 'my hero' before Alec moved off with his saddle towards the weighing room.

After a couple of steps, Charlotte appeared at his side with her microphone.

'Did you think your chance had gone when you got cut off on the final bend?' she asked.

'Not at all,' Alec replied, telling a white lie. 'I was always confident we could pick up the other runners.'

'Will you be speaking to Pat Duggan about the incident?' Charlotte continued.

'Why should I? These things happen in racing.'

'But what if it had cost you the race?' Charlotte persisted.

'But it didn't!'

'So how does it feel to have made so many people happy?'

'Absolutely great!'

And with that, Alec incurred Charlotte's father's wrath once again by putting his free arm around Charlotte's narrow waist and in front of millions of television viewers, lifting her up and whirling her around in a circle before putting her down and disappearing into the weighing room.

After he had weighed in, Alec went back outside still wearing Victor's black and white check silks for the presentation of the trophies and photographs. A large crowd had waited for this and as owner, trainer and jockey went up for their prizes, they were each greeted with a huge cheer.

After the ceremony, Victor asked Alec if he would mind putting in an appearance in his box as he knew that his guests would like to meet him.

Alec did not have a ride in the next race and said that he would be happy to do so.

Meanwhile, Robin had been on the phone to his head lad, Barry Jones. Barry had congratulated his boss and told him that the whole yard was celebrating after watching the race on TV. The beer was already flowing.

'Never mind the beer,' Robin had said, 'If you look under the desk in my office, you'll find a couple of crates of champagne which I hid there in case this happened. Put as many bottles as you can in the fridge and we'll have a party when Caroline and I get back. Make sure the rest of them don't get too pissed before we get back!'

However, before Robin could finally relax and enjoy his triumph, he had one more not unimportant duty to perform.

As he had suspected might happen, the stewards wanted an explanation about House of Cards' huge improvement in form. Robin had spent weeks worrying about whether he had judged the horse's preparation correctly. Now he was worried about whether he had overdone it! Far from having about a stone in hand of the other runners House of Cards would probably have won the race even if he had been carrying top weight of twelve stone rather than ten stone five.

Anyway, Robin had prepared what he was going to say and wittered on about the horse being better suited by a longer distance and a tougher track. He hinted that the conditional jockey who had ridden him at Market Rasen hadn't 'made enough use of him' and that anyway none of his horses were running well at that time. It all sounded pretty unconvincing to Robin and the stewards listened stony faced. But since they could not prove otherwise they decided to 'record' his explanation. He had got away with it!

10

Frank Morris was still sitting at his desk with his head still in his hands when his bookkeeper, Lennie Cohen walked into the office. Cohen sat down in the chair on the other side of the desk and folded his arms.

'Well,' Morris asked him, 'how bad is it?'

'You know how bad it is,' Cohen replied, 'I told you to lay some of the money off.'

'There's no way that fucking race was straight!' Morris raged.

Lennie thought it a bit rich of Frank Morris to complain about a bent horse race. What he was annoyed about was that he hadn't been in on the action.

'And as for that little bastard Duggan!' Morris continued, 'What a cock up he made!'

'Come on, Frank, Duggan did his best. The whole world saw him try to shut Hammond out! The only way he was going to stop House of Cards winning was to kick Hammond out of the saddle and he could hardly do that could he?'

'Why not?' Morris grumbled.

'Never mind that now, Frank. How are you going to pay out? Unless you pay pretty quickly, you're finished as a bookie.'

'There's only one thing I can do and that's to borrow the money.'

'Where the hell are you going to borrow that sort of money without collateral?'

'There are people I can go to but they're going to want an extortionate rate of interest and if I don't pay up, I'm dead.'

'But the way things have been going, there's no way the business will be able to finance such repayments.'

'Then there's only one thing I can do. We'll have to go back to the old ways.'

Lennie winced. 'Times have changed, Frank. It won't be so easy now.'

'We'll do it just long enough to get out of this mess,' Morris replied.

Morris had started his bookmaking firm several years previously with a few betting shops. After a time, he had sold the shops to concentrate on credit bookmaking for punters who wagered large stakes. He had soon gained a reputation as a 'gambling' bookmaker. Most bookmakers try to produce a balanced book on a race so that they make a profit whichever horse wins. Of course, that is not always possible and by and large a bookmaker will make a smaller profit or even a loss if a fancied horse wins but a much larger profit if an outsider wins. Overall, however, he should make a steady profit.

Frank Morris was not content with this and would often run an unbalanced book. If he decided that a particular fancied horse was unlikely to win, he would offer his customers more generous odds on that horse than his competitors thus attracting a disproportionate amount of money on that horse. If he was really confident that the horse was going to lose, he would shorten the odds on the other fancied runners so as to discourage bets on them.

If the horse duly lost then he made a huge profit on the race. On the other hand, if it won, he made a huge loss.

However, Morris was not prepared to rely solely on his own view of the formbook. That way he would end up losing like most of his own clients. Providing he knew that one preferably fancied horse in the race would not be winning, that was enough for him.

Consequently, he had developed a team of three or four jockeys who from time to time, usually in the bigger handicaps where there was a strong ante-post market, were prepared to ensure that their horses did not win.

Apart from the very top boys, jump jockeys do not make large sums of money and even jockeys quite well known to the racing public struggle to make ends meet. Morris had not found it hard to find either embittered jockeys whose careers had not developed the way that they had hoped or corruptible youngsters to whom four figure sums for throwing the odd race were a fortune.

Once under his control, Morris found that if any jockey showed an unwillingness to continue the arrangement, the threat of extreme violence either to himself or a loved one worked wonders.

In fact, he had only had to carry out his threat once. After breaking one jockey's legs so badly that he never rode again, none of the team had ever refused Morris again.

However, as time went on, better security and blanket coverage of all races made it more difficult to stop races on a regular basis. Morris found himself running a respected business used by many racing industry insiders. His team of jockeys either retired or faded into obscurity with the notable exception of one who like Morris went on to achieve success and respectability – Pat Duggan.

So Morris decided to abandon his old ways and run a straight business.

To begin with, the business thrived and made a reasonable profit but eventually greed got the better of Morris and gradually he went back to his old method of gambling by taking in disproportionate sums on horses he was convinced would lose, only without the inside information that he had had previously.

Sometimes, he had come out on top but on other occasions, he had suffered huge losses and the flat season which was just coming to an end had been disastrous for him. Many bookmakers had suffered due to the firm ground and in consequence the unusual quantity of winning favourites, particularly in the big races. Morris had tried to gamble his way out of trouble and failed spectacularly.

He had seen House of Cards as a way of easing his increasing financial problems. When the big bets had started coming in at long odds, he had known immediately that some sort of coup was being planned. However, even if the horse was being prepared for the race and his previous form could not be trusted, he still could not see the horse winning such a valuable handicap.

Lennie had warned him to lay off some of the money on to other bookmakers but Morris had been too greedy. By the time the public gamble took off, it had been too late anyway.

So Morris had taken out the insurance policy of offering Duggan money to try to make sure the horse did not win.

Now, rather than his problems being solved, he faced paying out hundreds of thousands of pounds and the only way he could do that was to put himself in hock to some very dangerous people.

'But which jockeys are you going to approach?' Lennie asked. 'There's no one left now apart from Duggan and he's hardly going to co-operate now. He's champion jockey for Christ's sake! Accepting a bonus if House of Cards didn't win is one thing but stopping his own mounts is an entirely different thing.'

'Don't worry about that. Duggan won't have any alternative but to co-operate. I'm going to make him an offer he won't be able to refuse. In fact, given Duggan's position, I doubt we'll need any more jocks on board. He rides a lot of fancied horses in the big races and we can probably make do with only two or three a month given the amount of money we can pull in on those races. Given that some of them will have lost anyway, it probably won't even dent his title chances.'

'I'm not sure he'll see it that way.'

'Leave Duggan to me. In the meantime, I'd better give Dave and Chris a bell and tell them they're back in business.'

11

When Alec entered the box, a cheer went up and he was immediately surrounded by Victor's guests who all wanted to congratulate him and shake him by the hand.

He accepted a glass of sparkling water as Victor introduced him to his guests individually. Nicola was one of the last to be introduced and Alec held on to her hand a little longer than with the other guests. He had agreed to come up to the box as a courtesy to the owner but he was now very pleased that he had.

After exchanging a few pleasantries with the other guests, it was not long before Alec managed to involve himself in a conversation with Nicola and Sol and after a short while Sol withdrew discreetly leaving Alec and Nicola together.

'So, do you often cause such an uproar as well as humiliating the runner up?' Nicola asked.

'No, not at all,' Alec replied. 'I may have been riding the horse but the uproar has really been caused by your host and his friends betting so much money on the race. As for Pat Duggan, the other jockey, you must have seen what he tried to do to me. I was just paying him back.'

'Anyway, it was pretty exciting stuff. This is my first trip to the races and like everyone else here I've made a nice profit! It's a pity it's not always this easy.'

'That race was made more exciting because of the money

riding on it. I'm not riding in the next race but if you want to see an exciting race you should watch the one after that.'

'Why? What's so special about it?'

'It's a novice chase over two miles. What you've just seen is a hurdle race for fairly experienced horses. Chases are over much bigger fences. The horses are all inexperienced and as they will be racing over the minimum distance, they'll all be going hell for leather. This course tends to produce some pretty dramatic action in that type of race.'

'Will you win?'

'I've got a good chance. But who knows?'

'Should I have a bet on you?'

'Why not! But don't complain if it loses!'

'Don't worry. I've already made enough on you today and I was only planning to have a modest bet. What's the horse's name?'

'Skin Flick'

Nicola prayed that she was not blushing but Alec was already changing the subject.

'How do you know Victor then?'

'I don't. I came with Sol.'

'How do you know him?'

'He's my boss. I'm his personal assistant.'

'What line of work is that?'

'He runs a theatrical agency.'

Alec and Nicola continued to talk and took no interest in the next race at all. This was most unusual for Alec who nearly always watched the races in which he did not have a ride, particularly at the bigger meetings. They only parted when Alec said that he had to go get changed for the next race.

When he had gone, Sol joined Nicola.

'You two seemed to be getting on well.'

'He's easy to get on with.'

'He was obviously interested in you. But who wouldn't be?' Nicola changed the subject.

'He's given me a tip for the next race. Would you put £50 on it for me?'

'Sure. What's the name of the horse?'

'Skin Flick.'

'Priceless!' Sol said as he made for the stairs.

Alec found himself thinking about Nicola as he went out to ride but put her out of his mind when he joined Martin Saunders and Skin Flick's owners in the paddock. Alec had ridden for the Saunders stable for over ten years and as retained first jockey for most of them. He knew Martin's horses better than anyone's and that all his novices were well schooled. However, after a couple of easy victories around smaller tracks, Skin Flick was taking a big step up in class. He could see that the owners, a retired doctor and his wife, who had had a number of horses with Martin, were nervous.

'We just hope you both get back in one piece,' Mrs. Robson said.

'He's jumped fine so far,' Alec reassured them. 'We wouldn't be coming here if we didn't think he could handle it. He's got a good chance.'

The public too thought that Skin Flick had a good chance and as Alec went down to the start, he was being quoted as 3 to 1 second favourite of nine, although undoubtedly some of the money had been wagered as a result of the 'Alec factor' particularly in view of what had occurred earlier with House of Cards.

Alec had been right about the pace of the race. Some of the runners took off at what he considered to be a ridiculous pace and he decided to hold up Skin Flick at the rear of the field. As often happens in novice chases, the field had thinned out by the time the runners had negotiated the railway fences down the back straight before turning for home and there were only five runners left standing.

As the field turned into the straight and approached the infamous Pond fence, the race was between three horses, Skin Flick, Sandbank, the favourite, and Jimmy O'Brien's mount, Ratcatcher. They took the fence together and by the time they reached the last fence, they were still virtually neck and neck with all three jockeys riding for all they were worth.

Alec was sufficiently confident with Skin Flick's jumping to go for a big jump at the last. With his heart thumping with exhilaration, he gave his mount a slap and Skin Flick soared over the fence. Sandbank went with him but Ratcatcher, a neck behind, also took off at the same time, a fraction too early. He caught his front legs on the fence and somersaulted over the fence landing on his back. Jimmy was catapulted from the saddle and from the stands it looked as if he was being thrown through the air like a rag doll. Fortunately for him, he went one way and the horse went the other.

Once again, that day, there was a collective gasp from the crowd but then a sigh of relief and a cheer as Jimmy got up and the horse struggled to his feet.

Meanwhile Alec was throwing everything at Skin Flick up the final hill. Johnny Carr, Sandbank's jockey, was putting in no less an effort and they flashed past the winning post with whips flailing, locked together in a tremendous finish.

'Photograph, photograph!' The public address system announced.

Up in the box, Nicola and most of the other occupants had nearly shouted themselves hoarse. The word had gone round that Alec had been confident and they had all put some of their House of

Cards winnings on Skin Flick. Nicola had never seen such a thrilling sporting event. Alec had been right. This race had been far more exciting.

Alec and Johnny, who were both exhausted, touched hands after they had brought their mounts to a halt.

'I think you've got it,' Johnny said.

'I'm not so sure,' Alec replied.

But as he was being lead back to the winner's enclosure, the announcement was made that Skin Flick had won by a short head, the minimum winning distance.

The crowd roared their approval even though the favourite had been beaten and judging by the reaction when Alec reached the enclosure, a lot of people had backed Skin Flick.

The scene was a little more restrained than when House of Cards had won but Dr. and Mrs. Robson were beaming with pleasure as they stepped forward to congratulate Alec and pat their still steaming horse.

12

The first thing Alec did after weighing in was to check how Jimmy was after his fall. In fact, Jimmy had escaped with only a few bruises and had declared himself fit for his remaining ride of the day. Alec found him back in the changing room where they indulged in some light hearted banter about whether Ratcatcher would have got up to beat the other two horses if he had not fallen. They agreed however that the form looked good and that maybe they would all meet again in the Arkle chase, the championship race for two mile novice chasers at the Cheltenham Festival in March.

The second thing he did was to go back up to Victor's box where he was hoping to talk to Nicola again. As he anticipated, he received a warm welcome from the guests who were now celebrating Skin Flick's victory in addition to that of House of Cards. It was a good ten minutes before he could get Nicola on her own. Fortunately, the next race on the card was for amateurs and once again he had a break until the final race of the day.

'Sorry to cut it so fine,' Alec said, 'but at least that was a bit more exciting than the previous race.'

'I thought it was terrific,' Nicola replied. 'I was shouting my head off. But what about the horse that fell? I saw the horse and jockey get up but are they OK?'

'Yes, they're fine. In fact, Jimmy, the jockey who fell, reckons he would have beaten me but for the fall. Fat chance!'

'If I'd been in a fall like that I would never want to get on a horse again.'

'For us it's all in a day's work. Don't worry about Jimmy. He may have a few bruises but his pride is more bruised than his body!'

'Do you often get finishes as close as that?'

'Not as often over jumps as you do on the flat, where the races are shorter and quicker.'

'Do you know in a situation like that whether you've won or not?'

'Not always. The outcome can depend on which horse was nodding its head towards the line at the time. In that race I thought I might just have got there but I couldn't be certain until the announcement was made.'

Alec tried to steer the conversation towards Nicola but she seemed reluctant to talk about her own life and content to question Alec about racing and his way of life.

Nevertheless the conversation flowed and Alec found Nicola to be good as well as attractive company. He was hoping and indeed suspected that she felt the same about him.

After a while, they were interrupted by Robin North.

'Alec, I'm having a bit of a party back at my place this evening for all the staff and some friends. I do hope you'll be able to drop by.'

Alec only lived a few miles from Robin's yard in Upper Lambourn and had no other plans for the evening. Anyway, it would have been rude not to put in an appearance after Robin had pulled off one of the betting coups of the season, if not the last few years.

'I'd be delighted,' he replied. 'What time?'

'Why not call straight in on your way back? From what I hear the yard is already celebrating and the party should be in full swing by the time we get back!'

Robin then turned to Nicola.

'I'd be delighted if you and Sol could also join us, my dear, although I appreciate it's a long way in the other direction for you.'

'Thank you for inviting us,' Nicola replied, 'but Sol and I have to get back to London and I've got an early start in the morning.'

After Robin had moved on Alec asked Nicola what she had meant.

'I'm going on holiday with a friend,' she lied. 'We're hoping to enjoy a bit of sun'.

'Perhaps we could see each other again when you get back.'

Nicola hesitated.

'I don't know…'

'Perhaps I could come up to London and see you after a meeting at one of the nearby tracks?'

'I don't know that that's a good idea.'

Alec noticed a distinct cooling in Nicola's attitude towards him. Previously she had been animated and obviously enjoying herself. She had certainly not been flirting but Alec had had enough experience with women to know that she was interested in him. Why the sudden change?

'Why not? I don't mean to pry but if there's someone else, I'll withdraw gracefully.'

'No, no. It's nothing like that and it's not as if I don't like you, it's just…'

'What?'

'I don't know. I just can't explain. It's been really great to meet you and I will certainly make a point of following your results but I don't really want to start seeing someone at the present time and I have this feeling that if I see you once, that won't be the last time.'

'Bad experience?'

'Yes, something like that. I hope you understand.'

Alec understood that she was interested in him. She had

virtually admitted it. She obviously had some hang up but he did not give up that easily.

'At least give me your phone number. I promise I won't pester you. In fact, I won't phone you for a month or so. You may feel differently then.'

Nicola smiled.

'You're persistent, I'll give you that. But no, I won't change my mind. Anyway, from what I've heard about you this afternoon, you won't lack for female company.'

By this time, Alec had to depart for the final race and felt he should say goodbye to Victor and the other guests. Victor and some of the others said that they were going on afterwards to Robin's house so he would see them later. They all wanted to know what Alec thought of his chances in the final race, a novices handicap hurdle.

'No more than an each way chance I'm afraid,' he replied.

With that he had to dash off. He glanced over one last time at Nicola but she avoided eye contact with him.

Once again Alec found himself thinking about Nicola as he changed into his colours for the last race only this time the excitement that he had felt previously had been replaced with a feeling of disappointment. He was not used to rejection but what bothered him more was the prospect of not seeing her again.

He had been right to be cautious about his chances in the last. His mount had been up with the leaders turning into the straight but then faded to finish in fourth place. However, that was not the reason that he felt rather flat as he changed after the race despite his earlier successes.

Soon after the last race, Nicola and Sol said their goodbyes and returned to Sol's car for the journey back to central London. Sol was in high spirits having made a tidy profit on the afternoon but he noticed that Nicola was fairly quiet. He had noticed that she had been that way since Alec had left the box to go and ride in the last race.

'You and Alec Hammond seemed to be getting on pretty well,' he commented.

'He was more interesting than the rest of them,' Nicola replied.

'So why the long face?'

'What do you mean? I'm fine.'

'Come on, you seemed to be really enjoying yourself until the last race.'

'So?'

'You then went all quiet and couldn't wait to leave.'

'Was it that obvious?'

'It was to me.'

'Look, it's nothing. I don't really want to talk about it, OK?'

'If you say so.'

Sol let the subject drop for a while but then asked, 'Did Alec Hammond ask you out then?'

'What if he did?'

'No reason. I'm just making conversation.'

Nicola did not reply.

'Well, did he?' Sol persevered.

'I can't see it's any business of yours but as a matter of fact he did. Is that good enough for you?'

'Frankly, I would have been surprised if he hadn't.'

Nicola made no further comment.

'Did you accept then?' Sol continued.

'No, I didn't.'

'Why not?'

'That's none of your business, Sol. Just because he was good company does not mean I have to start going out with him.'

'I agree. But that doesn't answer the question.'

'And I've told you, it's none of your business.'

Sol shrugged.

'OK. But you seemed a good match to me. Particularly as you got on well and so obviously fancied each other.'

Nicola looked across at Sol in the driving seat.

'Yes. But there's one thing you're forgetting, Sol. One fairly important ingredient that's necessary for a relationship – honesty. He thinks I'm your personal assistant and that I'm going on holiday with a friend tomorrow. Just about everything I told him about myself was a lie. What sort of basis do you think that is to start a relationship? Or do you think I should tell him the truth and see whether he's still interested?'

'He might be.'

'What? In sex? Like virtually every other man I've met. You saw him today. He's a hero. Everybody loves him. He couldn't possibly afford to get involved with someone like me. He may have a reputation as a bit of a lad with women but he's still the 'housewives' choice' when it comes to the Grand National!'

'OK. Don't tell him, but what's the harm in lying about your job? When was the last time you had anything approaching a normal relationship? You deserve a bit of fun.'

'And what if he found out?'

'Why should he?'

'Someone could easily recognize me.'

'I don't think that's very likely. Only the most ardent fans would have any chance of recognizing you off screen. Anyway, you usually wear dark glasses in public and less flamboyant clothes and make up.'

'You've seen my films?' Nicola felt disappointed, and ashamed.

'Only a couple. I have to know about my clients' work. It's part of the job.'

'I suppose so. Anyway it would be too risky.'

She and Sol then lapsed into silence for the rest of the journey. Sol thought about asking Nicola about her trip the following day but wisely guessed that she would not be particularly keen to talk about it.

On arriving back at her flat, Nicola had something to eat and then packed her bag for the next day. Usually, she looked forward to working in glamorous locations as a welcome change to some claustrophobic studio but on this occasion she had no desire to go anywhere. She tried to watch some television but found it difficult to concentrate. Her thoughts kept straying to her afternoon at Sandown and how for once, she had really been able to enjoy herself, even if only for a brief period. But now the after effects of the champagne she had drunk, her encounter with Alec and the conversation in the car with Sol had all combined to make her feel very down. She decided to go to bed early but it was a long time before she eventually cried herself to sleep.

13

On the way back from Sandown, Alec tried to persuade Jimmy to accompany him to Robin's impromptu party.

'I'm sure they'd be delighted to see you,' he said. 'After all you've ridden winners for both Robin and Victor.'

'No thanks. I think I'll give it a miss. I'd feel a bit out of it with everyone else celebrating how much money they've won. You go on alone. You're the hero of the hour!'

'To be honest, anyone could have won on House of Cards. All I did was to nearly cock it up when I got myself blocked by Duggan! I couldn't believe how much I had in hand!'

'Shaw and the North stable must have won an absolute fortune!'

'I think they did. There was a lot of celebrating going on up in Shaw's box.'

'Has Shaw shown his appreciation yet?'

'He said he would be thanking me 'in more tangible form' in due course when they dished out the trophies.'

'I'm sure he will. I told you earlier that he can be pretty generous. So what was it like up in the box?'

'It would have been fairly tedious but for this absolutely stunning woman.'

'What was she doing there?'

'She'd come with some friend of Victor's but they weren't

together if you see what I mean. She worked for him. He was some sort of show business agent.'

'He could still have been shagging her.'

'I hardly think so. I think she had more class than that! She didn't strike me as the type to sleep with her boss. She's got more taste.'

'What? You mean she fancied *you*?'

'Well, I thought she did but when I asked her out, she said no. She wouldn't even give me her telephone number.'

Jimmy was highly amused.

'What, you mean Alec Hammond struck out for once?'

'It's not funny, Jimmy. I really liked her.'

'She's probably got someone else. Someone like that is bound to have a boyfriend.'

'No. I asked her about that.'

'So she lied.'

'Why lie about something like that? It would have been the simplest way out for her just to tell the truth. I don't think she was lying to me. I think there was something else, some sort of bad experience or something.'

'Maybe she was a lesbian!'

'Hardly! Lesbians don't look like that – except maybe in blue films! Anyway, I'm sure she fancied me.'

'Yeah, yeah, Alec, I'm sure she did. There must be another explanation for her refusing to go out with you and to give you her phone number! Perhaps she prefers short divorced Irishmen!'

'Oh yes! That must be it. She must have seen you in the paddock and realized I was only second best!'

'There you are then!'

'As a matter of fact, she did inquire about your health after your rather spectacular fall but only because she felt sorry for you!'

'Don't knock it! I've had a lot of success with women because they feel sorry for me!'

After dropping Jimmy off at his home, Alec called in at his own home to change and to check his messages on the answerphone before going on to the party. There were one or two calls that he had to make about riding arrangements the following week and by the time he reached Robin's home, it was nearly eight o'clock.

By that time, the party was in full swing and a number of people, particularly the stable staff who appeared to have been drinking since House of Cards' victory, were already distinctly merry.

Robin lived in a large old house attached to the yard which he had inherited from his father. The place seemed to be heaving with guests. Apart from the stable staff and their various spouses, partners and friends, Alec recognized a number of other members of Lambourn's racing community. From the way they were celebrating, it appeared that the stable secret about House of Cards had leaked before the odds had fallen too dramatically and a large number of people had good reason to be celebrating.

The usual mode of entry to Robin's house was through the large kitchen at the back and as soon as Alec had entered, a cheer had gone up and a number of people started slapping him on the back. Someone thrust a glass of champagne in his hand and someone else proposed a toast first to House of Cards and then to Alec.

Alec remained in the kitchen for about twenty minutes not only because there were so many people who wanted to speak to him but also because it was so packed that he would have had difficulty progressing to another room.

He then heard his name being shouted from the door and looked over to see Victor struggling through with a crate of booze. Alec pushed his way over and Victor ushered him outside.

'I've just been down to the pub to get some more supplies,' he said, 'give me a hand to unload it, will you? I suspect that you and I are probably the only two here who are still sober. Anyway, I wanted the chance to talk to you on your own'.

Victor led Alec over to his Bentley. The boot was open and contained a number of crates and boxes. Alec thought it rather incongruous that this wealthy businessman and the stable's principal owner should be fetching the drinks like this. Victor must have read Alec's thoughts.

'I can't remember the last time I actually went out and bought booze for myself,' he said, 'but it was clear that Robin hadn't got enough in.'

'You could have got one of the staff to get it,' Alec replied.

'None of them are in a fit state to drive. I only had a couple of glasses of champagne at the course as I was driving. Besides, maybe I'm feeling a bit guilty.'

'Why's that?'

'Between you and me, I had planned to remove my horses from the yard if House of Cards didn't win today. If that had happened, some of the staff may have lost their jobs.'

'That's a bit drastic isn't it? Taking the horses away because of one race even if you had lost a lot of money.'

'It's not the money. I haven't been happy with the situation for some time. Apart from the fact that the horses haven't been running well, there's another…er complication which has developed.'

'And House of Cards' victory resolves that?'

'No. Not at all. But I can hardly take the horses away now, can I? I'll just have to deal with the other complication.'

'Anything I can help with?'

Victor laughed at this.

'Actually, you probably could! But after today, I could hardly pass the problem on to you!'

Before they removed the drink from the boot, Victor opened the passenger door and removed a bulky looking brown envelope from the glove compartment.

'Alec, here's the 'more tangible thank you' I was talking about this afternoon. Lock it away in your car before we go back inside.'

Alec thanked Victor and did as he said. Jimmy had been right. Victor was a generous owner in victory. Alec later found that there were ten thousand pounds in the envelope. He also heard that there had been a thousand pounds for the conditional jockey who had ridden House of Cards at Market Rasen in his previous race, managing to avoid being placed.

After helping with the drink, Alec decided to circulate and managed to negotiate a passage out of the kitchen to the rooms beyond. The rooms downstairs were nearly all full of people, most of whom Alec knew and even those he did not know all seemed to know *him* and want to chat with him.

Alec stopped to talk for a few minutes to another local trainer and as he was about to move on he heard a low husky voice behind him.

'Ah, Alec, there you are. I've been looking for you.'

Alec turned round to face Caroline North who had a mischievous grin on her face and was obviously more than a little tipsy. Alec saw that she had changed out of the outfit that she had been wearing at the races into a short low cut leopard print dress. She was teetering in white high heeled shoes and clutching a glass of champagne in one hand, she put out her other hand and took hold of the lapel of Alec's jacket to steady herself.

'Hello, Caroline. What can I do for you?' Alec replied.

'Do you really want me to tell you? In front of all these people?' she giggled.

Alec found himself gradually backing away and at the same

time looking around to see if anyone was watching them. Fortunately, no one appeared to be paying them any attention and the noise level was such that no one was likely to be listening.

'What's the matter, Alec?' Caroline continued. 'You're not shy are you? Come on, I've seen the way you've looked at me.'

The truth was that Alec did find Caroline attractive in a rather brash and brassy way. The two of them had often flirted with each other and Caroline had on more than one occasion hinted at her availability. Alec had been momentarily tempted but he was not so stupid as to embark on an affair with the wife of one of his principal trainers. Many a jockey's career had nosedived after being caught having an affair with his trainer's wife. Quite apart from that, he had heard rumours that she had spread her favours to a number of people in the racing world and was to put it bluntly 'bad news'.

'A man can look at an attractive woman, can't he?' Alec said, trying to make light of the situation. 'No harm in a bit of window shopping, is there? But that's as far as it goes if the goods are not for sale.'

'Wouldn't you like to handle the merchandise, though? Just to see what you're missing?'

'I don't think that would be a good idea.'

Caroline appeared not to hear Alec above the noise and signalled that he should repeat himself by indicating one of her ears. However, as he bent down towards her, she suddenly put her arm around his neck, pulled him further down and kissed him. Alec immediately jerked backwards and Caroline giggled.

'Relax, Alec. No one's looking and even if they are, what's wrong with the wife of a trainer who's just pulled off a massive betting coup giving the jockey a thank you kiss at the celebration party?'

Alec had to admit that this made sense and wondered whether

he was being a bit uptight about the situation. After all, he appeared to be just about the only person present not under the influence of alcohol. Maybe, she was doing no more than tease him.

'I'm sorry,' he said. 'I think I've got a bit of catching up to do so far as the booze is concerned!'

'Well we can soon remedy that.' She reached out and took a half full bottle down from the mantelpiece and then topped up her own and Alec's glass.

'Cheers,' she said and clinked glasses with Alec.

By this time, the room seemed to have become even fuller, causing Alec to be pushed closer to Caroline than he thought wise. It was also difficult to hear what she was saying. Thus, when she suggested moving to another room where it was less crowded, he was happy to agree.

She led him across the room out into the hall. There were a number of people in the hall but it was not nearly as crowded and Alec would have been content to remain there. However, Caroline walked straight across the hall to a door on the other side and Alec had little option but to follow her. He was in two minds as to what he should do. His head was telling him to bring someone else into their conversation and then discreetly withdraw but he had to admit that another part of his anatomy was not being so sensible.

Caroline opened the door and led Alec through it. He saw that they were in a snooker room but what was of immediate concern to him was the fact that there was no one else in the room.

'There's no one else here,' Alec remarked.

'Well spotted, Einstein!' Caroline replied, 'Robin wouldn't let guests use this room as someone might spill drink on his precious snooker table.'

Alec stood by the table with his heart thumping. He was uncertain whether this was nerves, anticipation or a combination of both. He knew that he should leave the room immediately. Unbeknown to him, he was experiencing similar feelings to those experienced by Charlotte at his house a few days earlier.

Unfortunately, just like Charlotte, he did not leave the room.

'Why have you brought us in here?' he asked.

Caroline turned to face him.

'I've got something I want to show you,' she replied.

However, unbeknown to both Alec and Caroline, Robin and Victor had also taken the opportunity to escape from the other guests.

Having been on the verge of removing his horses from Robin, Victor had had a complete change of heart following House of Cards' victory and had instead decided to increase his string. He and Robin had been discussing these plans in Robin's study. Victor had told a delighted Robin that he wanted him to start looking for another three horses. He also said that he wanted Alec to ride his horses when available. Robin had no problem with that and the two of them were just toasting their new plans as Alec and Caroline had entered the snooker room.

The study led off from the snooker room at the opposite end from where Alec and Caroline had come in.

Had Caroline not drunk so much and not been so intent on getting Alec where she wanted him, she might have wondered why the lights were already on in the snooker room. She might also have noticed that the door at the other end of the room leading into the study was ajar. As it was, she had only one thing on her mind.

'What is it?' Alec said.

'This.' And with that Caroline hoisted her dress up until it was round her waist, revealing that she wasn't wearing any knickers. Before Alec could say anything or react, she placed one hand on his chest and pushed him back against the snooker table thrusting one of her legs between his thighs. Alec was completely taken by surprise and ended up on his back on the table whereupon Caroline climbed up and sat astride him as she started unbuckling his belt.

Whatever temptation Alec may have had earlier, Alec was not prepared to be effectively raped on the snooker table with a party going on next door.

'Stop it, Caroline,' he gasped. 'This is madness.'

'Don't be such a wimp!' Caroline retorted. 'You ride my husband's horses, well now it's my turn to ride you!'

At that, Alec put his hands on her knees and pushed her as hard as he could. She fell over backwards and landed in an ungainly heap on the floor. Alec struggled to his feet and then nearly died of shock when he saw Robin standing at the other end of the room with a look of complete horror on his face and Victor standing behind him, looking slightly amused.

Robin and Victor were standing at the other end of the room by the now fully open door to the study staring at the scene before them. For a moment there was silence but Caroline was the first to react. As she lay on the ground, she saw the expression on Alec's face as he looked beyond her towards the other end of the room. She turned her head to the left and saw her husband surveying the scene whereupon she jumped to her feet pulling her dress back into position as she did so.

'Thank God you're here, darling,' she said to Robin in a tone full of anxiety. 'Alec persuaded me to show him the snooker room and as soon as we got in here he made a grab at me. I tried to push him off but he wouldn't take no for an answer. He must have had too much to drink.'

Alec could hardly believe what he was hearing. He had thought that the situation could not get any worse but now he found himself accused of indecent assault.

'That's not true, Robin,' he said 'I'm completely sober. It was Caroline who brought me in here and then tried to make a pass at me. I had to push her off. That's how she ended up on the floor.'

Even as he said it, Alec realized that the chances of Robin believing him rather than his wife with whom he was well known to be besotted were slim. Caroline had obviously had the same thought.

'That's ridiculous!' she scoffed. 'You're not going to accept his word against mine are you? Everyone knows his reputation with women. He thinks he can have anyone. Do you seriously think I'd be interested in a jockey?'

However, confident though Caroline sounded, she was beginning to have some doubts as to the position. She could not understand why Robin continued to stand there seemingly frozen to the spot with a fixed expression on his face. He seemed uncertain how to react, not just through shock but as if he was weighing up whom to believe.

The truth was that Robin desperately wanted to believe his wife but could not reconcile that with what he had seen with his own eyes. In fact, he and Victor had heard the whole exchange between Alec and Caroline and when they had walked through the door they had been confronted with the sight of Caroline's bottom as she had sat astride Alec on the snooker table. He knew that she was the one who had been making the running and that it was Alec who had pushed her off. He just didn't want to believe it.

Caroline eventually forced him to react.

'Well what are you going to do about it? I've been attacked in my own home!' she shouted,

'Aren't you going to throw him out?'

'Be quiet, Caroline. I suggest you go upstairs and sober up.

81

We'll talk about this later. I'm afraid I saw exactly what went on,' Robin replied.

'As for you, Alec, it's clear that my wife has had far too much to drink but I cannot believe that she would have acted in the way she did unless you led her on. She must have got carried away by the excitement of today's events and you must have taken advantage of her and caused her to behave entirely out of character. I'd therefore be grateful if you'd leave my house. In the circumstances it would not be appropriate for you to ride any more of my horses.'

At this, Victor decided to intervene for the first time.

'Now wait a minute, Robin. You saw and heard what I saw. On what basis do you say Alec led Caroline on?'

'Victor, I'll thank you to keep out of this,' Robin replied. 'This is a matter that doesn't concern you.'

'I think it does. What have we just been discussing? I've agreed to send you more horses and you agreed to put Alec up whenever he was available.'

'You can hardly expect me to use Alec now.'

'What, because you're clutching at straws to find a way to blame someone else for your wife's behaviour? I might have had some sympathy if Alec had betrayed you but he hasn't.'

'How do you know?'

'Open your eyes, man. There's only one person betraying you.'

'Hah!' Caroline interjected. 'That's rich coming from you!'

'What do you mean by that?' Robin said, looking at Caroline and then at Victor.

For a moment there was silence. Then Victor spoke.

'I'm afraid she's right. I've been uncomfortable about the situation for some time and have been meaning to do something about it. Perhaps that time has come. I should tell you, Robin, that had House of Cards not won today, I was planning to remove my horses from the stable. I would have justified the decision on the basis that things haven't been going too well recently but the main reason would have been to resolve an unfortunate situation which has developed.'

'What 'unfortunate situation'?' Robin said. 'What on earth are you talking about?'

'Don't listen to him, Robin….'

'Shut up, Caroline. It's time your husband found out what a slut you are.'

'You bastard…'

'What are you saying, Victor?' Robin pressed him.

'I was wrong when I said Caroline was the only one betraying you here but I'm afraid the other person is not Alec but me.'

'You mean…'

'Yes. Caroline and I have been having an affair for some weeks; although 'affair' probably dignifies the relationship too much. The truth is we've been meeting purely for sex.'

Alec could hardly believe what was unfolding in front of him, although he now knew what Victor had been referring to earlier. He felt desperately sorry for Robin who looked as if his world had come to an end.

'I'll quite understand if you want me to remove my horses,' Victor continued.

Caroline made one last ditch effort to save herself.

'I only did it for you, darling. Victor was going to take his horses away if I didn't. I knew the yard couldn't stand that.'

'So how do you explain all the other lovers, then?' Victor asked. 'I'm sorry, Robin, but the fact is she's been sleeping around since you got married and as usual the husband is the last to know.'

At that moment Caroline knew she had lost.

'Who can blame me for looking for a real man when I've had to put up with likes of you two?' She snarled defiantly. 'You're both as pathetic as each other…'

Her outburst was interrupted by a resounding smack and Caroline ended up on the floor again in a similar position to where she had been after Alec had pushed her off.

This time, Robin, whose blow had put her there, sounded cold and determined as if any former doubts had been firmly put aside.

'Go upstairs and pack your bags. I want you out of this house tonight and I don't want to see you here again.'

Caroline scrambled to her feet and with her head spinning from shock as well as the force of the blow staggered to the door and left the room.

After she had gone, Robin slumped into a chair set back from the snooker table and put his head in his hands. Victor went back into the study and came back with a glass of brandy which he handed to Robin. Alec wondered whether he should stay or go. Victor was obviously thinking the same thing.

'Would you prefer us to go?' he asked Robin.

Robin did not appear to hear.

'I've been a complete fool, haven't I?' he said. 'But after my first wife she was like a breath of fresh air. I guess I always knew it was too good to be true.'

Victor and Alec looked at each other.

'Robin, you may want time to think, but we need to talk about what we were discussing earlier,' Victor said.

Robin looked up at him.

'Why? Are you changing your mind?'

'No, not at all. I thought you might want to now.'

'Why should I? I've got nothing left but the yard now. I should be grateful to you for opening my eyes to what a fool I've been.'

Robin then looked across at Alec.

'Alec. I owe you an apology. Victor was right. I'd seen exactly what had happened. I was wrong to accuse you of leading her on.'

'Don't worry about it,' Alec replied. 'I'm sorry how things

have turned out after such a good day. Perhaps it would be better if I left now but I can assure you that no one will hear about what happened in here from me.'

'Thank you, but there's no need for you to leave. You're welcome to stay and have another drink. You probably need one almost as much as me!'

Alec smiled and walked to the door. As he reached it, Robin said 'Oh, Alec. There's one more thing before you go. Are you OK to ride House of Cards again next week before the handicapper gets hold of him?'

'My pleasure!' Alec replied as he left the room.

Alec was relieved to leave the room and it seemed strange to be back in the crowded rooms where the guests were all enjoying themselves completely oblivious to what had transpired between their hosts. No doubt the racing rumour mill would soon be working overtime but no one was going to hear a thing from Alec.

Alec decided that he was no longer in the party mood. It had been a long and eventful day and although it was still quite early he made his way through the throng towards the kitchen door. Just as he was about to leave, he heard a familiar voice behind him.

'Hey, Alec. Don't tell me you're sneaking off already!'

He turned round and smiled when he saw Charlotte.

'What are you doing here?' he asked.

'Celebrating like everyone else. News of a party travels fast. So where have you been hiding yourself then?'

'Er… I've just been discussing future plans with Robin and Victor. Victor's thinking of increasing his string.'

'And now you're going?'

'Well, it's been a long day. I thought I'd get away from the noise. Everyone else is drinking and I've still got to drive.'

'Me too. But it's too early to go to bed. Why don't I follow you back to your place and we could watch a film…or something?'

Alec thought about the day he had had, House of Cards, Skin Flick, the time he'd spent with Nicola, her refusal to see him again and what had just gone on in the snooker room. He looked at Charlotte's smiling face and the invitation in her eyes. He really could do with a quiet night in alone.

'Why not?' he said 'but who said it's too early to go to bed!'

14

Pat Duggan was still feeling very pleased with himself when he arrived back at his cottage in Somerset after Fontwell races on the following Monday. Not only had he ridden a treble but in two races he had had the satisfaction of getting the better of Alec Hammond in tight finishes. That had made up to some extent for Hammond beating him on House of Cards at Sandown on Saturday.

He went into the kitchen and was in the process of checking the messages on his answerphone when he heard a car pull up on the gravel at the front of the house. Pat lived alone in a fairly isolated position in a village not far from his main retaining stable. He did not have many friends and casual, uninvited visitors were rare. He looked out of the window and saw a large silver Mercedes. He could see that there were three occupants but it was not until Frank Morris got out of the front passenger seat that he realized who they were. His good humour disappeared immediately.

Frank Morris had known that Pat Duggan was riding at Fontwell that day and had decided to approach him with his 'proposition' when he got home. He had been waiting at the side of the road for about half an hour waiting for Duggan's BMW to pass by as he had wanted to make sure that Duggan was alone. Morris certainly did not want anyone to see them together and did not know how far he would have to go to persuade Duggan to co-operate with him.

Morris was accompanied by two 'employees', Dave Marsh and Chris Higson, who were both pleased that Morris was reverting to what they viewed as 'the good old days' when their intimidatory skills had been put to good use. In recent years, in between spells in prison, their only decent work for Morris had been in talking to losing punters who had been showing a reluctance to pay up. This sort of thing was far more fun.

'Dave, you come with me,' Morris said. 'You can stay in the car, Chris. I don't think I'll need both of you for this.'

Pat was horrified when he saw Morris get out of the car accompanied by an even larger man who got out of the rear. He recognized Dave Marsh from years ago and he did not seem to have changed at all, tall, broad, with a face like a boxer who had had too many fights and dressed in a long black leather coat. Pat assumed that they had come about his failure to prevent House of Cards winning. Hadn't they seen the race? Surely they must have realized that there was nothing else he could have done?

He heard the bell ring, shortly followed by loud knocking. He decided not to answer. Maybe they would go away. But he then heard Morris shouting through the letter box.

'Come on, Duggan, open this fucking door. I know you're in there. Do you think we're stupid? Apart from the fact your car's here, we saw you arrive.'

After a short pause, Morris continued.

'If you don't open this door now, we're going to kick it in. We haven't come about House of Cards if that's what you're worried about. I know you did your best. There's something else I want to talk about.'

Realizing he had little choice and hopeful that they had not come to give him a beating, Duggan went out into the hall and opened the door. Morris and Marsh immediately pushed past him and found their way to the sitting room at the rear of the cottage.

Not the largest of jump jockeys, Duggan was completely dwarfed by his visitors but now that they were in, he did his best not to appear intimidated.

'What the hell do you want, Morris, barging in here like this?'

Morris smiled. A large bull of a man, he stood there in his brown cashmere coat and looked around.

'Relax, Pat. That's no way to greet your old business partner. Do you mind if we sit down?'

'As if I have a choice,' Duggan replied, gesturing towards the chairs. 'What's this all about?'

Morris sat down but Marsh went over to the windows and remained standing, leaning against the window ledge. Duggan sat down facing Morris but felt distinctly uncomfortable about Marsh being behind him.

'As I said, you've nothing to worry about,' Morris said 'But I've got a proposition for you.'

'What sort of proposition?' Duggan asked suspiciously.

'I want to resurrect our previous relationship.'

'You've got to be joking. I finished with that sort of thing years ago.'

'You were prepared to take my money to stop House of Cards.'

'That was different. Trying to block another horse if the opportunity arises is not the same as stopping your own horse. There's no way I'm getting involved in that again. Do you realize who I am? I'm the champion jockey for christsake. I don't need your money and I don't need the risk involved! Anyway I thought you'd moved on as well, running a respectable business.'

'So I did but I'll level with you, Pat. Things haven't been going so well recently and House of Cards was the final straw.

I need an edge and I need it now. Nothing permanent. Just for a few months.'

'House of Cards wasn't my fault.'

'I know. It was that cheating bastard Robin North, who must have engineered a ridiculous weight for the horse somehow. But the fact is, I need your help and I'll make it worth your while. I'm not talking about anything regular. Just the knowledge that in certain races, ones with a big ante post market, a particular horse won't be winning. No more than two or three horses a month. They may not have won anyway so it's hardly likely to dent your championship prospects.'

'I'm not interested. Get someone else.'

'There is no one else and you fit the bill perfectly riding so many high profile horses.'

'Tough. I'm not doing it.'

Until then, Morris had seemed almost affable but realizing Duggan was going to be difficult, his expression and his tone changed.

'This isn't a matter for negotiation, Duggan. One way or another you're doing it.'

'Yeah. Well give me one good reason why I shouldn't report this approach to the Jockey Club as soon as you leave.'

Morris reached into his pocket and produced a hand held dictating machine. He switched it on and put it on the coffee table in front of him. He then sat back to listen to a recording of the telephone conversation in which he had offered Duggan £5000 to stop House of Cards winning. Duggan's voice was heard clarifying that he would get the money providing the horse lost even if he did not have to do anything.

Duggan went cold. It wouldn't have been so bad if he had not actually done anything but he had made a blatant attempt to stop House of Cards seen by everyone at the course not to mention millions on TV. At the time, he was given the benefit of the doubt as to whether he had been entitled to shut the door on Hammond but he realized that this could finish him.

'This is not the only tape I have of you,' Morris said. 'I have numerous taped conversations of you agreeing to stop horses in the old days. I like to have an insurance policy. You never know when it might come in handy. There's more than enough to get you warned off for life, not to mention prosecuted.'

'But you can't use the tapes without implicating yourself.'

'True. But I'm finished anyway unless I do something pretty drastic so you see I've got nothing to lose. You've got everything to lose. You've got no woman, no friends. All you've got is racing and the respect it brings you. Take that away and you're nothing.'

'I still don't believe you'd expose yourself.'

'Maybe I wouldn't need to. Maybe the tapes will remain as a bit of extra insurance.'

'What do you mean by that?'

'Let me make it simple for you. You have a choice. Either you agree to help me, in which case all you have to do is to make sure the occasional horse does not win for which you will be well rewarded. Or you refuse, in which case your career is over anyway.'

Duggan felt beads of sweat around his head as Morris signalled Marsh to step forward. Marsh then opened his coat to reveal a battered looking baseball bat.

'You must remember what happened to Sammy Morgan?' Morris continued. 'Well, if I'm not mistaken, this is the very bat that was used on him. Isn't that right, Dave?'

'Certainly is, boss,' Marsh replied, and with that he brought the bat down with all his strength on Duggan's television, shattering plastic and glass together.

By this time, Duggan was quivering with fear. He was well aware of what had happened to Sammy Morgan. He had been found in his home with his legs smashed to pieces. He had been too frightened to say what had happened to him and had never ridden again. There were all sorts of rumours but Duggan knew that Morgan had tried to stop working for Morris and had refused to stop a horse.

Morris stood up and both he and Marsh looked down at Duggan cowering in the chair beneath them.

'I'm sorry we had to get to this, Pat, but what's it going to be? Are you going to help me or not?'

'OK, OK,' Duggan stammered, 'You've made your point. I'll do what I can.'

Morris leaned over him.

'You'll do exactly what I tell you. And if you change your mind or double cross me in any way at all, I won't just break your legs, I'll kill you. Do you understand?'

Duggan nodded quickly. Morris and Marsh stared down at him for a moment longer as if assessing whether he meant it. They then turned round and left the house slamming the door on their way out.

15

Despite Charlotte's nubile and available charms, Alec found himself thinking about Nicola a lot over the next few days. There had certainly been a mutual attraction between them. Of that, Alec was in no doubt and he could not recall any woman making such an impression on him at their first meeting. He had also believed her when she had said that there was no one else in the background. Why then the absolute refusal to allow Alec not only to see her again but even to have her number?

There were only two people that Alec trusted enough to discuss his problems. One was Jimmy and the other was Martin Saunders. This was definitely not a problem to be discussed with Jimmy as the nature of their relationship was such that problems with the opposite sex were never treated seriously. Alec therefore decided to raise the matter with Martin.

Alec had ridden for Martin's stable since he was twenty-one and two years later had become stable jockey after the previous incumbent had retired. A year later, Alec had won his first championship and Martin had become champion trainer for the third time in his career.

Everything seemed to be going well for them professionally but tragedy was to strike both of them within the next year.

First, Alec's parents were killed in a car crash and then six months later Martin's wife died of cancer at the age of forty-two.

Alec was living in Martin's house at the time and had helped Martin cope with the running of the stable following his loss. Even though he had moved out to his own property about five minutes drive away two years later, Alec still regarded the stable as home and would turn up for breakfast whenever he could, even if he was not due to ride out. He was also a regular visitor at the end of the day when he and Martin would sit down and talk over the day's events and the horses in the stable.

Alec raised the subject of Nicola on Thursday evening after they had arrived back from Uttoxeter where they had shared a winner. They were sitting in Martin's study at the time sipping whiskies.

Martin could not help smiling. He had been on at Alec for some time about settling down. He was aware of Alec's relationship with Charlotte as nothing much escaped his attention. He had warned Alec that her father would go mad if he found out. Alec had assured him that they were only having fun and that there was no question of her getting hitched to a reprobate jump jockey rather than one of the chinless wonders her father had in mind. Alec had amused Martin by saying that he was doing the family a favour by giving Charlotte a chance to sow her wild oats.

Now, here was Alec apparently smitten by some unknown beauty who had turned him down.

'Are you sure it's not just a case of her not fancying you?' he asked. 'You can't expect every woman to fall for the Hammond charms.'

'Honestly, Martin, I know when a woman fancies me and when she doesn't. Nicola was definitely giving me the green light.'

'Maybe she was just flirting.'

'No way. In fact, she wasn't flirting at all. She was far too classy for that.'

'Well, if she'd just had a bad experience in a previous relationship, maybe she just wasn't interested in seeing anyone whether she fancied them or not. Perhaps if you wait a while, she might be more receptive.'

'But how do I get in touch with her again?'

'I'm sure you'll find a way if you're really determined!'

'Yes…Actually, I've got an idea.'

On Saturday, Alec went to Chepstow where he had a number of rides including House of Cards in the three mile handicap hurdle. After his easy victory at Sandown, it was inevitable that he would be re-handicapped for future races and it was likely that he would be raised about a stone and a half. However, because the weights had already been set for the Chepstow race, House of Cards only had to carry a seven pound penalty for his victory and it made sense to run him again before the handicapper could bring him up to a more appropriate weight.

However, there was no betting coup on this occasion as House of Cards started at the prohibitive odds of 9 to 4 on. Neither Victor nor Robin bet at those odds and they had to be content with the prize money which House of Cards collected with the minimum of fuss.

After the race, Alec asked Victor if he could have a word in private with him. They arranged to meet in the owners bar after the next race when Alec had a gap between rides.

Alec found Victor at a table in the bar and was relieved to find him alone.

After chatting about Victor's horses for a few minutes, Victor asked what he could do for him.

'Well, I was wondering if you could help me get into contact with one of the guests in your box at Sandown last week?'

'You mean the lovely Nicola?'

'Well, yes.'

'I thought you two seemed to be getting on well and I can't think that any of my other guests would be of any interest to you. You should have asked for her number at the time.'

'I did. But she wouldn't give it to me.'

'That does surprise me. Everyone was commenting on how well you were getting on. Why do you think we left you on your own without interruption?'

'I thought we were getting on too. But she said she didn't think it would be a good idea if we saw each other again despite the fact that according to her there is no one else in her life.'

'But you won't take no for an answer?'

'Well, I don't intend to hassle her or anything like that. I thought I might leave it for a bit and then give her a ring.'

'I wouldn't leave it too long if I were you or she'll be snapped up by someone else!'

'No. But can you help?'

'I can't give you her number because as you know she came with one of my guests. But I can give you Sol's number. He should be able to help you providing he hasn't got designs on her himself! Although, that didn't appear to be the case as he was giving you as much room as everyone else.'

'That would be really great.'

'I tell you what. I haven't got Sol's number with me now but if you give me your number I'll ring you later and if you're not there I'll text you or leave a message with his number.'

Victor was as good as his word and phoned Alec with Sol's number later that evening. Alec felt a little guilty as he had to lean across Charlotte to take the call.

16

Alec knew that Nicola was due to be away for a fortnight and decided to leave it for another week before attempting to get into contact with her.

Thus, just over a week after Victor had given him the number, Alec dialed it about an hour before he was due to set off for Taunton races. Sol's receptionist answered the call.

'Miller Enterprises. Can I help you?'

'Yes,' Alec replied. 'Can you put me through to Nicola James, please?'

'I'm sorry. There's no one here of that name. Are you sure you've got the right number?'

Alec read out the number he had dialed and the receptionist confirmed that that was the number of Miller Enterprises but that no one of that name worked there.

'I see', Alec continued. 'Are Miller Enterprises some sort of agency for the entertainment business?'

'That's correct.'

'Well, do you have an employee by the name of Sol? I'm afraid I can't recall his last name.'

The receptionist chuckled.

'We have a Mr. Sol Miller but I would hardly describe him as an employee. He owns the business.'

'Oh, I'm sorry. But that is the gentleman I had in mind. Would it be possible to have a word with him?'

'May I ask what about?'

'Er, it's a private matter.'

'I'll see if he's available. Who shall I say is calling?'

'Alec Hammond. We met at Sandown races about three weeks ago.'

'I'll see if he's available.'

After a gap of about thirty seconds, the receptionist came back on the line.

'I'm putting you through now.'

Moments later, a male voice came on the line.

'Hello. Sol Miller here.'

'Hello, Mr. Miller. It's Alec Hammond here. We met at Sandown races.'

'Yes, of course. I'm hardly likely to forget you, Alec. What a day that was! I won a packet on your horses. To what do I owe this pleasure? You're not phoning me to give me another tip are you?'

'I'm afraid not. Actually, I was trying to get into contact with Nicola but your receptionist says she doesn't know her. That's why I asked to be put through to you.'

For a moment, Sol was puzzled, but then the penny dropped.

'Well, she doesn't. Nicola doesn't...What I mean is that the receptionist you spoke to is a temp and doesn't know Nicola. Nicola isn't here today so they won't have met.'

'I see. Can you tell me when Nicola will be back, then?'

'Um...I can't say for certain. Probably not today.'

'Perhaps I should phone back tomorrow?'

By now, Sol was thinking rapidly. Clearly, Alec had got his number somehow, possibly from Victor, and assumed that Nicola would be working there. Sol could only stall him for so long before he realized that Nicola did not work there. The simplest thing would be to give Alec Nicola's home number but he knew that Nicola had already refused to give it to him. Would Nicola thank him if he gave Alec the number? On the other hand, what if Alec discovered that Nicola did not work there? He would wonder why everyone was lying about such a seemingly innocent piece of information. If Sol had had his wits about him at the start, he could have said that Nicola had moved on or had got a job abroad but he had endorsed the lie that Nicola still worked there. Anyway, Sol was still of the view that Alec might be good for Nicola and cheer her up a bit. He decided to give Alec the number and if Nicola wanted nothing to do with him, she would have to tell him. That would at least resolve the situation one way or the other.

'Look, Alec, Nicola is always out and about. It might be better if I gave you her home number.'

'That would be great.'

Sol gave Alec the number and Alec said that he would phone her later.

After the conversation had finished, Sol decided that he had better warn Nicola what he had done. However, there was no reply and her answerphone was not switched on. Sol resolved to try later but in the event forgot.

17

Alec waited until the evening before trying Nicola's number, figuring she was more likely to be home after office hours. For reasons that he could not explain, he felt really nervous. The phone only rang a couple of times before it was answered.

'Hello.'

Alec recognized her voice immediately and the butterflies in his stomach increased. Given his experience with women, he was surprised at his nervousness. He hadn't felt this way since as a young conditional jockey many years previously he had plucked up the courage to ask out a stable lass who was rumoured to fancy him. Somehow, he felt that with Nicola, it would take more than a half of mild in the local pub and a pound spent in the condom dispenser in the gents before they sneaked into an empty stable together.

'Hello, Nicola. It's Alec Hammond here.'

Alec would have felt better if he'd known that Nicola experienced a similar feeling as soon as she heard his voice. Nicola's thoughts were racing. How had he got her number? How was she going to deal with this? She'd tried to put Alec out of her mind since their meeting at Sandown but had not been entirely successful. At work, she had closed her eyes and imagined that she was with him rather than some steroid enhanced moron with only half a brain. She had even taken to checking the racing pages to see if there was any mention of him. She had found that there frequently was. Nevertheless, she was still certain that she had made the right decision. Alec represented a world that was simply unattainable for her and she knew that if she started to see him, it would end in tears. Why then was she so pleased to hear from him? Why had her heart jumped at the sound of his voice? Why did she feel breathless?

'Alec? How are you?'

'I'm fine. I hope you don't mind me calling you like this.'

'No. Not at all. But how did you get this number?'

'I got your work number from Victor, and Sol gave me your home number.'

Work number? And then Nicola realized what had happened.

'I see. Sol doesn't like his staff taking calls at work. I wouldn't ring there again if I were you.' What are you saying, she thought, it's up to you to make sure he doesn't ring anywhere again!

'He seemed fine about me calling. I think he was hoping for another tip!'

'That sounds like Sol.'

'By the way, how was your holiday?'

Great, she thought, I'll send you the DVD. That should go down a storm in the jockeys' changing room!

'Wonderful. It's just what I needed. Sun, sea and relaxation.'

'No holiday romance, then?'

'Hardly.'

'Come on! I bet you met lots of eligible admirers!'

It depends on your definition of 'met' and 'eligible', she thought.

'Not at all. That was the last thing on my mind.'

'Anyway, I was wondering if you'd changed your mind about getting together some time?'

'Look, Alec. I'm flattered that you should go to the trouble to find out my number but I thought I'd made myself clear about that.'

'I'm not suggesting anything heavy. I just thought we got on well and it might be fun to spend some time together.'

'I'm sure you're not short of female company.'

'Maybe not. But most of the people I meet are connected with racing in one way or another. It would make a change to spend some time with someone outside the industry.'

Snap! Nicola thought. But it's easier for you than me!

'I really don't think it's a good idea.'

'Did you enjoy the day at Sandown?'

'You know I did.'

'Well I've got an idea. On Saturday, there's a big meeting at Newbury when one of the biggest steeplechases of the year is being run. It's a great day out and you can get a train direct from Paddington that takes you straight to the course. Why don't you come down with a friend and enjoy a day at the races and we can have a drink between races? If you feel like it we could all go out for a meal afterwards. If you don't want to, I won't be offended.'

You've got it all worked out, haven't you? Nicola thought. But she had to admit that what Alec was suggesting was tempting. On Thursday, a Russian 'actress' was flying over to make a film with Nicola. Lana had become one of Nicola's closest friends in the business and they had appeared in films together a number of times. Nicola had said that Lana could stay on after the shoot and spend the weekend with her. Going to the races on Saturday afternoon might be fun and better than trawling round the crowded shops with Lana. Could Lana be trusted to keep her mouth shut and dress a little less outrageously than she usually did?

'As a matter of fact,' she said 'I've got a friend staying for the weekend and she might like the idea of an afternoon at the races. I could give her a call and see if she fancies it.'

'Great. I could arrange for one of my friends to join us!'

'Now wait a minute. Don't get carried away. We might come to the races but I'm not sure we'll be doing any more than that.'

'No, no. I understand. But just in case you do, what's your friend like?'

'She's Russian.'

'Russian! How do you know her?'

'She's some sort of model, a client of Sol's.' Nicola was already beginning to regret the whole thing.

'A model? So she's attractive then?'

'Very.'

'I take it she speaks English?'

'With a thick accent.'

'How tall is she?'

'Why on earth do you want to know that?'

'Well, you remember the jockey who had such a spectacular fall at Sandown?'

'Yes.'

'He's only five feet five!'

'Well, Lana is about five feet nine! And she always wears ridiculously high heels!'

'So she should get on fine with a short Irishman with a thick accent?'

'Don't start fixing up any dates!'

'No. Of course not. As if I would!'

Nicola could not help smiling to herself. Alec's boyish enthusiasm was infectious and suddenly a foursome with Lana was beginning to appeal to her. The truth was that Lana was tremendous fun and game for virtually anything. If anyone was going to cut this short on Saturday, it would have to be Nicola.

'I suggest you don't tell her that her blind date is a few inches shorter than her!'

At this point, Nicola laughed as well.

'No promises, Alec. I mean it!'

They carried on talking for another half an hour although Nicola was careful to steer the conversation to what Alec had been doing in the last three weeks rather than herself. She found herself in fits of giggles when he told about the events at the party at Robin's house after House of Cards' victory. Alec had not told anyone else the story but did not see any harm in telling Nicola as she was hardly likely to gossip given that she did not move in the same circle as the people involved. He did however omit to tell her about how his evening had ended.

At the end of the conversation, Alec said that he would ring on Friday evening to confirm that Nicola and her friend were going and to give her the travel details.

That night, in contrast to the last time when she had spoken to Alec, Nicola went to bed feeling happier than she had for a long time although she knew that she might be going down a very dangerous path. Just how dangerous, she could not possibly have foreseen.

18

The last Saturday in November. Hennessy Gold Cup day. Alec woke early, full of anticipation for the day ahead. Although it was still dark, the forecast was for a fine late Autumn day.

A bumper crowd was expected at Newbury for the first major steeplechase of the season. The flat season had come to an end two weeks earlier and for the next five months the racing press would be concentrating on jumping.

The Hennessy Gold Cup is a handicap run over three miles two furlongs, the same distance as the Cheltenham Gold Cup. Because of the lack of championship races and top class conditions races for staying chasers as well as the prize money available, the big handicaps like the Hennessy attract a top quality field comprising not just handicappers but also horses likely to run in the King George and the Cheltenham Gold Cup later in the season. Even winners of those races often contest the biggest handicaps not just because of the money on offer but because their connections want to enhance their reputations. To be viewed as a 'legend' requires more than winning the championship races. A horse needs to show that he can give up to two stone to his rivals and still win as Arkle and Desert Orchid did. In this respect, the jumps program differs markedly from the flat where the top class horses never compete in handicaps.

Obviously, the better class horses are set to carry the most weight and this can be a tough task for a relatively young and inexperienced horse fresh out of the novice stage in a large field of runners largely comprising seasoned campaigners.

It was for this reason that the decision had been taken not to expose Deep Secret to such a gruelling race at this stage of his career as a bad experience could do severe damage to his development.

Nevertheless, the Saunders stable had another candidate for the race in the form of North Thorseby and Alec was confident that the horse would run well. The ten year old had run third in the race the previous year before winning a valuable three mile chase at Ascot later in the season. He had not won in his two prep races this season but had run well and Martin felt that he was spot on for the race. Set to carry ten stone twelve pounds, he was third favourite in the ante-post market at 8 to1.

However, the prospect of riding North Thorseby was not the only reason Alec was looking forward to the day ahead.

The previous evening, he had telephoned Nicola as arranged and she had confirmed that she and her friend, Lana, would be coming down from London by train to the races although she had emphasized that they may well be going straight back afterwards. Unlike their previous conversation, this one had been fairly short and Nicola had seemed a little distant but Alec was confident that her trip down would be a success.

Jimmy O'Brien was also looking forward to the day. He had landed the ride on the main Irish challenger in the race, Don't Tell The Boss, a top class chaser almost certainly destined to run in the Cheltenham Gold Cup the following March. Set to carry eleven stone ten pounds, the horse was currently 10 to 1 in the market although Jimmy fancied that the odds should be shorter.

Jimmy had also been warned by Alec that if he played his cards right, he could end the day with a date with a Russian model. Alec had told Jimmy all about Nicola and that his chances of a proper date with her could depend on Jimmy working his Irish charm on her Russian friend. Jimmy was confident that he would make an impression and was not at all fazed to hear that Lana was a lot taller than him.

'She'll learn that big things can come in little packages,' he'd told Alec. 'Don't you worry. We'll be making a real night of it.'

Pat Duggan was not looking forward to the day. He was riding another fancied contender, Zulu Warrior, but a week earlier he had received a call from Frank Morris who had told him bluntly that Zulu Warrior was not to win.

Duggan had been furious. Since Morris' visit a month previously, Morris had only called him twice telling him to stop horses in relatively low grade handicaps for which Duggan had been paid £5000 each time. However, as far as Duggan was concerned the Hennessy was a different matter. Quite apart from his share of the significant prize money which he might be forfeiting, the Hennessy was one of the most prestigious races of the season, a race which every jockey wanted to win.

He had objected strongly but Morris was adamant and made it perfectly clear what would happen to Duggan if the horse won. The Hennessy was a huge betting race and to know that one of the fancied runners was not going to win was extremely valuable to Morris.

Morris had sweetened the pill a little by offering £10000 but Duggan was very nervous about stopping a horse in such a high profile race.

19

Svetlana Sahkova was a very imposing woman as well as a larger than life character. Standing at five feet nine inches without her high heels (which she rarely took off, even in bed!), she had high Slavic cheek bones, Cleopatra style long black hair and cat like blue eyes.

But for her looks, she would undoubtedly have remained where she was born, in a small town about a hundred miles from Moscow, working as a lowly paid factory worker like both her parents. However, like Nicola, Svetlana had discovered at a young age the effect that sex can have on men although in her case she learned to use sex to exercise power over men, rather than the other way round as had occurred for Nicola with her stepfather.

At the age of sixteen, she had been working in the same factory as her mother when a representative of the consortium who owned it made a visit from Moscow. This man had picked her out and had her taken to his hotel room. Svetlana was under no illusions as to why she was there. By that time she had already had several lovers and she realized that this man could be her ticket to the bright lights of Moscow. The following day, she left for Moscow with him never to return.

Her new lover found her a room and although it was nothing special, it seemed like luxury compared to what she had been used to.

When her lover had tired of her, he had set her up with one of his friends and this process continued with Svetlana being kept by and provided with gifts by a succession of new rich Russian 'businessmen'. She only had to provide one thing in return and although she did not consider herself to be a prostitute, she came to regard sex as nothing more than a commodity for sale like everything else in the new world of capitalism prevailing in Moscow.

However, despite her improved circumstances (as she saw it), she hankered for more and her chance came when one of her lovers invited her to Budapest for the weekend.

Svetlana had never been outside Russia and was thrilled to visit a city which seemed much more appealing than Moscow and more like she had imagined western cities to be.

What she did not know at the time was that in the new era of freedom in the former eastern bloc, Budapest had become the porn capital of the world. In their rush to join the capitalist world, many eastern and central European countries, repressed for so long in the communist era, turned to anything to make money. Lower production costs and an endless supply of beautiful girls prepared to do anything to escape poverty meant that the industry thrived.

Shortly after her arrival in Budapest, her lover asked her whether she would be prepared to appear in a film while she was there. Svetlana was no fool. She realized that this was why she had been invited on the weekend but unlike many of the western girls who go through agonies deciding whether to accept such an offer, she accepted without hesitation. In her mind this was her passport to fame and fortune and she knew she had the attributes to be a star. After all, it would not be the first time that she had had sex in front of other people and to her it was no different from some of the drunken orgies she had had to attend back in Moscow.

Thus, she made the film and never looked back. In a world

which she saw as glamorous, she did indeed become a star, changing her name from Svetlana Sahkova to Lana Sahkov.

Because of her amazonian looks, she soon began to specialize in roles which required her to dress in outrageous leather gear and boots in contrast to Nicola who tended to play softer more feminine roles. As Nicola put it, Lana usually dressed up like a triple X rated Wonderwoman!

Over the years, Nicola and Lana had become friends and had done many scenes as well as films together. Nicola did not count many people as friends either within or outside the industry but Lana was an exception. She was always fun to be with and made Nicola feel better about herself. Unlike most of the western girls, Lana had absolutely no hang ups about what she did and indeed seemed proud of it, boasting that she never had to fake an orgasm. As she had reminded Nicola many times, she could have ended up like her mother but now she lived in a luxury apartment in Hamburg, had money and her own fan club.

Nicola sometimes wished that she could be more like Lana and had been feeling that way when Alec had phoned on Friday evening. She had seemed subdued on the phone because she was arranging to meet a man who would surely have been appalled if he had known what she and Lana had been doing with each other that afternoon under the glare of lights and cameras.

Lana predictably thought that the situation was amusing and suggested that they should give Alec and his friend a re-run after racing and satisfy what she believed every male's fancy to be. On this occasion, Nicola did not see the joke and began to wonder whether she was making a big mistake in introducing Lana to Alec.

As if able to read Nicola's mind, however, Lana promised that she would be on her best behaviour and in particular would stick to the script which she had been given. She even promised to dress in a suitable way for the Members Enclosure of a British racecourse on a major race day.

20

Alec drove the short distance over to the Saunders stable where he had breakfast with Martin and Martin's head lad, Bill Ryan. Bill had been in the business even longer than Martin and had worked for Martin since Martin had first started training. No one knew the horses better than Bill and Martin had often told Alec over the years that he would not be able to cope without Bill and his wife, who had worked as Martin's housekeeper since his wife had died.

Apart from North Thoresby in the Hennessy, the stable had two other runners at Newbury that day and each of them was discussed in detail.

Bill was worried that the ground would be too firm for North Thorseby and the other two admitted that it was a concern. The autumn had so far proved to be unseasonably dry and although good ground was forecast for Newbury, North Thorseby had shown his best form when the ground was on the soft side of good.

'One thing in our favour is that the Hennessy is usually run at a good pace and there are a couple of frontrunners in the field. So it should be a good test of stamina,' Bill remarked.

'I suggest you let the frontrunners go if they set off too fast but stay up with the leading group, Alec. Try to take it up some time after the cross fence to take the sting out of the horses waiting behind,' Martin said.

Later that morning, as Jimmy was driving Alec up the M4 towards the Newbury exit, it was not just the racing that Alec was thinking about. He had told Nicola to take an early train so that he could meet them well before the first race for a drink and then show them round so they could see where to bet and where the best places were to stand during the races before the place became too crowded. He was going to advise them to place their bets on the Tote rather than get involved with the scrums that could occur around the bookmakers on busy race days. Alec was aware that at Sandown, Nicola had not left Victor's box and had relied on others to place her bets. If she wanted to bet at Newbury, she was going to have to do it herself. He could hardly do it for her if he wanted to keep his licence!

Alec and Jimmy often travelled together when they were both riding at the same meeting. On this occasion, they had decided that Jimmy should drive so that they had a fourseater car available if the girls were on for something after racing.

Jimmy interrupted Alec's thoughts.

'So what do reckon my chances are with this Russian babe?'

'Chances of what?'

'You know what I mean. These eastern women are all on the lookout for someone from the West, aren't they?'

'I think you're too late for that. I gather she lives in Hamburg now.'

'Hamburg! Ever been there?'

'No.'

'Best red light area in Europe. Much better than Amsterdam!'

'You would know!'

'What sort of a model did you say she is?'

'For God's sake, Jimmy, you've got a one track mind!'

'No, seriously, what sort of stuff does she do?'

'I don't know. You'll have to ask her.'

'What are we going to do with them after racing?'

'Assuming they want to do anything, I think we'd better go up to London for the evening. There's not much down our way. Anyway, we don't want to have to take them all the way back to London at the end of the evening.'

'They could always stay!'

'You're taking a lot for granted!'

Nicola and Lana were travelling in the opposite direction by train, which had been a matter of complaint by Lana. She had become accustomed to being chauffeured everywhere in a luxury car and was not used to public transport. She had insisted on travelling first class and been appalled at the cost of the tickets.

It was probably just as well that they had chosen to travel first class as they would certainly have been out of place in standard class with many of the ordinary racegoers, some of whom were already tanking up with cans of lager. The noise coming from adjoining compartments was confirming Lana in the view that she had formed on other visits to England that rather than the civilized, genteel place that she had imagined, England was in fact a nation of yobbos. Of course, it did not occur to her that these were just the sort of people who after a few pints and a curry would settle down to watch one of her films.

Lana had promised Nicola that she would dress like an 'English lady' for the Members Enclosure and although that wasn't quite the result, Nicola was aware that things could have been decidedly worse.

Lana had chosen to wear a cream top which emphasized her surgically enhanced bust size although fortunately it was not too low cut. She was also wearing a smart knee length brown skirt and high heeled brown leather boots. The only problem was the slit in her skirt which, if she sat in a certain way, showed enough leg to reveal the top of her stockings (Lana claimed never to have worn tights in her life). On top of everything, she was wearing a long fur coat.

Nicola had warned her that such a coat could provoke abuse from some members of the public who disapproved of such garments. Lana simply could not understand this and said that if anyone abused her, she would poke them in the eye with her long and very pointed fingernails.

Nicola winced, knowing that she meant it, but consoled herself with the thought that they should be safe in the Members Enclosure.

For her part, Nicola was dressed in Chanel suit, cut only a couple of inches above the knee, a brown leather coat and brown high heeled shoes.

21

On arrival at the course station, Nicola and Lana made their way towards the entrances together with the other racegoers. Alec had given her instructions as to which entrance to head for so as to buy their passes for the Members Enclosure.

Although the crowds were not heavy at that time, there were a number of early arrivals and the two women attracted a number of stares en route to the entrance as well as one or two comments from some of the men. Mostly they were put off by a withering stare from Lana but one young man was a little more persistent.

Walking beside them, he said, 'you two look as if you can do with the company of some real men. Why don't you join me and my friends for a drink?'

Nicola ignored him in the hope that he would go away but Lana stared him up and down and said contemptuously in the hearing of his friends in her thick accent:

'Why don't you drop dead, sonny? We'd eat you and your friends for breakfast!'

The chastened young man beat a hasty retreat.

Once inside the course, they found their way to the bar which Alec had described.

Alec and Jimmy had already arrived after dumping their riding gear in the changing room. They had taken a quiet table in a corner and ordered a bottle of champagne in an ice bucket with two glasses and two glasses of mineral water for themselves.

Alec had given Nicola a big build up with Jimmy but they were both shocked when Nicola and Lana walked through the door. The bar was still half empty but the excited racecourse chatter from the other occupants ceased as they entered and every head turned towards them.

'Bloody hell!' Jimmy muttered, 'I've died and gone to heaven! Is that them?'

'It certainly is,' Alec replied.

'What a pair of absolute crackers!'

They both stood up as Nicola and Lana approached the table.

'Hi, Nicola, you made it then,' Alec said as he leant across and kissed her on the cheek. 'Can I introduce you to Jimmy?'

Jimmy shook her hand and Nicola then introduced Lana. Alec shook her hand but Jimmy took her hand and kissed it in an exaggerated gesture which brought a warm smile from Lana.

'What a pleasure to meet such a beautiful lady! Now I know what they mean by the luck of the Irish!' he said.

'We took the liberty of ordering some champagne,' Alec said. 'I hope that's OK.'

He handed them both a glass.

'How was your journey?' he asked.

'Adequate.' Lana replied. 'I had to deal with a couple of peasants on the way who had ideas above their station but a glass of champagne more than makes up for that.'

Jimmy suggested that Nicola and Lana might want something to eat before a queue developed and after they had looked at the menu went to fetch a couple of smoked salmon sandwiches. When he returned Lana asked why Alec and Jimmy were not eating.

'I wish we could!' Jimmy said, 'but we can't risk it because of the weights. All I've had today is coffee and water. Perhaps I'll make up for it after racing.'

The conversation flowed easily and Alec noticed that Jimmy was pouring on the Irish charm and seemingly making a good impression on Lana.

Lana was also particularly impressed by the fact that every now and again they were interrupted by people asking for Alec and Jimmy's autographs. She was tempted to remark that someone might recognize her and 'Susie' and ask for their autographs but did not think that Nicola would appreciate such a comment.

After a while, when the girls had finished the champagne, Alec and Jimmy showed them round outside and gave them a crash course on how to place bets. By this time, the course was filling up and Nicola and Lana agreed that they would stick to the Tote and remain in the Members Enclosure as much as possible. They agreed that Alec and Jimmy would look for them in the same bar between races but that they might not always turn up as they both had a full book of rides and had owners and trainers to deal with.

As luck would have it, one of the people they bumped into was Charlotte who greeted Alec effusively but gave Nicola and Lana a frosty stare.

'I take it I won't be seeing you after racing today?' she asked Alec.

'Er..probably not,' Alec replied.

Charlotte put her hand on Alec's face.

'There's no need to look so embarrassed,' she said, 'I've always known you were a rogue. That's why I like you…among other things!'

To her annoyance, Nicola felt a pang of jealousy even though she could hardly expect someone like Alec not to have other girlfriends. Her annoyance was because she had been determined to avoid that sort of feeling about Alec.

22

After Alec and Jimmy had gone to change for the first race, Nicola and Lana decided that Nicola would bet on Alec's mounts and Lana on Jimmy's. After each race, they would return to the bar for a drink unless either Alec or Jimmy had won in which case they would walk over to the winners' enclosure to cheer them in. Nicola had told Lana all about her Sandown trip and how exciting it had been.

The first race was a disappointment because Alec and Jimmy both finished unplaced. The only consolation for them was that with no weighing in and no trophies to receive they could sneak off to join the girls for a while.

Then, Alec won the second race, a handicap hurdle, on a horse trained by Robin North at 8 to 1. By the time he could get away, Jimmy was already in the bar with Nicola and Lana. As he entered, a loud cheer went up from the racegoers in the bar many of whom slapped him on the back or shook his hand as he walked through.

Nicola was delighted as Alec's horse had paid out at 10 to 1 on the Tote and she and Lana were already well into another bottle of champagne that she had bought with her winnings.

There was a longer gap before the feature event of the day, the Hennessy, but Alec and Jimmy excused themselves fairly soon as they needed to concentrate on the task ahead.

Bill Ryan had been right. When the tapes went up, two of the runners shot to the front and soon opened up a gap of several lengths. Alec tucked North Thorseby into the group of runners immediately behind them, hugging the inside so as to take the shortest way round. He was not the slightest bit worried about the lead that the front two had as he was sure that they would both run out of steam.

Although some horses prefer to bowl along in front, it is never easy to make all the running in such a competitive race and the last thing such a frontrunner wants is another horse trying to do the same thing. Instead of relaxing and enjoying their lead, the two horses tend to take each other on usually resulting in them both running out of steam.

For about a circuit, there was little change in the order and Alec was able to keep North Thorseby in about sixth position. The horse seemed relaxed and was jumping well. However, Alec could now see that one of the two horses in front was struggling to maintain its position. The horse was off the bridle and its rider was giving it a couple of slaps with the whip. By the time they were halfway down the back straight, the horse started dropping back and North Thorseby and the other runners in the leading group soon passed it.

As they made the lefthand turn towards the Cross fence at the side of the course before the final straight, Alec could see that the leader was now struggling. He may have won the battle of the frontrunners but there was no way he was going to win the race.

Alec decided that it was time to make his move. He pushed his mount up into second place and after the Cross fence collared the leader.

Alec urged North Thorseby forward but soon realized that he was in difficulties. He had been hoping to draw two or three lengths clear but although his mount was trying his best, he was obviously not appreciating the ground. As they made the turn into the straight, Alec was aware of a number of horses breathing down their necks.

Jimmy had held Don't Tell The Boss up at the rear of the field for the first circuit and then began to make steady headway through the field. Like Alec, he had not been concerned by the pace set by the front two and was under instructions to make his challenge late.

When Alec made his move, Jimmy was in a group of about six horses behind him. The remaining horses still on their feet were too far back to play a part in the finish. Jimmy could see that Alec was already riding North Thorseby hard and at least three of the chasing back including his own horse were travelling better.

The two that Jimmy was particularly concerned about were the favourite, Gunners Pride, and Zulu Warrior but, at the second last, Zulu Warrior made what seemed to Jimmy to be only a slight mistake but which caused Pat Duggan to be unseated. The horse had been on the outside and Duggan appeared to slip off the side well away from the following horses.

As far as Jimmy was concerned, that only left Gunners Pride as a realistic rival. He decided to track Gunners Pride and try to take him on the run in.

Between the last two fences, Gunners Pride swept past the gallant but now struggling North Thorseby and his rider, Johnny Carr, asked him to put in a tremendous leap at the last. The horse landed full of running.

Jimmy also sent his mount past North Thorseby and jumped the last two lengths behind Gunners Pride. He could see Johnny in the drive position ahead giving his mount a few cracks of the whip.

Gunners Pride was responding to Johnny's strong driving but

Don't Tell The Boss also began to respond to Jimmy's urging. Alec could see Don't Tell The Boss gradually reeling Gunners Pride in. Then for several strides they were neck and neck up the run in.

The crowd cheered them on. Nicola (who had switched allegiance to Jimmy's mount when it was clear that Alec was not going to win) and Lana were jumping up and down with excitement.

Fifty yards from the post, the titanic struggle ended when Gunners Pride faltered and Don't Tell The Boss surged on to win by a length and a half. Jimmy waved his fist in triumph and the Irish (and Russian) contingent in the crowd roared their approval.

23

Jimmy and Don't Tell The Boss were cheered all the way back to the winners' enclosure and a huge roar erupted as they were led in. It occurred to Jimmy not for the first time that when you win a big race it always seems as if everyone has backed the winner.

After talking to the delighted connections, weighing in, giving post-race interviews and attending the presentation of the trophies, it was some time before Jimmy could escape and return to the bar.

The cheer that went up when he entered it was deafening and it seemed that a celebration party was already in full swing. Jimmy finally managed to make his way over to the table where Alec, Nicola and Lana had been joined by a number of new friends. Lana appeared to be in her element but turned away from her admirers to give Jimmy a hug and a kiss.

'My hero!' she purred and lifted him right off his feet.

However, while Nicola and Lana were being topped up with champagne by happy punters, there was still business to be attended to by Alec and Jimmy.

Alec managed to fuel the celebrations even more by completing a double in the last race on one of Martin's horses and the party in the bar continued long after racing had finished.

Alec was finally able to relax and have a drink. He felt a bit sorry for Jimmy who had won one of the biggest races of the season but could not afford to have more than one drink given that he was driving.

When people started to drift away, Jimmy asked Alec what the plan was for the evening.

Nicola had been having similar thoughts. She had long since realized that there was no way in which she and Lana were going to return to London alone by train. Lana had drunk twice as much as her and she knew that in this mood Lana was not going to settle for a quiet night in. Besides, Nicola had to admit that she had not enjoyed herself so much for ages and saw no reason to ruin everyone's evening.

Thus, when Alec suggested that he and Jimmy drive them back to London for an evening out, she readily accepted.

Lana was suitably impressed by Jimmy's Mercedes, considering it to be a far more congenial means of travel than the train and the high spirits continued during the car journey during which a discussion began as to what they would do when they got to London. At that point, Alec confessed that in anticipation that this situation might arise he had taken the liberty of booking a table at a fashionable restaurant for nine o'clock.

Lana was delighted.

'And then?' she said.

'Well, I hadn't thought that far,' Alec replied.

'What about a club?' she asked.

'Aren't you a member of Nirvana, Alec?' Jimmy asked.

'Yes, I am. We could go there if you like.'

Nirvana was one of the most exclusive clubs in London, frequented by numerous celebrities. Alec had been a member ever since he had won his first championship.

Lana had heard of the club but had never been there.

'Oh, yes! We must go there!'

'Let's see how we feel after the meal,' Nicola said, alarm bells ringing at the prospect of being seen at such a location.

But Lana was not to be deflected.

'Don't be silly, we must definitely go there!'

They arrived back in London just after seven thirty and Lana insisted that they went back to Nicola's flat so that the girls could get changed. Nicola conceded that if they were going out to a restaurant and a club they would need to have a shower and change. As for Alec and Jimmy, they had already showered after racing and as jockeys riding at a major race meeting were suitably dressed in suits.

On arrival back at the flat, Nicola invited Alec and Jimmy to help themselves to the drinks cabinet while she and Lana got ready. Jimmy remarked that he would have to stick to soft drinks whereupon Lana intervened.

'It's unfair that you can't celebrate your win properly. Why can't they stay here tonight? They don't want a long drive back after going to a club.'

'Well, I don't know…,' Nicola replied. She had not anticipated this.

'That way, Jimmy can have a drink as we can leave his car here and take a taxi,' Lana persisted.

'Alec?' Jimmy said.

'That's fine by me but only if Nicola is happy with that.'

'No, no, I don't mind,' Nicola said 'You and Jimmy can crash out in one of the bedrooms and Lana and I will take the other.'

'If you say so,' Lana smirked.

It took the girls over an hour to get ready by which time Jimmy had done his best to catch up with everyone else by helping himself to the gin and slimline tonic. When they finally appeared, his reaction was not dissimilar to the reaction he had had when he first saw them. Alec too was staggered by the 'makeover' for a night out on the town. They had looked glamorous at the racecourse but this was something different again. In fact, he was somewhat surprised by the change in Nicola's appearance. At Sandown and that afternoon, she had been elegantly dressed and made up but here was an altogether different look. She was heavily made up, particularly around the eyes, and her blond hair, which normally fell loosely around her shoulders had been given pink streaks to match her dress and heavily spiked up with gel. She was wearing a low cut backless dress in a pink satin material with a jagged diagonal hemline starting at the knee on one side and ending just below her hip on the other side. She had matching high heels.

While Alec thought she looked sensational, Nicola was less comfortable with her look but had deliberately chosen it to alter her appearance as it was not a look that she had used in her films. Her worst nightmare was to be out with Alec and to hear the words 'Hello Susie'.

Lana had sprayed silver glitter in her hair and extended her eye make up to increase her Cleopatra look. She was wearing a tiger print dress showing an outrageous amount of her enhanced cleavage. The dress was as short as was possible without being arrested. In six inch high ankle boots, she towered above Jimmy.

'Wow!' Jimmy exclaimed.

'You like,' Lana growled while doing a twirl.

'You bet!'

Lana gently scratched Jimmy's cheek with her long red painted nails.

'Maybe you stroke the pussy later, eh?'

Jimmy was rendered speechless as he, Alec and Nicole all wondered whether Lana's mastery of English slang was such that she realized what she had said.

24

They had one more drink before leaving the flat to look for a taxi. Nicola as always found Lana's high spirits to be infectious and they were all laughing and joking as they got into the back of the taxi.

The two girls sat on the bench seat and Jimmy sat down in the middle and put an arm round each of them. Alec perched himself on one of the pull down seats and faced them. In that position he found it difficult to know where to look but was relieved to see that both girls were wearing knickers.

Perhaps not surprisingly, the taxi driver had barely looked at the men when he had picked up his fare but once they were on their way he turned back towards the gap in the perspex barrier between himself and his passengers.

'Hey, aren't you Alec Hammond?' he asked.

'That's right.'

'And that's Jimmy O'Brien isn't it?'

'Yes.'

'Out on the town then to celebrate his win?'

'We certainly are.'

'Looks like you're in for quite a night!'

'You could be right about that!'

The restaurant was a lively trendy place and one of the in spots to be seen. Alec had never been there before but his profile was such that he had had no difficulty booking a table. They were welcomed effusively by the general manager and decided to go straight to their table. As they passed through the bar area, they attracted a number of stares but when they were led into the dining area, the hubbub of conversation dipped almost to nothing as the other diners watched as they were led to their table. How many people recognized the two jockeys (or maybe even the two 'actresses') was difficult to tell but it occurred to Alec that the sight of Lana, six foot three in her heels, being accompanied by Jimmy several inches shorter, and the way the two girls were dressed was bound to attract attention.

When he sat down, Alec had a quick look round. There were one or two faces he vaguely recognized. Perhaps he'd seen them on the television or something but there was no mistaking that his party was the centre of attention.

After a couple of minutes, a waiter appeared with a bottle of champagne and an ice bucket.

'With the compliments of the gentleman sitting over there.'

The waiter indicated a large man with a beard sitting in a party of eight about four tables away.

They all looked over at him whereupon the man raised his glass at them and shouted across at them:

'Nice one, Jimmy! I won two grand on your horse this afternoon!'

Once again, the noise died down and then started up even louder as people obviously discussed the new arrivals.

As the meal progressed, the atmosphere became more and more lively as the drink flowed. As word spread a number of people came over to the table to congratulate Jimmy and they lost count of the number of bottles that were sent over.

When they left about two hours later, a number of the diners cheered and called out good wishes to them. None of them had ever experienced anything like it, not even Alec who was more used to the celebrity lifestyle than the others. Jimmy was well known in racing but not to the public at large; Lana was used to attention from men but again not the public at large and Nicola went out of her way to keep a low profile.

They had asked a waiter to call them a taxi and when it arrived, the waiter led them out of the restaurant and opened the door of the taxi. Alec passed the waiter a tip and immediately told the taxi driver to take them to Nirvana.

On hearing this, the waiter watched the taxi leave and then took out his mobile phone and called the number of a tabloid newspaper.

Nirvana was everything Lana had expected. She had been taken to all the best clubs in Moscow but most of them were little more than brothels for wealthy businessmen. The clubs in Hamburg and other European cities were also pretty tacky but here she was at one of the most famous clubs in the world, frequented by film stars, sports stars, pop stars and even the younger members of the royal family.

Alec had been greeted warmly by the door staff as 'Mr. Hammond' and they had also been pleased to welcome 'Mr.O'Brien'. On entering the premises, the first person they met was a well known England football international whom Alec knew fairly well. In fact, Alec, though not a frequent attender, seemed to know a lot of people there and there were clearly a number of racing fans as many of them were keen to meet Jimmy.

By this time, the four of them were more than a little merry. Alec was amazed that Lana was even standing given the amount she had knocked back since midday. She soon became the centre of attention on the dancefloor, insisting that Nicola should stay with her after Alec and Jimmy started flagging and returned to their table.

When the girls returned to their table, Lana sat down on a sofa next to Jimmy and put one arm round him and started stroking his thigh with her other hand. Alec and Nicola were sitting on a similar sofa and Alec leant across and put his arm round Nicola. She felt a tremor of excitement and tried to relax but despite the drink she realized that things were going far further than she had ever intended.

After a while, she said that she was going to the Ladies and indicated to Lana that she wanted to her to accompany her.

'This is where they have a serious discussion about us,' Jimmy said.

Alec smiled.

In the Ladies, Nicola came straight out with it.

'Are you planning on sleeping with Jimmy tonight?'

Lana looked at Nicola as if she was mad.

'Of course. I like him. We've had a great time. Why the hell not?'

'I'm not going to sleep with Alec.'

'Why ever not? It's obvious you both want to.'

'That's not the point.'

'Why not? You weren't serious about that separate rooms stuff, were you?'

'I was actually.'

'But there are two double beds.'

'I'm sure we'll manage for one night.'

'We would,' Lana grinned. 'But I'm not sure they would!'

'What do you mean by that?'

'They're as straight as they come.'

'So am I!'

'It didn't seem like that on Friday! Or all the other times before!'

'What are you suggesting?'

'You seemed like you were enjoying yourself.'

'I was acting!'

'Oh really? Well, you deserve an Oscar! Look, Nicola, I've done everything you asked and Alec has no idea what we do, but you're taking it a little bit too far in trying to portray yourself as the sweet English virgin. Do you think sleeping with him on the first night might ruin a beautiful relationship because he'll lose respect for you? I thought you said a proper relationship would be impossible anyway.'

'I did.'

'Well, in that case, enjoy it while you can!'

Nicola had to admit that Lana had a point.

'Anyway, I don't see why Jimmy and I should suffer because of your hang ups. I've had a tremendous evening and I'm feeling very…what is it you English say…horny. If you insist on sharing a bed with me, then you will have to 'stroke the pussy' but no offence, I'd rather it was Jimmy!' Lana grinned, and with that she flounced out of the Ladies.

They eventually left the club at about three o'clock. As they stepped outside, Alec had his arm round Nicola. He said something that amused her and at that moment, a camera started flashing. None of them took much notice as they piled into the back of a taxi for the journey back to Nicola's flat.

During the journey back, Alec again sat on one of the pull down seats. Jimmy and Lana were all over one another and Alec was in no doubt what they would be doing back at the flat. He wondered if it would be the same for himself and Nicola. He certainly hoped so. He leaned across and took Nicola's hand.

Nicola smiled when Alec took her hand although the smile masked her confusion. Since the conversation with Lana, she'd been worrying what would happen back at the flat. She knew that Lana was probably right but she could not shake off the feeling that she was heading for disaster.

On arrival at the flat, Jimmy and Lana had scarcely got through the door before they headed for the spare bedroom without saying a word.

'Well, they didn't take long!' Alec said.

He put his arms round Nicola and bent down to kiss her. She didn't resist. As their lips met, a tear ran down her cheek. One way or another, she had never been so certain that she was making a big mistake but she took his hand and led him to her bedroom.

On the following day, Alec and Jimmy did not return to Lambourn until late afternoon. They had all risen late and then gone out to lunch before dropping Nicola and Lana back at Nicola's flat and saying their goodbyes. Alec promised to call Nicola that evening and Jimmy asked Lana to let him know next time that she was in the country.

On the journey back, both men were in good spirits despite still feeling slightly hung over but while Alec was content to sit back in contented silence, delighted with how the weekend had turned out, Jimmy could not stop talking.

'Jesus! What a woman! She was insatiable!'

'So you didn't get much sleep then?'

'You're joking! What about you?'

'None of you're business!' In truth, Alec had not had too much sleep either but for some reason he did not feel like discussing it with Jimmy.

Fortunately, Jimmy was too wrapped up in his own adventures to press Alec too hard.

'I found out what she models. Stockings! I'm not surprised with legs like that!'

Alec grunted.

'And,' Jimmy continued, 'you'll never guess what she's got on her stomach!'

'What?'

'She's got a tattoo of a snake which begins just below her tits and goes all the way down to her…'

'What?'

'You know!'

'I don't!' Alec laughed.

'I thought the thing was going to bite me!'

'Do you think you'll see her again?'

'No. I don't think she's the relationship type. Still, it's been a great weekend, one I'll never forget! What about you? Do you think you'll see Nicola again?'

'Oh yes, definitely!'

25

On Monday morning, Frank Morris was staring intently at a tabloid newspaper when Lennie Cohen walked into his office. Morris did not look up.

'So what's so interesting?' Lennie asked.

Morris pushed the paper across his desk.

'Have a look at that.'

Lennie turned the paper round and the only thing of possible interest that he could see was a picture of Alec Hammond and Jimmy O'Brien leaving Nirvana in the early hours of Sunday morning with two extremely glamorous women on their arms. All four of them were laughing and were obviously having a good time.

'What, this picture of Hammond and O'Brien out on the piss?'

'Yeah.'

'Well they were presumably out celebrating O'Brien's win in the Hennessy. What about it?'

'Do you recognize the women they're with?'

Lennie looked at the picture again.

'No. But Hammond and O'Brien are lucky bastards to have pulled a pair like that. O'Brien probably needed a stepladder to communicate with the one he's with. Then again maybe he preferred to be level with her tits!'

'There's nothing even vaguely familiar about them?'

'No. Why the interest?'

'There's something about them. Particularly the blonde.' Morris took the paper back. 'Maybe I'll ask Dave and Chris. So how are we doing?'

'Don't Tell The Boss was a good result for us. We took a lot of money on Duggan's mount and not a huge amount on anything else.'

Confident that Duggan's mount, Zulu Warrior, was not going to win, they had lengthened the odds on that horse to attract money and offered slightly worse odds than were generally on offer for the others so as to deter bets on them.

'Unfortunately, though,' Lennie continued, 'it's not enough. We've been doing OK since Duggan's been back on board but we're not taking enough money for you to be able to repay what you owe or at least not within the time you've got.'

'Half the money's got to be repaid by Easter.'

'Not possible. Particularly as you're pushing Duggan as far as you can.'

'What about the ante-post market?'

'What about it? You can only use Duggan when you're sure of what he's riding. So it doesn't work with races months or even weeks in advance.'

'Never mind Duggan. The only way I'm going to survive is to take as much money as I can and if that means offering very favorable odds on some horses, that's what I'll have to do.'

'With no control over the outcome of the race? That's too risky.'

'If I don't do something, I'm dead, so what have I got to lose?'

'Well you'd be better off sticking to races where there are only a limited number of fancied runners. In open races with large fields like the National and the Tote Gold Trophy, laying against one runner is not likely to be much use. The big Cheltenham races like the Gold Cup and the Champion Hurdle would be better.'

'OK. Let's look at the Gold Cup. Bring me details of the current odds on offer.'

Lennie left the room and returned a few minutes later with two pieces of paper. He handed one to Morris and kept the other copy for himself.

'Those are the best prices on offer at the moment: 3 to 1 last year's winner, Backpacker, 5 to 1 Don't Tell The Boss, 6 to 1 Gunner's Pride, 6 to 1 Deep Secret, 8 to 1 Dungannon. The rest are 12 to 1 or longer. Unfortunately, Duggan is unlikely to get the ride on any of the leading five.'

'Backpacker hasn't run yet this season.'

'No. He's had a slight setback but he's due to return in the New Year. The connections seem positive. You'd be mad to bet against him. He only had three runs before winning last year and was very impressive.'

'OK. What about the others?'

'Well I thought Don't Tell The Boss was pretty impressive in the Hennessy.'

'So did I. And Gunner's Pride wasn't far behind.'

'Deep Secret beat Dungannon in the Sun Alliance at the last festival but he's only run once this season at Wincanton.'

'He didn't beat much and he's barely out of the novice stage.'

'But he was a bloody good novice!'

'True. But they ducked the Hennessy.'

'We'll know more about him after the King George.'

'I'm not waiting that long.'

'What do you want to do, then?'

'Offer Deep Secret at 8 to 1.'

'You can't do that! Two points longer than the best you can get now. That's crazy!'

'You're right, Lennie, that's crazy. Make it 15 to 2!'

'Are you serious?'

'Just do it.'

'OK. You're the boss. But you'd better pray that Hammond doesn't win his first Gold Cup.'

'Hammond won't be winning the Gold Cup on Deep Secret. Leave it to me. I'm going to find a way to stop Deep Secret from winning if it's the last thing I do. In fact, if I don't find a way, it probably will be the last thing I do!

26

Lennie Cohen was a man who liked to keep things neat and tidy and in a bookmaking context that meant keeping a balanced book. He had not been particularly happy when Morris had had to revert to his old ways and 're-employ' Duggan in a bid to repay his debts but this new tactic of singling out a horse in big race months in advance and offering ridiculously generous odds in the belief that the horse would not win worried him deeply.

Of course, not all bookmakers keep balanced books. Some are prepared to back their own judgment on a race if they either fancy or do not fancy a particular horse and organise their book accordingly. That was what had caused Morris to get into difficulties in the first place. However, no one in their right mind offered the sort of odds that Morris was offering in a race like the Gold Cup three months before the race was due to be run.

Lennie had to admit though that in the short term the tactic appeared to be working. When word got round as to the odds that Morris was offering on Deep Secret, the firm had taken a flood of money on the horse. In the first week, they took five individual bets of £10000 alone and very little on any other horse.

Lennie had approached Morris and almost begged him to shorten the odds on Deep Secret but Morris wasn't interested. All he would say was, 'Trust me, Lennie, Deep Secret won't be winning the Gold Cup'. Lennie knew better than to argue too forcefully with Morris but the state of the firm's book on the Gold Cup was beginning to keep him awake at nights.

Meanwhile, back at the Saunders stable, while the Gold Cup remained the horse's ultimate target, preparations were in hand for Deep Secret's run in the King George V1 chase at Kempton Park on Boxing Day.

Apart from the Gold Cup, which is the highlight of the Cheltenham Festival in March, the King George is the only other championship race for three mile steeplechasers, the sport's Christmas showpiece and only just behind the Gold Cup in prestige. Indeed, many followers of the sport actually think it's a better race. Whereas the Gold Cup is run over three miles two furlongs over a tough undulating left hand course, the King George is run over two furlongs less over an easier flatter right hand course. It does not necessarily follow that a horse suited to one race will also be suited to the other. Stamina plays a bigger part in the Gold Cup whereas speed is often the deciding factor in the King George. This has sometimes meant that in a mediocre year, particularly when the ground is soft, the Gold Cup has been won by a horse which in other years would be rated no better than a good 'handicapper'. Such a horse has been able to slog his way through the Cheltenham mud which has blunted the speed of higher rated horses. In contrast, a look at the list of past winners of the King George shows that the race is almost invariably won by a horse of real class.

Because Kempton is a flat course where stamina is not always so important, the race is often contested by top class horses which would have no chance in the Gold Cup. Thus, the horses which normally run over two and a half miles or even two miles might have a crack at the race, running against established three milers. Therefore the King George often brings together horses which would not normally run against each other and this adds to its fascination.

Of the leading Gold Cup contenders, Deep Secret was the only one running in this year's King George. Backpacker, who had completed the King George/Gold Cup double the previous year, was out of action till the New Year. The unseasonably dry autumn had caused the Irish contingent of Don't Tell The Boss and Dungannon to stay at home and contest a race at Leopardstown where the ground was softer. Gunner's Pride, whose main strength was stamina, had opted for the longer distance of the Welsh National on slightly easier ground at Chepstow.

Alec, Martin and Bill Ryan were also concerned about the good to firm ground at Kempton but had seen no reason to pull Deep Secret out of the race. They were all of the view that if you had a potential champion in your stable then the only place to be on Boxing Day was Kempton even if the conditions were not ideal. Deep Secret was in fine form at home and after ducking the Hennessy for perfectly sound reasons (despite some comments in the racing press) they were not about to duck the King George.

Despite the absence of Deep Secret's main market rivals for the Gold Cup, the race had still attracted a top quality field. There were two French runners from a stable which had had considerable success with their runners in England but Alec and Martin had identified Cutting Edge as the main danger. Cutting Edge was almost certainly the best chaser over two and a half miles in the country. Unfortunately for his connections, the racing calendar provided no championship races over two and a half miles and whereas he did not have the speed to compete with the top two mile chasers he did not have the stamina to contest the big long distance chases.

However, this year he would never have a better opportunity

than at the King George with the track and the ground giving his connections every reason to believe that under those conditions their horse would get the three miles.

The bookmakers agreed and in the weeks leading up to the race Deep Secret and Cutting Edge were generally quoted as 2 to 1 joint favourites.

27

Nicola normally dreaded Christmas. It usually involved sitting at home in her lonely flat wondering what it would be like to have a family Christmas. She did not consider that Christmases with her mother and stepfather qualified as the sort of family Christmas that she imagined other people had. In the past, she might have gone out with some of her fellow performers but she found that equally depressing with everyone pretending that they were having a good time and the men in particular not the sharpest wits that she ever encountered.

This year it was different.

Against her better judgment, she had allowed the relationship with Alec to continue and despite her misgivings, she had found as Christmas approached that she was happier than she could ever remember.

She had been shocked to see her picture in the papers after the Hennessy weekend and was relieved that she had taken steps to change her appearance. At first she had vowed never to see Alec again. However her resolution had lasted until she had next heard his voice on the telephone. Nevertheless, she had learned her lesson. There were to be no more high profile visits to night clubs. Dinners in quiet country pubs or evenings watching television at Alec's house became the routine. When she visited racecourses to watch Alec ride, she invariably wore dark glasses whatever the weather, kept her collar up and her hair tucked away. She had also told Sol and her other industry connections that she wanted no more work for the time being. How could she do what she did while she was seeing Alec?

Alec always spent Christmas at Martin's house and this year he had invited Nicola to join them. She was going down to Alec's house three days before Christmas when the racing industry began its short break. She was then travelling up to Kempton with Alec and Martin on Boxing Day. She was already beginning to feel like one of the 'family' as Martin and the whole stable had made her feel very welcome.

About a week before Christmas, Nicola had lunch with Sol and he was delighted to hear about how her relationship with Alec had developed.

'So you've forgiven me for giving him your number?'

'To be honest, I'd forgiven you the moment I heard his voice!'

'And you're obviously enjoying a normal relationship?'

'I'd hardly call it a normal relationship. I hate the deceit involved. When I'm with him I'm happy, when I'm not with him I'm worried about how it will all end.'

'Who says it's going to end?'

'How can it last? Happy ever after is not an option. I couldn't marry him or even move in with him with such a lie hanging over me and if I tell him the truth, it would ruin everything.'

'You don't know that. He may be shocked but he may understand if you tell him everything you've been through.'

'He won't.'

'How can you be so sure?'

'Alec's a traditionalist at heart as are most of the people in the world of jump racing. I've got a small tattoo on the back of my left shoulder which I had done when I was sixteen and he doesn't even approve of that!'

'Did he say so?'

'No. He's too polite but I could tell. He asked why I had it done and I told him it was something I did when I was a teenager.'

'So?'

'Well, why ask why I'd done it if he approved of it? Alec is the sort of guy who doesn't like tattoos on women whatever the current fashion. He probably thinks they're common.'

'You're reading a lot into this!'

'Believe me. I haven't yet met a man prepared to accept my background and he's less likely to than most men. He seems to have put me on some sort of pedestal and thinks I'm a class above most of the women he meets!'

'You probably are.'

'You're kidding! You can't stoop any lower than I have!'

'Maybe it's too early, but one day he may understand. You've only known him a few weeks.'

'It seems like longer.'

'What are you going to do then?'

Nicola shrugged.

'Enjoy it while I can. Even though I know the sensible thing is to walk away before I get in too deep.'

'How deep are you in now?'

'That's the problem. I've already fallen in love with him.'

28

As Christmas approached, Nicola found herself looking forward to spending a few days at Alec's house and having him all to herself for a change. Apart from the occasional Sunday morning, Alec was invariably up at the crack of dawn either ready to set off for some distant racecourse or to go over to Martin's stable to ride out and have a working breakfast with Martin and the other stable staff. On days when she saw him at the races and then returned to London, they had little opportunity to spend time together. Alec had told her that if she thought his schedule was hectic, she should have seen what it was like when he was chasing the championship. He had explained the effort and stamina that it took to try to chase every winner possible regardless of the distance involved and the poor prize money which might be on offer.

Pat Duggan was of course still chasing the championship and was involved in a close three way struggle with two other jockeys. There was therefore no opportunity to ease off at all and he had to go wherever there was the best chance of riding a winner. Sometimes that meant travelling to a course at the opposite end of the country if the prospects were better there than at a more local course. Because the championship was based simply on the number of winners ridden, he might have to give up the ride on a fancied runner in a lucrative race at one course to ride odds on runners in low grade races at one of the smaller tracks.

Since the prize money for such races was so low, Duggan could find himself earning less for riding a double in such races than he would have for riding one winner of a better class of race. Further, since odds on shots were by no means certain to win, he had on occasions travelled all the way to a course like Wetherby or Sedgefield only to return home empty handed and find that his rivals had ridden winners much nearer home.

Nevertheless, Duggan had known what he was taking on and could have coped with all the stress involved in chasing the championship. After all, he had managed to cope the previous season and had gone on to win the championship. What he was finding difficult to cope with was the additional stress brought about by his renewed 'arrangement' with Frank Morris.

In truth, Morris had not had to put much pressure on Duggan in his younger days to stop horses from winning. It was a relationship which had suited them both and Morris had not had to resort to the threats that he had issued to other jockeys at that time to keep them on the payroll.

Duggan was a young up and coming jockey who wanted the kind of lifestyle that he saw more senior and better established jockeys enjoying. He was easily seduced by the money on offer and his relationship with Morris came to a natural end when Morris decided that he no longer needed to take the risk of bribing jockeys just as Duggan was achieving the success that brought increased financial rewards. They no longer needed each other.

Duggan was not a popular man in racing circles but he had talent and had acquired the status and respect which goes with becoming champion jockey. Having reached the top, the last thing he had needed was the re-activation of a relationship from his past which he had done his best to forget about particularly since Morris rarely attended race meetings personally.

Duggan now bitterly regretted agreeing to accept £5000 to try to prevent House of Cards from winning. Maybe if he had told Morris that he wasn't interested, Morris would not have come to see him afterwards? On the other hand, if Morris really was in trouble, it had probably not made any difference.

Now, he was locked into an arrangement to which he could see no end. Duggan was in no doubt as to what would happen to him if he did not co-operate. The racing world had been stunned when Sammy Morgan had had his legs broken so badly that he never rode again. The police investigation had got nowhere with Sammy claiming that he had not seen who had attacked him. There had been various rumours but so far as Duggan knew, no one had connected Morris to the incident. Duggan had known that Sammy was one of the Morris team of jockeys and was desperate to end his relationship with Morris. He was also in no doubt that Sammy had kept his mouth shut because of some further threat by Morris, probably directed at Sammy's family.

Quite apart from the threat of violence, there was the additional threat of exposure through the tapes Morris had of their conversations so all in all Duggan saw no way out. He could not face the disgrace that would follow any exposure by Morris after all he had achieved, not to mention the likely prison sentence.

He dreaded the calls made by Morris to stop this horse or that horse. Although as Christmas approached, Duggan had only had to stop half a dozen horses, he realized that he no longer had the nerve for that kind of thing. Times had changed. Security at racecourses was better. All races were filmed and scrutinized in a way which had never happened previously.

Duggan had been terrified of an inquiry of his riding of Zulu Warrior in the Hennessy. The horse had been going so well that he had panicked and virtually jumped off him. As it happened, he doubted whether Zulu Warrior would have got near Don't tell The Boss and Gunners Pride on the run in but he had had some difficult explaining to do to the connections of the horse afterwards. He was convinced that the trainer was now no longer using him as much as in the past.

He was becoming paranoid about people suspecting what he was doing. He was sure that the worry was affecting his riding, thus resulting in fewer bookings and less winners. He felt that instead of leading the championship by two, he should be a dozen ahead.

The pressure had been increased recently when Morris had been furious to find that Duggan had turned down the ride on a horse that he usually rode to ride better fancied runners at a different course. The horse had been about 5 to 1 in a competitive handicap hurdle and Morris had been banking on Duggan being available to stop it.

As Christmas approached, Duggan was glad of the opportunity to have a few days off even if it meant spending it with what had increasingly become his only friend – Mr. Jameson, very often drunk straight from the bottle.

29

Christmas was everything that Nicola had been hoping it would be and Christmas Day itself made her feel like part of one large happy family. Alec always spent Christmas day at Martin's house where Annie Ryan and her daughter cooked lunch for Martin, Alec, the Ryan family and all the stable staff who had not gone home for Christmas.

Martin's house was open to all from about eleven o'clock onwards and by the time lunch was served, there was a tremendous atmosphere with the men helping themselves to Martin's plentiful supply of drink and children running about playing with their new toys.

Nicola was happy to help with the preparation of the vegetables and with laying the various tables that had to be used and was amazed at the way Annie was able to cope with feeding a full Christmas lunch to so many people.

So far as the men were concerned, the main topic of conversation was the stable's runners on the following day at the Boxing Day race meetings and in particular how Deep Secret would get on in the King George. Nicola took the opportunity to learn a little more about everyone's background from Annie, explaining that Alec was not the best person from whom to find out about such matters.

'Typical man!' Annie said. 'Their conversation revolves around sport and all the other things that men talk about! They pretend they're not interested in the sort of things women talk about but when there's the slightest bit of gossip, they're the worst of the lot!'

Nicola learnt that Martin had a daughter the same age as herself, Melanie, who lived and worked in America. She had only been eighteen when her mother had died. She had gone out to America in her gap year before attending university to stay with Martin's brother who farmed out there. She had liked it out there so much that when she had finished her degree, she had gone back and found herself a job.

'I'm surprised Alec never mentioned her', Nicola said.

Annie looked at Nicola and then looked away quickly.

'Well, there you are', she said. 'Typical man!'

'How often does Martin see Melanie?'

'He goes out there once or twice a year when racing's quiet, but that's not so easy now that we have all year round jump racing although it's not so busy in the summer months.'

'Doesn't she come back here at all?'

'She hasn't so far. To be honest I think her mother's death hit her hard. She didn't come home a lot during her university vacations either. It was such a happy home before Mary's death. Afterwards, Martin had the stable to occupy himself with but Melanie went to boarding school and didn't have too many friends around here. I'm sure she'll return one day.'

After Martin and Bill Ryan had carved the two huge turkeys that Annie had cooked, the food was laid out for everyone to help themselves before finding a spot in the large house where they could sit down and eat.

Alec and Nicola were two of the last to serve themselves and, after pushing aside some dishes of vegetables, sat down at the kitchen table.

Nicola had taken what for her was an enormous portion and felt guilty when she saw how little Alec had on his plate. By now, Nicola was getting used to Alec's constant battle to keep his weight down and the only occasion that she had seen him eat a full meal had been in London after the Hennessy Gold Cup with Jimmy and Lana. Alec had told her subsequently that he had paid for that by eating virtually nothing the following week. However, in the three days leading up to Christmas, Alec had eaten reasonably well, albeit with regular trips to his sauna, and here he was on Christmas Day making do with one slice of turkey, one small roast potato and a few peas.

'Christmas Day may be the beginning of the holiday for most people,' Alec explained, 'but for us it's the end. Tomorrow is the busiest day of the year for race meetings and the next week until New Years Day one of the busiest weeks; particularly as the winter has been so mild so far and there are unlikely to be any cancellations because of the weather!'

'I suppose you can't risk being overweight for Deep Secret.'

'Deep Secret's no problem at all! Because it's a championship race, all the runners will be carrying eleven stone ten. I could eat like a horse, if you'll excuse the pun, and still do twelve stone. It's the other races I'm worried about, the handicaps where I have to do under eleven stone including all my riding gear!'

'What happens if you turn up and find you're too heavy to make the weight?'

'That depends. If your horse is right at the bottom of the handicap on ten stone and you weigh in at a pound or two overweight, that's not too disastrous but if you can't do say ten stone five that would be unprofessional and the trainer would not be too impressed!'

'Don't the trainers know what weight different jockeys can do?'

'Yes, usually. They know that these days I struggle to do under ten and a half stone! Although I did make an exception for House of Cards.'

'I noticed that Billy had a full plateful.' Nicola was referring to Billy Johnson, the stable's conditional jockey. 'And you told me previously that he gets a five pound allowance because of his inexperience.'

'That's right. But Billy's young! I could do nine stone nine at his age. It gets a lot harder when you get older and even more difficult at my height when you get past thirty!'

After lunch, Nicola helped with the clearing away while Martin, Alec and the rest of the stable staff went back to work. Apart from Deep Secret and two other runners at Kempton, the stable had runners at two other meetings on Boxing Day. Although Martin had long since made all the necessary arrangements, he wanted to make absolutely sure that everyone knew what they were doing and where they were supposed to be. As he was going to Kempton, he had arranged for his travelling head lad to supervise the runners and look after the owners at one meeting and for Bill Ryan to make a rare racecourse appearance at the other. As head lad, Bill usually remained at home to look after the stable but was good with owners and sometimes helped out at the races at busy times.

Later that evening, back at Alec's house, Alec and Nicola curled up on Alec's sofa to watch television but Nicola could tell that Alec was not really concentrating on what was on. In his mind, he was already riding in the King George.

30

As was usually the case, Alec did not sleep particularly well the night before a big race and for once his lack of sleep was unconnected with the presence of Nicola beside him. He jumped out of bed at 5.30 am raring to go and took Nicola breakfast in bed after he had restricted himself to a cup of black coffee and half a slice of dry toast. Nicola playfully tried to undo the cord to his dressing gown when he put the tray down and for a fleeting second he was tempted to get back into bed. However, he was strong enough to resist and half an hour later, he arrived at Martin's stable having told Nicola that they would pick her up later on their way to Kempton.

The yard was already a hive of activity. Alec found Martin in the kitchen giving Billy Johnson his riding instructions for the stable's two runners at Huntingdon. As Huntingdon was the furthest course, the horsebox for the runners at that course was setting off first. Kempton was next and the runners for Wincanton for whom an outside jockey had been booked would set off last.

After the horseboxes had left and Martin was satisfied that the yard was running smoothly under the direction of a senior lad, he followed Alec back to his house where they picked up Nicola and dropped off Alec's car. As ever, Nicola looked stunning and although he was going to be busy, Martin was pleased that he would be looking after her for most of the day as Alec had a full book of rides.

During the journey to the course, Nicola sat in the back of Martin's Mercedes while Alec sat in the front discussing race tactics with Martin. The discussions lacked the humour that she had become used to when listening in on such conversations and she was aware of the tension that both men were feeling.

Alec had explained how much the King George meant not only in it's own right but as a pointer to Deep Secret's prospects in the Cheltenham Gold Cup.

The Boxing Day meeting at Kempton always draws a huge crowd and this year was no exception particularly as it was such an unseasonably fine day. Nicola had been worried about turning up at such a high profile televised meeting and spending the day in the company of one of the leading trainers. During her previous attendances at race meetings, she had tended to tuck herself away and keep out of the limelight. However, Alec and Martin had insisted that she should accompany Martin rather than spend most of the time on her own and since she was staying with Alec and had been a guest at Martin's house, she could hardly refuse. Nevertheless, she was relieved at the sunny weather because it gave her the perfect excuse to wear a large pair of sunglasses.

Arriving at the course early meant that Alec again bumped into Charlotte, although this time he was on his own as he was on his way to the weighing room while Martin had taken Nicola off to check on the arrival of the stable's runners.

While the rest of the television crew might have thought that Charlotte was asking Alec about his prospects for the afternoon had they seen them talking together, that was not what Charlotte was interested in.

'A little birdie tells me you're still seeing the same woman I saw you with at Newbury?'

'Oh really,' Alec replied with a smile. 'What if I am?'

'Well, for you to still be seeing the same woman must be some sort of record!'

'It's only been a few weeks. I saw you for a similar period!'

'I'd hardly call that a relationship. We ended up in bed a few times!'

'Well? I didn't hear you objecting!'

'I wasn't! Anyway, I've heard that you and your new friend are scarcely apart!'

'That's not wholly accurate but do I detect a little jealousy?'

'Hardly! Anyway, I'm seeing someone else myself.'

'What? Someone Daddy would approve of?'

'Oh yes. The right background, plenty of money and useless in bed!'

Alec laughed.

'I'm only joking! He's not that bad but if you do get fed up with your new friend, you could always give me a call…'

With that and a mischievous grin, Charlotte turned and walked away swinging her hips in what appeared to Alec to be a deliberately provocative gesture.

The afternoon started badly for Alec. After two frustrating seconds, his mount in the third race fell when in a challenging position.

Up in the stand, Nicola gasped with the rest of the crowd but while their attention quickly turned to the closing stages of the race, she tried to see whether Alec had been hurt.

'Don't worry. He's OK,' Martin said beside her.

'How do you know?' Nicola asked.

'Because,' Martin said, while continuing to look through high powered binoculars, 'he's just thrown his whip to the ground in anger and he's walking off looking very cross indeed. He's annoyed about the fall and losing the race when in a good position rather than his health! It's only his pride that's hurt!'

Nicola was still not convinced.

'But after a fall like that, will he be in a fit state to ride Deep Secret in half an hour?'

'Providing he hasn't broken anything. These jump jockeys are tough. A fall like that is all in a day's work.'

After the race, Nicola accompanied Martin while he supervised Deep Secret's saddling and did not see Alec until he walked out with the other jockeys to the paddock where Martin, Nicola and Deep Secret's owner, Mary Pickering, were waiting.

Mary Pickering was a delightful woman in her sixties whose husband had had horses with Martin for years. Sadly, he had died two years previously before Deep Secret had started his chasing career so he had had no idea that the rather moderate hurdler that he owned was going to become one of the country's leading chasers. In fact, he and his wife had never owned a horse remotely good enough to contest a championship race.

Mary, a racing enthusiast herself, had decided to continue in racehorse ownership and was thrilled that one of her husband's horses had gone on to be a star.

She had always had a soft spot for Alec and was delighted to meet Nicola.

'It's about time Alec settled down,' she had said. 'I know he's one for the ladies but I've never known him to bring someone to the races to be looked after by Martin while he rides! You must be special!'

However, by the time they had walked out to the paddock, the small talk had ceased to be replaced by obvious tension in both Martin and Mary.

When Alec arrived, he was sporting a large bruise to the side of his face and the beginnings of a black eye following his fall. Nicola wanted to say something but realized that was the last thing on Alec's mind as they all watched the imposing looking Deep Secret being led around the paddock by his stable lass.

Martin went through the riding instructions for the umpteenth time, largely, Nicola thought, to relieve the tension. She had heard them so many times that she could have given them herself.

Alec was to remain up with the pace throughout the race and then take it up three out and try to draw the sting out of the main danger, Cutting Edge, who would be held up at the rear to conserve his stamina before coming late.

Despite the fact that the ground conditions were in Cutting Edge's favour for his first attempt over three miles, Deep Secret had edged ahead in the betting and was being quoted as 13 to 8 favourite with Cutting Edge at 9 to 4 and one of the French runners at 7 to 2.

After a few minutes, the announcement was made for jockeys to mount. Alec was relieved that the action was about to commence and that all the waiting and anticipation was over. Mary wished Alec luck as Martin gave him a leg up into the saddle. The stable lass led Deep Secret to the gate and Alec felt the tension disappear when he and Deep Secret went out on to the track and cantered down to the start.

As soon as the tape went up and the race began, Alec realized that he was in trouble. Although there were no specialist frontrunners in the fourteen strong field, he and Martin had banked on the race being run at a reasonable pace. However, none of the other runners seemed willing to take the lead and the field proceeded at a ridiculously slow pace with all the jockeys holding up their mounts in the hope that someone else would take up the running.

Alec knew that this was playing into the hands of his main rival, Cutting Edge, who was being held up at the rear of the field to conserve his stamina over a distance greater than his optimum distance. In contrast, Deep Secret needed a true test of stamina not only for his own benefit but also to ensure that the stamina doubts of Cutting Edge and one or two other runners were tested to the full.

After two furlongs of the field dawdling along and Deep Secret fighting for his head just behind the reluctant leaders, Alec decided to abandon his riding instructions and seize the initiative. He swept Deep Secret to the front and they were soon bowling along about ten lengths ahead of the rest of the field setting a punishing pace. Most of the other runners responded but when Alec managed a sneaky look behind, he saw that Cutting Edge's wily jockey, Mick Stannard, was still holding his horse up well behind the others.

Up in the stand, Martin had seen the problem immediately and was willing Alec to take up the running. He breathed a sigh of relief when Alec appeared to read his thoughts and went clear at the front. Deep Secret had never made his own running before and Martin did not know how it would suit him. But one thing was clear. If the race had proceeded as it had been, he would have had a little chance of coping with the finishing speed of a specialist two and a half mile horse. So much for all their planning and his riding instructions! But that sometimes happened. No matter how carefully you planned your tactics, they could all come to nothing if events did not turn out as you had anticipated and a good jockey like Alec had to have the courage to take the initiative in that situation, and quickly!

Alec continued to set as fast a pace as he dared and by the time they were in the back straight before the right hand turn for home, the field was well strung out. Deep Secret appeared to be enjoying himself at the head of affairs and was jumping well. As they rounded the turn, one of the French horses broke free from the small group immediately behind and closed the gap on Deep Secret to about three lengths. Alec stole another glance behind and saw that the French jockey was having to ride his mount hard to maintain his position. Alec was more concerned by Cutting Edge, whose jockey still had him on the bridle and who was making steady progress through the other tiring runners.

By the time Alec had turned into the straight and was approaching the second last, the French runner was beginning to drop back. Alec urged Deep Secret forward but the horse, though galloping on bravely, seemed unable to quicken after setting such a punishing pace for so long.

Before the last fence, Alec was aware of the bright red colours of Cutting Edge behind him on his outside. He asked Deep Secret for one final leap. The horse responded but Cutting Edge also put in a fine jump and loomed up alongside Deep Secret on the run in. For a moment, Alec thought that Cutting Edge was going to go on and win comfortably but then he realized that he was beginning to falter.

The pace set by Deep Secret and the effort required to make up the ground had resulted in Cutting Edge finding little off the bridle. Mick was now riding for all he was worth and for the first time went for his whip as the two horses ran on towards the post neck and neck. Alec was reluctant to hit a tired horse but there is only one King George and in a last desperate effort to gain the day, set about Deep Secret in a manner which brought him a reprimand from the stewards afterwards. But it was enough. Fifty yards from the post, Deep Secret finally wore down his rival and passed the post a neck ahead.

Alec entered the winners' enclosure on Deep Secret to another hero's welcome. The crowd was ecstatic. They had just seen one of the races of the season and most of them appeared to have bet on Deep Secret, backing him down to clear favourite largely because of Alec's personal following.

As he was led over to the winner's spot, Alec was delighted to see that Nicola was there too with Martin and Mary Pickering.

Caught up in the excitement of the moment, Nicola had, without thinking, gone down with Martin and Mary to join in the celebrations. Although she did not know it then, it was the biggest mistake of her life.

Had she thought about it, she would have realized that far from keeping a low profile she was putting herself on live television in front of millions of viewers. Further, she only just managed to avoid being interviewed herself. After Alec had dismounted, he gave a brief interview to Charlotte before going to weigh in. Charlotte then collared Martin and Mary and in the course of the interview mentioned to Martin that she understood that Alec's girlfriend was there to see his triumph.

'Indeed she is,' said Martin, completely oblivious to Nicola's desire for anonymity, 'Now, where's she got to?'

At that, both he and Charlotte turned round to look for Nicola and bring her into the conversation but Nicola had seen the danger and retreated into the background. Unfortunately for her, the damage had already been done.

Sitting in his office, Frank Morris had watched not only the race but also the post race celebrations with a great deal of interest. He opened a drawer in his desk and pulled out a month old copy of a tabloid newspaper already turned to a particular page and stared intently at a photograph. He then rewound the recording he had made of the race, not to the race itself but to the scenes in the winners' enclosure afterwards. He let the tape run until he had the best view of Nicola before freezing the picture.

After staring at the image for several seconds, he could scarcely believe what or rather whom he was looking at.

'Gotcha' he said, with a look of triumph on his face.

31

How to interpret racing form is largely a matter of opinion and opinion was divided on the merit of Deep Secret's win in the King George.

Some commentators applauded his performance in a race which had not been run to suit his style of running but others were more critical of the narrow margin of his victory at level weights over a horse running over a distance half a mile longer than he had ever run before and who according to his connections would now be reverting to races over the shorter distance.

The bookmakers' confusion was further complicated by results elsewhere. Don't Tell The Boss won well at Leopardstown, beating Dungannon by a similar distance to Deep Secret's margin of victory over the same horse at the previous Cheltenham Festival. Gunners Pride won the Welsh National at Chepstow.

In the event, they reacted predictably by shortening the odds on all three horses for the Gold Cup, thus bringing Deep Secret in to 5 to 1.

Regardless of what other commentators may have thought, Alec and Martin and everyone else at the Saunders stable were delighted with Deep Secret's performance. With the exception of Cutting Edge, on whom Mick Stannard had ridden a brilliant waiting race, the other runners had been beaten out of sight and it had been Deep Secret's first race in two months. The stable was convinced that Deep Secret would improve for the run and anyway would be much better suited by the longer distance and tougher course at Cheltenham. Martin decided that the horse would have one more run before the Festival, probably in a three mile chase at Sandown.

Frank Morris was still not convinced that Deep Secret was a potential Gold Cup winner but was confident that the horse would not be winning the Gold Cup however good he was. Armed with the knowledge that he now had, he had devised what he considered to be the perfect plan to ensure that Deep Secret would not win, regardless of the merit of his King George win.

Consequently, he was all smiles when a worried Lennie Cohen came into his office.

Lennie had come in to tell his boss that they were now dangerously exposed on Deep Secret in the Gold Cup and that in order to balance the book, they needed to shorten his odds drastically.

'Don't worry, Lennie,' Morris beamed. 'Everything's under control.'

'How can you say that when we've taken a fortune on the horse and virtually nothing on any other runner? The horse has just won the King George, for God's sake!'

'Well, let's hope he wins his prep race as well. I gather Saunders intends to run him at Sandown next.'

Lennie looked at Morris as if he was mad.

'If he wins at Sandown, he'll be challenging for favouritism, particularly if anything happens to any of his rivals, and your theory that the horse isn't up to it won't be looking too clever.'

Morris shrugged.

'So maybe I was wrong about the horse. Maybe he's better than I thought. That doesn't mean he's going to win the Gold Cup.'

'He'll have a damn good chance!'

'Not this year!'

'What do you mean?'

'I mean that if Hammond and Saunders think this horse is going to give them their first Gold Cup then they'll have to wait till next season, not this one.'

'How come?'

'Just wait and see, Lennie. Stop worrying. Deep Secret will not be winning the Gold Cup this year. Of that you can be sure! You can shorten the odds a bit so it doesn't look too suspicious but continue to offer at least a point better than the opposition.'

'It'll be your funeral if the horse wins. Quite literally!'

'There'll be no need for any funerals!'

32

Nicola returned to Lambourn with Alec and Martin after the Boxing Day meeting at Kempton although Alec and Martin were due to return there on the following day when they had a runner in the Christmas Hurdle. She had told Alec that she was off work between Christmas and the New Year so he had invited her to stay with him for the whole period even if she did not want to go racing every day. Nicola had been happy to agree as she had nothing much to do in London particularly since she had stopped her real work altogether. She now realised that whatever happened between her and Alec in the future, she would never be able to go back to that way of life.

Martin had been delighted to find out that in addition to Deep Secret's victory, Billy Johnson had ridden his first ever double on the stable's runners at Huntingdon and one of the stable's runners at Wincanton had also won so the stable had had its most successful Boxing Day ever.

To celebrate, he said that he would take Alec, Nicola and Billy out to dinner and managed to persuade the landlord of a local pub to squeeze them in.

The pub was full of people from the racing world and most of them came over to their table to offer their congratulations. Nicola was also the subject of considerable interest as word had spread that Alec had a stunning new girlfriend. She hoped that the people she met were as respectable as they seemed and did not have one of her films on their shelves at home!

Once again, she felt sorry for Alec who simply picked at his meal while everyone else including Billy tucked in enthusiastically.

'Just you wait till you're older, Billy,' Alec said enviously as the young jockey crammed food in his face. 'You won't be able to eat like that if you want to continue in this game!'

'It's just as well you're not riding tomorrow!' Martin added.

'Don't worry, boss, I've never let you down yet.'

'You'd better not! It's bad enough an old hand like Alec putting up overweight but I won't tolerate it from a conditional!'

'Anyway,' Billy continued, 'only a couple more wins and my allowance will be cut. Then I should have even less problems with weight.'

'You may not be so much use to me then!' Martin joked. Conditional jockeys are given a weight allowance in most races until they have ridden a certain number of winners. This encourages trainers to use such jockeys and gives them valuable experience. However, once the conditional has ridden enough winners, he loses his allowance and then has to compete with more senior jockeys on level terms. Some jockeys find the transition tough as without the weight allowance, they find that trainers who had previously used them prefer more experienced jockeys.

Nicola then asked after Jimmy.

'He went to Ireland to ride Don't Tell The Boss,' Alec replied. 'He won as well so I expect he's celebrating too...probably a bit more raucously than this if I know Jimmy!'

'Of course, I'd forgotten! He could be your main rival in the Gold Cup, couldn't he?'

'He could indeed,' said Martin, 'and nothing would give Alec and me greater pleasure than to beat him into second place. He's never stopped reminding us of the time when we had the favourite for the race and he pipped us on an outsider!'

After the meal, Alec took Nicola back to his house and Martin and Billy returned to the yard.

Despite all his exertions that day, Nicola found that Alec still had plenty of energy left and as she lay in bed afterwards she reflected that she had never been happier. It occurred to her that Alec would have been far better at her game than she would have been in his! Although deep down she still believed that it could not last indefinitely, she was determined to make the most of it while she could. Who knows? Maybe her past could remain buried forever. Or maybe she was kidding herself!

Alec was also reflecting on how well things were going. What more could he ask for? A woman he had really started to care about and a horse that might win the Cheltenham Gold Cup. Add to that the fact that he was riding as well as ever, the continuing stability of Martin's yard which he still viewed as home and friends like Jimmy O'Brien, and Alec had every reason to be optimistic about the New Year.

Little did either of them know of the disasters that awaited them almost as soon as that New Year began.

33

The mild spell extended into the New Year and very few race meetings were lost due to the weather. This meant that Alec was as busy as Nicola had ever known. She continued to refuse all offers of work and with time on her hands was a frequent visitor to meetings within a reasonable distance of London.

On the Friday after New Years Day, she drove up to Towcester to watch Alec ride.

On the same day, Jimmy O'Brien was riding at Ludlow. After five rides which yielded one winner, he sat in the jockey's changing room with a towel wrapped round him contemplating his afternoon before taking a shower. Although his winner had only been in the selling hurdle, he was reasonably happy with his efforts as in truth none of his other mounts had had much chance. He was also pleased to be getting away early as the last race on the card was restricted to conditional jockeys. What he would give for another date with Lana...

His daydreaming was interrupted by the shrill tone of a nearby mobile phone. The phone continued to ring and Jimmy saw that it was lying on the bench opposite. Assuming that it belonged to one of the jockeys in the shower, he picked it up intending to take a message for one of his colleagues. He would not have wanted one of his colleagues to miss a ride for the following day because he could not be bothered to answer the phone.

'Hello,' he said, but before he could say another word, a harsh voice with a south London accent boomed in his ear.

'Duggan?' but without waiting for confirmation the voice went on, 'Katies Cousin in the two fifteen at Chepstow tomorrow. Make sure it doesn't win. Usual terms.'

Jimmy was stunned.

'Well, have you got that, Duggan?' the voice continued impatiently.

Jimmy just stood there stunned, not knowing what to say or do when the phone was suddenly snatched out of his hand.

'What the fuck are you doing with my phone, O'Brien?'

Jimmy looked up and saw Duggan standing in front of him with a towel round his waist. Duggan put the phone to his ear to find that the caller had disconnected.

Jimmy did not reply.

'I asked you a question, O'Brien. What were you doing with my phone?'

'Nothing,' Jimmy stammered. 'It rang, so I thought I'd take a message. I didn't know it was yours.'

'How dare you answer my phone!'

'You'd have been grateful for the message if it had been some one offering you a ride!'

'They'd have rung back. Who was it then?'

'No one.'

'What do you mean, no one? It must have been someone!'

'I mean I don't know who it was. He must have got cut off when you grabbed the phone.'

'In future, just mind your own damn business!'

At that, Duggan turned his back on Jimmy and having no wish to continue the conversation nor be in Duggan's presence, Jimmy walked off to the showers.

After he had gone, Duggan tried to see who had called but

received the message that the caller had withheld his number.

Duggan finished dressing before Jimmy returned, packed his bag and left the changing room. As he was walking towards his car, his phone rang again.

'Hello,' he said.

'Duggan, what the hell's going on?' Morris demanded.

'What do you mean?'

'You cut me off. I assume you couldn't talk when I rang.'

'Was that you ten minutes ago?'

'Well who the hell did you think it was?'

'I didn't speak to you.'

'Yes you did. You answered the phone!'

'That wasn't me. I was in the shower. Jimmy O'Brien answered the phone.'

Frank Morris went cold.

'O'Brien? I thought it was you!'

'Yes. O'Brien. I suppose all paddies sound the same to you!'

'What the hell was he doing, answering your phone?'

'I was in the shower!'

'Jesus!'

'What's wrong? You didn't say anything, did you?'

'No, no, of course not. Why, what did he say?'

'He didn't know who it was. He said the phone got cut off.'

'Why the hell did you leave your phone out for him to answer?'

'I couldn't take it in the shower, could I? Anyway what's the problem if you didn't say anything?'

Morris didn't reply.

'Christ, Morris, you didn't say anything stupid did you? Because if you did, O'Brien will report it!'

'Calm down. I didn't say anything. As he said, we got cut off.'

'Well, what did you want then?'

'To tell you to stop Katies Cousin tomorrow. On the usual terms, of course.'

'I need more notice than that!'

'You're riding the horse aren't you?'

'Yes, but that's not the point!'

'Just do as you're told, Duggan. I'm not in a mood to argue with you.'

With that, Morris put the phone down. At that moment, any reluctance on Duggan's part was the least of his worries. He knew very well what he'd said on the phone to O'Brien. Duggan had been right. Morris had heard an Irish accent and assumed that he had been talking to Duggan. Now he had to take immediate action to try to repair the damage. He had to hope that O'Brien kept his mouth long enough for him to put his plan into effect.

Morris dialled another number.

Dave Marsh answered on the second ring.

'Where are you?' Morris demanded.

'At the snooker hall.'

'Is Chris there too?'

'Yes.'

'Good. We've got a problem that needs sorting now.'

Morris explained briefly what had happened and what he wanted done.

'We're on our way,' Marsh said.

171

34

When Jimmy returned to the changing room after his shower, he was relieved to see that Duggan had already gone. His head was still spinning as a result of what he had heard on Duggan's phone. He had no idea whose voice it was but he was sure of what he had heard. Duggan was being instructed to stop a horse and the caller's reference to 'the usual terms' could only mean that Duggan was a willing and regular accomplice.

Jimmy did not like Duggan and was aware that Duggan had had a bit of a dodgy reputation when he was younger. However, he could not understand why he would want to get involved in such a risky business when he was at the top of his profession and chasing his second championship.

Jimmy knew that he had to do something but what? Report the matter to the Ludlow stewards? He did not know the caller's identity and if he reported what he had heard, Duggan would merely deny any involvement and say that Jimmy was either mistaken or motivated by spite. On the other hand, careful scrutiny of the recordings of races Duggan had lost when riding fancied mounts could be interesting. Jimmy recalled Duggan's somewhat surprising fall in Hennessy where Jimmy himself had ironically been one of the beneficiaries.

All these thoughts passed through his mind as he drove home from Ludlow racecourse.

Having seen no point in reporting the conversation immediately to the Ludlow stewards, Jimmy had decided that he would talk to Alec before he did anything. Having checked in the paper, he had seen that Alec had a ride in the last race at Towcester and had worked out that he would probably get home to Lambourn before Alec. He needed to talk to Alec in person rather than on the phone but left a message on Alec's mobile phone answering service that Alec should phone him as soon as he got home.

Jimmy lived on the outskirts of a village about three miles from Lambourn on one of the roads leading out of the village. As he approached his house, he did not see the car parked on the verge about two hundred yards away facing away from the village. Even if he had not been pre-occupied with what he had heard earlier, he would not have taken much notice if he had noticed the car.

Knowing that he was going to be driving out of the village to Alec's house later, he decided to leave his car in the road. As he got out of his car, his thoughts were interrupted by the sound of a car engine revving sharply. As he closed his car door, he looked back in the direction of the sound. The sound seemed to be getting closer but the road was dark and Jimmy thought that it was odd that he could see no headlights approaching.

Suddenly, he was aware of blinding headlights and a moment later, his left leg was shattered as he was catapulted into the air before being flipped back on to the bonnet of the accelerating car and striking his head on the windscreen. He then rolled off the bonnet as the car screeched to a halt.

The passenger door of the car opened and a man in a long black leather coat walked unhurriedly back to where Jimmy was lying in the road. He peered down at Jimmy but unable to see much in the darkness, he prodded Jimmy with his foot a few times whereupon Jimmy groaned. On hearing Jimmy groan, the man walked back to the car and said a few words to the driver. Once again, the driver revved up the engine but this time he put the car into reverse gear. The car lurched back over Jimmy. Once again, Jimmy was illuminated in the road by the car's headlights. On this occasion, the occupants could see that there was no need for the passenger to get out of the car for a second time.

As the car sped away from the scene, the passenger made a call on his mobile phone. The phone was answered on the first ring.

'Sorted', said the passenger before breaking the connection.

35

After Alec had finished riding at Towcester, he and Nicola had had a drink together at a local pub before beginning the journey back to Lambourn. Nicola was going to spend the weekend at Alec's house and followed Alec back in her car.

Before setting off, Alec had checked the messages on his mobile phone and had picked up the message from Jimmy asking him to ring Jimmy as soon as he got home. Alec detected a note of urgency in Jimmy's tone and wondered what it was that was concerning the genial and usually unflappable Irishman.

As Nicola was following him, Alec took the journey fairly slowly so it was quite late before they arrived back at Alec's house. As soon as he got in the house, he picked up the phone and dialled Jimmy's number. On getting no reply, he dialled Jimmy's mobile. Still no reply.

'I can't understand why I can't get him either at home or on his mobile,' Alec said. 'He's always available on one or the other!'

'He must be out with his mobile switched off.' Nicola replied. 'Try him later.'

'He was most specific that I should ring him the moment I got back.'

'Maybe he's on his way over.'

Half an hour later, there was still no sign of Jimmy and Alec still could not get through to him.

'I can't believe Jimmy would be out without leaving his mobile on particularly when he wanted to speak to me urgently. I think I'll pop over there.'

'What good will that do? We know he's not in. Wouldn't it be better just to wait for him to phone you?'

'Probably, but this is most unlike Jimmy. It's only a couple of miles. You stay here and if he rings, you can tell him I'm on my way over.'

As he drove over to Jimmy's house, it occurred to Alec that he was worrying unnecessarily but his heart sank as he approached the house and he knew that his instincts had been right.

The road leading out of Jimmy's village was a quiet road at the busiest of times but Alec found himself in a queue of cars waiting to get through and up ahead in the vicinity of Jimmy's house Alec could see that there were flashing blue lights. Alec pulled off the road and parked and then hurried past a line of about twenty stationary vehicles. As he got nearer the house, he could see that the traffic was being held up by a policeman. There were at least three police cars with their blue lights flashing and a whole section of one side of the road was taped off. The police were slowly letting traffic pass on the other side of the road by driving through on the grass verge.

Alec made his way to the barrier formed by the tape to be met by a policeman.

'Would you mind keeping back, Sir?'

'What's happened?'

'There's been an accident but I'd appreciate it if you'd keep well back while we continue our investigation.'

'I'm here to visit the owner of that house.'

The policeman hesitated.

'I see. Who would that be?'

'Jimmy O'Brien, the jockey. I'm Alec Hammond. He's a friend of mine.'

'Alec Hammond? I'm sorry, Sir, I didn't recognise you. Would you mind waiting here a moment?'

The policeman walked over to another uniformed officer who appeared to be supervising the investigation. The other officer looked over at Alec and then approached him.

'Mr. Hammond? I'm Inspector Harris. Could we have a word inside my car?'

The Inspector lifted the tape so that Alec could pass under it and led him to one of the police cars. Alec sat in the passenger seat and the policeman went round and sat in the driver's seat.

'What's all this about? Where's Jimmy?' Alec asked.

'I'm afraid I have some bad news for you, Mr. Hammond. There's no easy way for me to tell you this but I'm afraid Mr. O'Brien was killed in an accident earlier this evening.'

'What!' Alec was stunned. For a moment he thought there must be a mistake but as he looked at the Inspector's face, he knew there was no mistake. Alec looked away and after a pause asked how it had happened.

'That's what we're trying to find out, Sir. I'm afraid things are rather sketchy at the moment but we should know more when the accident investigators have finished. Unfortunately there were no witnesses. All we know for certain is that Mr. O'Brien was run down outside his house probably as he was on his way from his car to his home or from his home to his car.'

'But what about the vehicle which ran him down? Can't the driver tell you what happened?'

'I'm afraid it was a hit and run accident. The other vehicle has not been traced. Mr. O'Brien's body was found in the road by another motorist. Given the position of the body, the accident must have happened only shortly before it was found by the next motorist passing by.'

Alec could hardly take this in. After another pause, the policeman continued.

'Can you give us any idea of Mr. O'Brien's movements earlier today?'

'Yes. He'd been riding at Ludlow. Although I hadn't seen him because I was riding at another meeting. When do you think this accident occurred?'

'Probably about five thirty.'

'I think he was probably on his way from his car to his house then rather than the other way round.'

'Why do you say that?'

'Well, firstly he would probably have arrived home at about that time from the races and secondly, he was anxious for me to phone him when I got home, so I doubt he would have gone out again.' Alec went on to explain about the message he had received.

'Can you recall his precise words?'

'I can do better than that,' Alec said and took out his mobile. He keyed in the numbers for replaying messages and handed the phone to the policeman.

Inspector Harris listened intently.

'He does sound anxious, doesn't he? And you've no idea what he wanted to talk about?'

'None at all. That's why I drove over here. It's so unlike Jimmy to sound so anxious and I couldn't understand why I couldn't get hold of him. He's always available on the phone. It goes with the job."

'It looks like we know now, doesn't it?'

Inspector Harris promised to keep Alec informed about the progress of the investigation and as there was nothing more he could do, Alec drove home and gave Nicola the bad news. He then rang round Jimmy's closest friends. He was grateful when Martin offered to ring the trainers for whom Jimmy was booked to ride the following day so that they could make alternative arrangements. Martin also asked if Alec wanted to give up his rides the following day but although Alec was tempted, he felt that he would be better off working than sitting at home even if the racecourse was going to be a very sombre place once the news got out.

After he had finished his calls, Nicola remarked that Alec's intuition that something was wrong had proved correct.

'You don't think there's any connection between the accident and what Jimmy wanted to talk to you about, do you?'

'The thought has crossed my mind but I can't believe he was deliberately run down. It was probably kids in a stolen car who just panicked and drove off.'

36

Alec was right about the atmosphere at Chepstow the following day. It was as if the whole racing world was in shock at the news of Jimmy's death. There was a minute's silence before the first race.

Although Alec did his best to put on a brave face for the owners of the horses that he was riding when he met them in the paddock before the races and was able to perform while out on the track, the familiar thrill of riding a winner was completely absent when he beat the Pat Duggan ridden favourite into second place in the feature race of the day.

The usual banter in the weighing room was also absent as the other jockeys also tried to come to terms with the loss of their colleague. Jimmy had been very popular and everyone was going to miss him.

Alec was somewhat surprised to note that Pat Duggan appeared to be one of the most affected. Duggan had a haunted look and seemed lost in his own thoughts. Maybe Duggan had not disliked Jimmy as much as Alec had thought.

Shortly after Alec had arrived home, he was irritated to hear the doorbell ring. Not feeling like entertaining, he wondered who it could be.

On answering the door the door, he was confronted by a

stockily built man in his early fifties and a younger, fitter looking man.

'Mr. Hammond?' the older man said, and then without waiting for confirmation, continued, 'I'm Detective Chief Inspector Fuller of Berkshire CID. This is Detective Sergeant Green. I wonder if we might have a word with you about the death of your colleague, Jimmy O'Brien?' The policeman held out his identity card.

'Er, yes, of course. Come in.' Alec replied.

Alec led the two policemen into the living room and introduced them to Nicola, who offered to fetch some tea.

'Thank you, that would be very nice,' Fuller replied and he and his sergeant sat down at Alec's invitation.

'How can I help you?' Alec asked.

'We understand you spoke to our colleague, Inspector Harris, yesterday evening at the scene of the incident?'

'Yes, that's right. Have there been any further developments?'

'I'm afraid there have. We now have reason to believe that Mr. O'Brien's death was not an accident.'

Alec was stunned and had difficulty taking in this information. Nicola, who had brought some cups in on a tray, was equally shocked.

'What do you mean, not an accident?' Alec asked.

'I know this will come as a shock to you, but this is now a murder investigation,' Fuller replied.

'We believe that Mr. O'Brien was deliberately run down.' Green added.

'Are you sure about that? Who on earth would want to kill Jimmy?' Alec asked.

'That's what we were hoping to ask to you,' Fuller replied. 'As to your first question, we're quite certain that Mr. O'Brien was deliberately targetted. Forensic tests have revealed that after Mr. O'Brien was run down, the car was then reversed back over to him. He may well have survived the initial impact. It looks as though it was the reversing manoeuvre which killed him.'

Nicola put her hand to her face as Fuller continued.

'We found the vehicle burnt out in a field just outside Swindon. Unfortunately, there's no worthwhile forensic evidence but we've discovered that it was stolen in West London earlier that afternoon. Now, we know the time of Mr.O'Brien's death and we've been able to ascertain from the owner of the vehicle when it was stolen to within about ten minutes. The timings mean that whoever stole that vehicle must have driven immediately to Mr. O'Brien's house. Even then they must have driven pretty quickly to get there in time to intercept him when he returned from Ludlow races. So it looks to us as if someone not only wanted Mr. O'Brien dead but they wanted it done quickly. Why else steal a car and charge down the M4 in such a hurry?'

The policeman paused briefly.

'Which brings me to the purpose of our visit, Sir. Inspector Harris has told us about the message you received from Mr. O'Brien'

'Yes, he listened to it.'

'So we understand. You haven't deleted it, I hope?'

'No, my mobile's here.' Alec got up and fetched his mobile from the kitchen. He programmed in the number of his message retrieval service and handed it to Fuller. After listening to the message, Fuller handed the phone to Green who appeared to know how to have the message repeated and listened to the message himself.

'We'll need to get this recorded,' Green said, slipping the phone into his pocket, 'but we should be able to get the phone returned to you in a couple of days.'

'I'd appreciate it back a soon as possible. I need it in my line of work.'

'We'll have it delivered to the local nick Monday morning,' Fuller promised. 'Now, you told Inspector Harris that you were concerned by this message but had no idea what Mr. O'Brien wanted to talk to you about?'

'That's right. Jimmy's…was very easy going and nothing seemed to unsettle him. He coped with the disappointments we all suffer in this job better than anyone so it was unusual to hear him sound so agitated.'

'So agitated that you decided to drive over to see him despite the fact that so far as you were concerned he wasn't in?'

'Yes. After he'd left a message like that, I found it odd that he wasn't answering his home phone and his mobile was switched off.'

'Why go round to his house then? Did you think something may have happened to him?'

'No, no, nothing like that! I just felt there was something wrong. I certainly didn't fear for his safety if that's what you mean.'

'I was here as well,' Nicola chipped in, 'I thought Alec was wasting his time going round because I assumed Jimmy was out. But Alec has known Jimmy a long time and seemed to sense something was wrong.'

'What did you think it might be?' Fuller continued.

'I had no idea at the time and I still can't think of anything,' Alec replied. 'Do you think it's connected with his death?'

'Well, it's certainly a possibility. Here's a man who leaves you a message in a manner which is totally out of character and is then murdered before he gets to speak to you by someone who seemed to want him dead pretty quickly. A reasonable inference from that is that he was killed to prevent him from speaking to you. Did you tell anyone else about this message?'

'Only Nicola. No one else.'

'So maybe he was killed to prevent him talking to anyone about whatever was troubling him, not necessarily you,' Green said.

'But how did the killer know he was about to talk to someone?' Nicola asked.

'A good question,' Fuller said. 'Maybe something had happened which made the killer think Mr. O'Brien would be likely to talk to someone. Since the timings suggest that Mr. O'Brien did not stop for any length of time on his way back from Ludlow, maybe it happened there.'

Turning to Alec, he continued, 'Is it possible Mr.O'Brien got himself involved in something too deeply and decided to tell you about it?'

'What, you mean something crooked?'

'Well, it's not unheard of in the racing game.'

'Absolutely no way! Jimmy was as straight as a die. Everyone in racing will tell you that.'

'Perhaps he found out about someone else being involved.'

'That's possible but I'm afraid I've no idea what it could be.'

At that, Fuller stood up.

'Well thank you for your time, Mr. Hammond. You've been most helpful. If you think of anything else, here's my card. Please call me at any time.'

After the two policeman had left, Alec poured himself and Nicola a stiff drink and they tried to make sense of what they had been told.

A few miles away, Pat Duggan had also been hitting the whisky bottle but in a much bigger way. He sat slumped at his kitchen table, an empty glass and an empty bottle in front of him. Although he did not have the information that Alec and Nicola had been given by the police, he had been convinced from the first moment that he had heard about the hit and run 'accident' that it had in fact been no accident.

He had always known that Morris was capable of extreme violence but murder…that was something else. Duggan had never got on with Jimmy O'Brien but he hadn't deserved to die and Duggan felt guilty at his part in his death as well as fear for his own safety. He knew that he had to continue to do what Morris wanted but what about when his usefulness came to an end? Morris would know that Duggan could point the finger at him for Jimmy's murder. What if he decided to tie up a loose end? Duggan regretted not buying another bottle on the way home.

37

Jimmy's funeral took place the following week and it seemed as if everyone in National Hunt Racing had turned out, such had been his popularity. There was not enough room in the church for everyone and a large crowd stood outside listening to the service being relayed to them by speakers.

As Jimmy's closest friend, Alec had been asked by Jimmy's relatives who had come over from Ireland to say a few words about Jimmy and his life in racing. Alec found this a daunting experience but managed to produce a moving tribute to Jimmy which was greeted by a mixture of laughter and tears.

Alec noticed Chief Inspector Fuller and Sergeant Green at the back of the church and after the service he asked them if they had made any progress in the investigation. Fuller looked somewhat uncomfortable.

'Not as much as I'd hoped,' he admitted.

'What about your theory that something may have happened at Ludlow?'

'We've spoken to a number of people including the trainers he rode for that day and some of the other jockeys there that day. No one noticed anything unusual nor anything unusual in Mr. O'Brien's demeanour. Quite the contrary, in fact. A lot of people commented that he appeared to be on good form, cracking jokes and making everyone laugh.'

'That sounds like Jimmy all right but something must have happened between then and making the call to me.'

'I agree. But as yet we have no idea what it was.'

'Maybe he received a telephone call which disturbed him?' Alec suggested.

Fuller shook his head.

'We checked his phone records. He received a couple of calls from trainers before he phoned you but we've checked them out and are satisfied they had nothing to do with this. Besides, he was seen laughing and joking around after they were made so they hadn't upset him. The only calls he made himself apart from the one to you were also earlier in the afternoon as well.'

'So what now?'

Fuller shrugged.

'We keep digging. Given his good humour at the races, I'm now more convinced than ever that something happened late that afternoon which caused him to phone you. Maybe he stumbled on something in the car park as he was leaving. Maybe he overheard something. Whatever it was, it was enough to get him killed and whoever was responsible had enough clout to be able to arrange for his murder to be carried out at very short notice by London professionals.'

'That means something very heavy, not just some piece of racing gossip,' Green added.

Jimmy's wake at a local hotel was a fairly raucous affair as he himself would have wished but Alec was in a sombre mood when he returned home, unable to stop thinking about his conversation with the two police officers. It seemed clear that something had upset Jimmy at Ludlow but what could it have been? On the basis of the police investigation, it must have happened at the end of the afternoon. As Green had said, it must have been something

187

very serious. If it was serious enough to get Jimmy killed, people would have noticed a change in his demeanour.

Alec went into the kitchen and dug out his copy of The Racing Journal for that day from a pile of discarded newspapers. He saw that the last race at Ludlow that day was restricted to conditional jockeys. Jimmy had had a ride in the previous race, a seven runner chase. The chances were that the other senior jockeys who had not had a ride in that race had left the course some time before Jimmy. If as was likely Jimmy left the course after his last ride, he would have been showering, changing and packing his kit up at about the time the conditionals were going out to ride in the last.

The police had said that the trainers Jimmy rode for noticed nothing unusual about Jimmy. This would have included the trainer for whom he had ridden in his last race.

Alec decided to make some inquiries of his own. However efficient the police were, he knew the racing world better than them and most of the people present that day at Ludlow personally.

Later that evening when everyone would have arrived home from the funeral, Alec made some calls.

He started with the trainer of Jimmy's mount in his last race, a Welsh farmer for whom Alec had ridden in the past and who was only too happy to talk.

'Jimmy was in fine form before the race. I'd have certainly noticed if something was wrong. You know what he was like, charming the owners with his Irish blarney. They all loved him and I specifically remember him getting a laugh out of a rather po faced solicitor before that race. I also saw him after the race, of course, and everyone was delighted with the horse's second place.'

Alec then looked at the names of the jockeys in Jimmy's final race. He recalled seeing most of them at the funeral, including Pat Duggan, who had kept apart from everyone else and who had looked distinctly ill. Alec decided to leave him till last.

The first three calls proved unproductive. Alec then called a northern based jockey, Colin Sharp, who began by regretting that he hadn't been able to get down to the funeral.

'All the northern boys had wanted to come but we'd never have got there in time from Sedgefield.'

'I know. We managed to get a time which allowed a lot of people to get there but the wreath you all sent was much appreciated by the family.'

'So what's this call about, Alec?'

'I just wanted to ask you about the afternoon before Jimmy was killed. You rode in the last race with him, didn't you?'

'That's right. The police have already asked me about this but I didn't notice anything unusual. In fact, I walked out to the paddock with Jimmy before the last race and he was joking that he'd be lucky to get round on the horse he was on. In fact, he gave the horse a great ride and finished second.'

'What about after the race?'

'I finished third so I was next to him in the unsaddling enclosure. His connections were delighted to come second and Jimmy was all smiles.' There was then a pause. 'What's this all about, Alec? What's all this got to do with Jimmy's death?'

'Didn't the police tell you about the call he made to me either just before he left the course or shortly after he left?'

'No. They simply asked me whether I noticed anything unusual that day or anything odd about Jimmy.'

Alec told Colin about the call.

'Bloody hell! So that may have had something to do with what happened?'

'So it appears. That's why I'm making some inquiries of my own.'

'Well, I'd like to help but as I told the police, I didn't see anything unusual and Jimmy seemed his usual self.'

'When did you last see him?'

'I left before him. I remember he was still in the changing room when I left. The conditional jockeys riding in the last had already gone out.'

'Who else was there?'

'Pat Duggan was there and there may have one or two others still in the showers. Billy Jackson had already gone as he had wanted to get back for his kid's birthday party and Declan Kelly had gone with him as he wanted a lift.'

'Yes, I've already spoken to them. They didn't notice anything unusual either. So when you left, everything was normal?'

'Yeah. I recall Jimmy was having a few words with Duggan but there was nothing unusual about that. As you know, Duggan was one of the few people not to get on with Jimmy and they often had a go at each other. Mind you, not many people get on with Duggan! He doesn't come up our way much but when he does, he seems even more surly than usual.'

'Tell me about it!' Alec replied, 'He barely has a civil word for anyone these days! So what were Jimmy and Pat having a go at each other about this time?'

'To be honest, I didn't take much notice at the time but now I come to think about it, it was something to do with Duggan's mobile phone. That's it, I think Jimmy had answered Duggan's phone while he was in the shower and Duggan was telling Jimmy to mind his own business or something like that.'

'Really?' Alec hadn't thought anything of Colin mentioning that Jimmy and Duggan had exchanged a few words. As Colin had said, that was par for the course. But maybe there was something in this after all. 'So Jimmy answered Pat's phone? What did he say?'

'I don't think he said anything. I wasn't really paying much attention.'

'Think back, Colin, what exactly do you remember?'

There was a pause.

'I remember a phone ringing. I knew it wasn't mine so that's why I didn't take much notice. Jimmy answered it. I must have assumed it was his. Then Duggan came in and that's when he had a go at Jimmy.'

'And Jimmy didn't say anything on the phone?'

'I don't think so. He might have said 'hello' or something but I'm pretty sure he didn't say anything else. It all happened pretty quickly. Duggan came in and grabbed the phone from him and had a go at him. I then left.'

'Did you say anything?'

'Not that I recall. I might have shouted out 'goodbye' to anyone in earshot as I went out of the door but that's it I'm afraid.'

'How long was Jimmy holding the phone before Duggan intervened?'

'God, I don't know. Only a few seconds. Why is this so important?'

'I don't know that it is. But something happened to change Jimmy from his usual happy go lucky self to a worried man who was murdered two or three hours later!'

'I hardly think a few cross words with Pat Duggan would be responsible for that!'

'You're probably right, but supposing Jimmy heard something on the phone that he wasn't supposed to?'

'I honestly don't think there was time, Alec.'

'Well, something appears to have happened and if it didn't happen then, it could only have happened between there and the car park if Jimmy was fine till then. Whatever it was must have happened before he started driving home. He either heard or saw something pretty sensational!'

'Maybe someone offered him a bribe on the way to the car park?'

'Possibly. But why kill him? Surely you don't just kill a jockey who refuses to take a bribe?'

'What if Jimmy threatened to expose whoever tried to bribe him?'

'But everyone knows how straight Jimmy is. No one in their right mind would try to bribe him. And if they did, wouldn't they be more likely to approach him through some unknown intermediary rather than risk exposure?'

'I suppose so.'

'Did you tell the police about the incident with Duggan?'

'No. It never occurred to me that it might be relevant. It seemed such a trivial matter I didn't consider it unusual. Do you think I should have?'

'I don't know. Maybe. That's why I've been ringing round. To see if the police may have missed something because they don't know our world.'

'Should I ring them now?'

'Leave it with me, Colin. I'm in contact with the senior officer down here. I'll see if he thinks it's important. If he does, no doubt he'll get in touch with you.'

'I can't tell him any more than I've told you.'

Alec ended the call and considered what he'd learnt, if anything. Duggan? So he may have been the last person to speak to Jimmy before he was killed. Unless, of course, something happened afterwards.

Alec picked up the phone again and dialled the mobile number on Fuller's card. He had originally planned to phone all the jockeys who had ridden in the last race but decided to give Pat Duggan a miss and let the police deal with this new information. Fuller answered almost immediately and did not seem at all concerned about the lateness of the hour nor that Alec had managed to find out something that he had missed.

'Do you think it might be significant?' Alec asked.

'Possibly. I'd be interested to hear what Mr.Duggan has to say about it.'

'You mean this is the first you've heard about this, so Duggan didn't mention the incident to you when you spoke to him?'

'I'm not supposed to discuss with you what other people we've spoken to did or did not say to us but no, he didn't mention it. But then again, why should it have seemed any more important to him than Mr.Sharp?'

Alec had to admit he had a point.

38

Nicola had become so much a part of Alec's life that she had managed to quell her fears of exposure and really believe that she had put her past behind her. Of course, she should have known better but she had begun to think with her heart rather than her head.

Any notions of security were well and truly crushed at Huntingdon races the following week. She had driven up to the midweek meeting to watch Alec ride and as she wanted to get back to London before the A1 and the entry roads to London snarled up with rush hour traffic, she decided to leave before the last race.

As she walked back to the car park, she was thinking about what Alec had told her about the police investigation into Jimmy's death. After Alec had given Chief Inspector Fuller the information from Colin Sharp, Fuller had had the decency to tell Alec that morning the results of his inquiry into the matter.

Apparently, Duggan had made no attempt to deny that there had been words between him and Jimmy but had stated that the incident only lasted a few seconds and when he had left, Jimmy had seemed fine. He had admitted that they hadn't always seen eye to eye but hadn't seen any reason to tell the police about such a trivial incident.

When asked who had called him, Duggan said that it had been a friend of his brothers.

He knew this because he had rung back about ten minutes later. Duggan told Fuller that he'd met this man in Ireland but that he now worked on building sites in the UK. Somehow, he had got hold of Duggan's mobile number and rang him from time to time hoping for tips. Duggan had said that the man was a nuisance and had no idea where he was.

Fuller had checked Duggan's phone records and found that Duggan did indeed receive two calls at that time within ten minutes of each other, the first lasting only a few seconds and the second a couple of minutes. He had received calls from the same number about two or three times a month previously, none of them lasting very long. Unfortunately, the number was for an untraceable pay as you go phone.

Fuller did not feel that he could pursue the matter any further but Alec had told Nicola that so far as he was concerned it was all a little suspicious.

As Nicola walked through the car park towards her own car, she was turning this over in her mind. She was vaguely aware of a couple of people behind her but thought nothing of them until she heard the two words that she had been fearing above all others.

'Hello, Susie.'

The words had come from one of the two men behind her. She felt the blood drain from her face and her scalp began to sweat under the hat she was wearing. Nevertheless, she had the presence of mind to continue walking and not to react outwardly at all. How could anyone have recognised her dressed as she was, her hair concealed by a hat, a scarf, a long coat with the collar up and very little make up? Had the men made a mistake? After all, it was a fairly common name.

But there was no mistake. She could hear the men catching up with her.

'What's the matter, Susie, don't you want to talk to two of your biggest fans?'

'Maybe she's too posh for the likes of us now!' the other man said.

Nicola quickened her pace. She could see her car ahead, a convertible 3 series BMW. As she hurried along, she fumbled in her bag and found her keys. Unfortunately, she had to walk round to the other side of the car to reach the driver's door. That meant she had to face the men following her. Not to look up would have been unnatural and she was still harbouring the hope that she could make the men think that they were mistaken. Maybe they would even apologise.

Her heart sank when she looked up. These were just the sort of men who would be fans and they did not look the apologising types despite their broad grins. One was absolutely huge with a battered looking face and wearing a long black leather coat. The other was shorter but stocky with cropped hair and a single earring, wearing a leather bomber jacket and jeans. They were both in their early forties.

'That's better, darling,' the taller one said 'It's not very polite to ignore such loyal admirers.'

For a moment, Nicola couldn't decide whether to deny who she was or to try and appease them in some way. Maybe they'd go away if she gave them her autograph or something. But it was the 'something' that worried her. These men did not look as if they would be easily appeased.

'I'm sorry, I think you must be mistaken,' she said as firmly as she could.

'No mistake, Susie. We'd recognise you anywhere although we'd have to admit you're usually wearing less!'

Nicola managed to get the door unlocked and open but as she got in the car, the shorter man showed surprising speed to get round the front of the car and prevent her from shutting the door.

'Let go of it!' Nicola shouted, hoping that the man would back off as there were other people in the car park leaving early even if not in the immediate vicinity.

For a moment, the man glared at her and then he grinned, looking down to where Nicola's coat had fallen open as she had got in car, revealing her legs.

'We'll be seeing you, Susie,' he said as he released the door and allowed her to shut it.

Nicola switched on the engine and span the wheels on the grassy surface of the field which served as the car park in her haste to get away. As she drove towards the exit, she looked in her mirror and saw the two men staring after her, both with their hands in their pockets and both still grinning.

She then left the car park and turned right on to the short stretch of road leading to the A1. She turned left at the roundabout on to the A1 and drove as fast as she could to the nearest services where she parked away from the petrol pumps and burst into tears.

After composing herself, Nicola drove the rest of the way home and desperate for someone to talk to, phoned Sol.

Sol listened as Nicola told him about her encounter with the two men.

'I always knew something like this was going to happen. I knew it was too good to be true,' Nicola said tearfully.

'Hold on a minute.' Sol replied, 'It's not the end of the world. You'll probably never come across them again.'

'Then why did they behave so menacingly?'

'I thought you said they only said 'hello' and made a couple of remarks about being fans?'

'Believe me, Sol, they didn't behave like fans! Fans are usually pathetic guys who act as if they're proud to meet you. It's not what these men said as much as their attitude. Their whole demeanour was intimidating, threatening…it's difficult to describe if you weren't there. It's as if they wanted to let me know that I hadn't seen the last of them.'

'They didn't mention Alec?'

'No. Nothing like that.'

'Well, maybe they simply spotted you and followed you to the car park to check you were who they thought you were. If they haven't connected you to Alec, you've got nothing to worry about. They simply spotted Susie Stone at the races. So what? What can they do about it?'

'What if they saw me with Alec earlier?'

'If they had, and intended to do anything about it, they would probably have mentioned it. Come to think of it they probably wouldn't have approached you at all.'

'What do you think I should do?'

'What can you do? Just carry on as normal and hope you've seen the last of them. Although it might be sensible to avoid Huntingdon. They may live locally and be regulars there. The only other thing you can do is check tomorrow's tabloids!'

'That's not funny, Sol! What I am going to do is to avoid all racecourses for the next couple of weeks. I'll make some excuse to Alec and just visit him at his home.'

Nicola felt a little better after talking to Sol but found it difficult to stop worrying about what happened. Quite apart from the incident itself, she had been convinced that not even her biggest fans would be able to recognize her in her winter racing clothes wrapped up against the cold. She wondered whether she should cut and dye her hair as well.

That night, she slept badly and at one point woke up in a sweat having dreamt about one of the last scenes she had shot before meeting Alec. The scene had been filmed in a plush hotel suite. She had been playing the part of a rich woman 'entertaining' the two men who had just killed her husband at her request. The only difference in her dream was that the assassins were the men who had approached her that afternoon at Huntingdon. As they had started to paw her, she had woken up with a scream in a pool of sweat.

39

Alec, of course, was completely unaware of Nicola's worries but was missing Jimmy and increasingly frustrated at the lack of progress of the police investigation into his murder. He was however grateful to be able to concentrate on the hectic schedule demanded of a top jockey during the lengthy run up to the Cheltenham Festival.

Martin and Alec had decided to give Deep Secret one more run before the Gold Cup in a three mile handicap chase at Sandown in mid February and as Alec walked the horse back to the stable early one morning after giving him a workout on the gallops, he felt confident that this was the horse that could finally break their duck in the big race.

His thoughts were interrupted when he saw the flashing lights of an ambulance as he approached the yard and he knew something was seriously wrong when he saw the anxious and drawn face of Bill Ryan waiting for him at the entrance.

'What's going on, Bill?' Alec asked as the head lad led the horse over to his box.

Bill did not reply until Alec had dismounted and when Alec looked into his face, he saw that Bill was on the verge of tears.

'I'm sorry, Alec. It's Martin.'

Alec went cold.

'What's happened?'

'It looks like a heart attack. There's no easy way to tell you, but I'm afraid he's dead.'

Alec felt his legs go weak and he had to lean against the stable for support. He then sank down to his haunches and put his hands over his face. After a few moments, he looked up at Bill with tears in his eyes. Bill reached down and helped Alec up.

'But he was fine when I left the stable. What happened?' Alec asked.

'It must have happened soon after you left. Martin went into his office and Annie found him when she took him a cup of coffee. She called me and rang for an ambulance but he was already dead when she found him.'

'Where is she now?'

'In the house crying her eyes out. I left her to come and meet you.'

'We must get back to her.'

As they walked across to the house, Alec noticed that the stable staff had gathered in the yard. Lads and lasses alike had tears in their eyes.

'But he wasn't even sixty…' Alec commented.

'His father died from a heart attack at about the same age,' Bill replied. 'Maybe Martin should have had some sort of check up but you know what he was like about seeing doctors. If there was the slightest thing wrong with a horse he'd call the vet in, but he hadn't seen a doctor in years.'

They found Annie in the kitchen sitting at the table sobbing. When she saw Alec, she got up and threw her arms round him.

'Oh, Alec, I'm so sorry!' she said.

'Thanks, Annie. But you and Bill knew him longer than I did.'

'I know, but you were like a son to him, particularly after your parents were killed. He was so proud of you and what you've achieved since coming to the stable. And for you to lose Martin so soon after Jimmy…'

Alec sat down at the table.

'What do we do now?' he asked.

'Leave everything to me,' Bill replied. 'I'll go to the office and make the necessary calls and arrangements. As for the stable, it's too early to say what's going to happen to it but in the meantime, we have to carry on as best we can. As head lad, I'll take temporary charge. When I've made a few calls, I'd better say a few words to the rest of the staff. They may be upset now, but they'll soon start getting anxious about their jobs.'

'What about all the owners?' Alec asked.

'They'll all have to be rung. Hopefully, none of them will remove their horses until we know a bit more about what's going to happen.'

'Let me help you,' Alec said. 'There are dozens of people to be rung.'

'OK. We've got two lines. We'll make a list as to who is phoning who.'

'What about Melanie?'

'Yes, I'm not looking forward to that. It's still the middle of the night in America but I'll have to ring her soon as the news is bound to get out and the local press in Kentucky may pick up on it given she works at a leading yard over there.'

Once again, the whole racing world went into shock and mourning. For Alec, it was as if his whole world had collapsed. This time, he felt that he could not just carry on. Losing Jimmy had been bad enough but Alec's life had revolved around Martin and his stable. If Martin had looked on Alec as a son, Alec had looked on Martin as a father figure, friend and employer all rolled into one. Martin had made Alec's career. They had shared their triumphs and disappointments together. There had been so much to look forward to, in particular Deep Secret. For a time, Alec contemplated retiring. He refused all rides until after the funeral. Not that there were any from the stable anyway. As a mark of respect, Bill withdrew all the stable's runners until after the funeral had taken place.

Alec was grateful that Nicola was around but even she seemed detached and pre-occupied. Alec assumed that she too was in shock, as indeed she was, but she was also sick with worry. She could not bear the thought that on top of all his other problems, Alec might find out about her past. Nothing had appeared in any of the papers as she had feared, but the incident at Huntingdon had shattered her confidence and made her realise how vulnerable she was.

40

Although the stable had no runners, the rest of the routine at the yard had to go on.

On the afternoon before the funeral, Alec, Bill, Annie and some of the more senior staff sat in the kitchen at teatime. The mood was sombre and the conversation, such as it was, inevitably turned to the future of the yard. None of the owners had indicated that they intended to remove their horses but the staff all knew that it was only a matter of time unless something pretty dramatic happened ensuring the yard's continuity.

'Who could possibly take Martin's place?' said one of the older lads who had been at the stable longer than Alec.

'I could.'

The voice came from the open doorway and everyone in the room turned towards it. Despite having come straight from Heathrow after a long flight, Melanie Saunders looked immaculate. Her long brown hair cascaded around the fur collar of the long coat she was wearing and her high heeled boots made her look taller than most of the lads in the room. Annie could not help thinking that Melanie must have touched up her make up before making her entrance.

Melanie looked around the room with her deep brown eyes until she reached Alec. For a brief moment, their eyes locked to the exclusion of everyone else in the room.

A host of memories came flooding back to Alec, not all of them pleasant, but the moment soon passed and Melanie turned away to acknowledge the greetings and expressions of sympathy from the other people in the room.

Bill and Annie went over and hugged Melanie. Alec stood up and stepped towards her too.

'Melanie, I …'

But before he could get the words out, Melanie interrupted him.

'I know how much my father meant to you too, Alec. And you to him. He always told me what you were doing in every letter he wrote to me.'

Alec did not know whether he should hug her too but Melanie offered him her hand in what appeared to be a rather awkward and formal gesture. Her hand felt firm but cold and Alec could not help thinking about the last time that there had been any physical contact between them in altogether different circumstances.

When Alec had first joined Martin's stable as a conditional jockey, Melanie had been ten years of age. As Alec's career had taken off, Melanie had grown into a young woman. In those early years, they had been close, like brother and younger sister. He had taught her to ride, spent time with her when Martin had been too busy with the stable. She, perhaps not surprisingly, had idolised Alec. Her bedroom was plastered with pictures of him and stories about his triumphs. She had wanted to be a jockey like him and he and Martin had had to persuade her to finish her schooling.

As she grew older and developed into a stunning looking teenager, what had begun as a child's hero worship became a full blown crush.

This became a source of embarrassment for Alec, who was always worried that Martin might notice the way in which she flirted with him. Whether Martin noticed or not, he said nothing and Alec made sure that Martin never had any cause for concern even though Alec by then was beginning to acquire a reputation as a ladies' man.

Alec went out of his way to discourage Melanie and often when they were alone Melanie would tease him for being so stand offish.

'I'm not going to eat you,' she would say. 'If the press could see the great Alec Hammond now' she would laugh.

Matters came to a head at the party thrown by Martin to celebrate Alec's first jockey's championship. It was a huge affair. The house was full and the champagne was flowing. Alec was twenty four years old. Melanie was sixteen but that evening she looked much older, wearing full make up, high heels and a short low cut black dress. Only the ridiculous length of the dress and the way in which she seemed oblivious to the effect it was having on the men at the party gave any hint as to her true age.

By about half way through the party, Melanie had had far too much champagne as indeed had Alec and most of the people there.

Alec noticed that she was tipsy when she told him that there was a phone call for him. As all the rooms downstairs were occupied and noisy, she suggested that he take the call upstairs in her room.

Alec thought nothing of this and trotted upstairs to take the call. It was some years since he had been in her room and he noticed that the walls were still covered with his pictures as he walked over to the phone. When he picked it up, there was just the dialling tone. Puzzled, he put the phone down. As he did, he heard the door close behind him.

He turned round and saw Melanie standing by the door. Maybe because of the drink, he did not twig what was going on at first.

'There's no one there', he said. 'They must have hung up.'

'Oh dear, what a shame!' Melanie smirked and started to walk towards Alec. 'Never mind, I've got something I want to show you.'

By this time, Alec's heart had begun to beat faster and he realised that he had been set up.

'What?' he managed feebly.

'This', she said, and before Alec had a chance to react, she took one of his hands and thrust it up her dress.

Alec had thought back to that moment hundreds of times in the years that followed. He had felt a sense of guilt and betrayal although it had only lasted a second because the truth was that he had left his hand there for a fraction of a second longer than he should have. He could not forgive himself for the fact that for that fraction of a second he had been tempted.

At the same time, Melanie put her other arm round Alec's neck and kissed him. Alec then wrenched his hand away and pushed Melanie back.

'What are you doing?' he said.

'I would have thought that was obvious!' Melanie grinned.

She then slipped the shoulder straps off her dress and let it fall to the ground. Alec had already discovered to his horror that she had not been wearing any knickers. He now saw that she had no bra either. She was standing there stark naked save for her high heeled shoes.

By this time, Alec was beginning to panic. Melanie must have seen him glance over her shoulder.

'Don't worry,' she said. 'No one's going to come up here. I'll lock the door if you're worried.'

With that she walked back and turned the key in the door. She then walked back towards Alec.

'Would you prefer me to keep my shoes on?' she said seductively.

Alec backed away.

207

'I'd prefer you to put your clothes on. You've obviously had too much to drink. Hopefully by the morning you'll have forgotten all about this.'

'Oh no, I'm going to remember this for ever.'

'There's going to be nothing to remember apart from how you made a fool of yourself when drunk.'

'Playing hard to get are we? I know all about your escapades with other women. Now it's my turn.' Melanie had backed Alec against a wall and thrust her breasts out at him.

'But you're not a woman. You're a girl and you happen to be the daughter of my employer, a man who's trusted me with you since you were a child.'

'What's my age got to do with it? Most of my friends at school did it ages ago. I've been saving myself for you. Now I'm sixteen there's nothing to stop us.'

'Oh yes there is!'

Melanie reached for the zip of Alec's trousers but Alec pushed her away.

'Come on. Don't be so stuffy. You don't have to wear a condom. I'm not likely to get pregnant first time.'

Alec pushed her away again.

'That just shows how naïve you are.'

Suddenly, it seemed to dawn on Melanie that Alec was not going to play ball.

'But I've seen the way you look at me,' she said plaintively.

Over the years, Alec had been haunted by that too. He had made a point never to flirt with Melanie but perhaps she had caught him sneaking a glance at her more recently. He had certainly shared a ribald joke or two with some of the lads about her.

'You're mistaken,' he said.

'No I'm not. I know when a man fancies me.'

By this time, tears had welled up in her eyes.

'You screw lots of girls. You've even screwed some of the stable girls! What's wrong with me?'

'Nothing. You're just too young and it would be a betrayal of your father.'

By this time, Melanie was crying.

'But I love you. I always have. I thought you felt the same,' she stammered.

Maybe he did.

'I've always been fond of you but not in that way. I'm too old for you.'

'You bastard!' she screamed. 'I'd have done anything for you. How can you lead me on and then reject me like this?'

By this time, Alec had managed to get to the door. He unlocked it and looked back at Melanie, who by this time was sitting on the bed sobbing and trying to cover herself with her dress.

'Let's just forget all about this,' Alec said hopefully, as he opened the door.

Melanie looked up at him.

'I hate you!' she shouted and as Alec shut the door behind him, what he assumed was one of her shoes thudded into the door behind him.

Alec got what he wanted in one sense. The incident was never mentioned again. However, his relationship with Melanie changed completely from that time onwards.

No longer did she go out of her way to hang around with him. Indeed, she kept away from him as much as possible although she remained civil and friendly towards him when her father was around, probably, Alec thought, for her father's benefit.

The other change was that for the first time she started bringing boyfriends back to the stable. Martin had mixed feelings about this as most fathers would have, but commented to Alec one day, 'well, at least she seems to have got over that crush over you and is seeing people of her own age!'

Although Melanie tended to avoid Alec as much as possible, the one exception was when she had a new boyfriend, whom she would flaunt in front of him. Unfortunately, this never had the desired effect so far as she was concerned. She would introduce Alec dismissively as her father's jockey but instead of behaving equally dismissively, the poor youth would be so overcome at being introduced to such a celebrity that he would almost bow and touch his forelock, often stammering something about Alec being one of his heroes or worse, asking for Alec's autograph. No wonder none of them lasted long!

For his part, Alec always behaved as normally as possible but could not help feeling a twinge of annoyance at the thought of what these pimply youths were doing with Melanie and more to the point, that she was letting them do it just to spite him.

At the same time, Melanie's ambition to be a jockey faded. She finished her schooling and went away to university. From then on, she came back to the stable less and less, tending to spend the long vacations abroad and most of the other vacations staying with friends.

As soon as she graduated, she moved out to Kentucky to work as an assistant trainer in a racing stable and learn the trade. Martin had hoped that one day she might take over from him but that was anticipated to have been many years hence and long after Alec had retired. Now she was back…

Alec jerked his mind back to the present. Melanie had sat down at the other end of the table and was explaining her plans to take over Martin's licence. There was an air of excitement from the lads who saw that their jobs might be safe after all.

'How do you think the Jockey Club will react?' Bill Ryan

asked, bringing an air of reality back to the conversation. 'You've two years experience in a flat yard in America.'

'I don't think there should be a problem,' Melanie replied. 'Everyone knows that my father always ran this stable as a team effort. If we all pull together and persuade the owners to give it a try, then we can do it. I'm sure that's what Dad would have wanted and I do own the stable now!'

After a while, the lads drifted back to work where they could spread the news to the other employees. Bill and Annie also left leaving Alec and Melanie alone. For a few seconds there was an awkward silence, until Melanie broke it.

'You haven't said much about my plan, Alec. Don't you think I can do it?'

'Yes, of course I do!'

'I can count on you, can't I, Alec? You're a crucial part of the team.'

'Yes, yes, of course! What on earth makes you think you can't?' Alec smiled at this last comment but immediately regretted doing so. Melanie was not smiling. There was another pause, before Melanie again broke the silence.

'I hear you're seeing someone.'

'Er, yes, I am.'

'Dad told me in his letters that you'd been seeing her for a few months. That must be a record by some margin. He said you were good for each other and he was very fond of her too.'

'Yes. Well you'll be able to meet her tomorrow.'

'My, my! Is this a new mature Alec Hammond?'

'Maybe. What about yourself? Martin told me you were seeing one of the trainer's sons in the States.'

'I was. But I broke it off when I heard Dad had died and I knew I had to come back.'

'Just like that?'

'Well, it wasn't really going anywhere. There's no way I was going to stay there for ever. Look, I'm sorry, Alec. I haven't told you yet how sorry I was to hear about Jimmy. I know how much he meant to you.'

Alec looked down and put his hand over his eyes.

'Look I'm sorry if I gave the impression that I wasn't enthusiastic about your plans but I've just lost my two closest friends. Jimmy was murdered and now this. I just feel a bit numb at the moment.'

'Believe me, beneath this exterior so do I. But what do you tell someone to do who's just fallen off a horse?'

'Get back on again.'

'Exactly. As soon as the funeral's over, it's business as usual. Agreed?'

'Agreed!'

41

After the funeral, everyone at the yard worked extremely hard to keep the place going as Martin would have wished. Alec and Bill effectively ran the place but were impressed how hard Melanie worked to get to know the horses. Having been brought up in the stable and worked as an assistant trainer, she was well aware as to how to run the yard but before she could take over, she had to become familiar with nearly a hundred horses. Apart from watching them on the gallops, she spent countless hours studying the formbook, watching DVD recordings of races, and talking to the lads and lasses who looked after the horses, learning about each horse's individual characteristics. She also made a point of ringing all the owners to discuss plans for their horses and assure them that the Saunders yard intended to carry on as usual despite its tragic loss.

She was granted a temporary licence to the end of the season and none of the owners, most of whom had become personal friends of Martin, gave any indication that they were going to remove their horses.

As for Alec, he was grateful for the extra work as it gave him a new challenge and less time to dwell on Martin's death and the failure of the police to make any progress in their investigation into Jimmy's murder. He was also relieved that he and Melanie seemed able to work together although he had noticed that she and

Nicola were unlikely to become close friends. The two women were civil to each other but that was as far as it went and Nicola's visits to the stable became less frequent.

For her part, Nicola had sensed immediately a slight tension between Alec and Melanie and she realised that there had probably been some 'history' there. Indeed, from what she knew of Alec's past, she would have been surprised if there had not been. However, it had not affected her relationship with Alec and it was her past rather than Alec's which was causing her more concern.

Nevertheless, she had been growing more confident about that too. Following Martin's death, Nicola had started attending race meetings again, mainly to provide support for Alec, and although she had been very wary to begin with, there had been no sign of the two 'fans' who had accosted her at Huntingdon, nor any other incident which had caused her any concern. Maybe Sol had been right and that there really was nothing to be worried about.

On the second Saturday in February, Alec rode Deep Secret to a comfortable victory in the three mile handicap chase at Sandown, the race which had long been earmarked as his prep race for the Gold Cup at the Cheltenham Festival in just over a month's time. Despite giving away lumps of weight to a good field, Deep Secret had taken up the running at the Pond fence and then galloped away from his rivals up the stiff run in. The horse was immediately installed as three to one favourite for the Gold Cup and by close of business had been backed down to five to two.

The victory also gave the yard a tremendous boost. It was as if the cloud which had been hanging over it since Martin's death was beginning to lift and everyone's dream of winning the Gold Cup as a tribute to him came that bit nearer.

Frank Morris also watched the race with some satisfaction in the knowledge that the next part of his plan to make a killing on the Gold Cup was soon to be put into effect. Knowing that a fancied runner in any race was not going to win was one thing, but knowing that the favourite in the Gold Cup was not going to win was in a different league altogether.

42

Three days later, Nicola was in her London flat, looking forward to driving down to Taunton races and spending the rest of the week at Alec's house, when the doorbell rang. She lifted the entryphone in the hall and looked at the small screen. A man was standing there in what looked like a blue uniform and wearing a blue and red baseball cap.

'Yes?' she said.

The man held up a small package.

'I've got a registered delivery for Miss James. I need a signature,' he replied.

Nicola had not been expecting a delivery but assumed that a production company was sending her a DVD of a film that she had made before she had met Alec. She usually received a complimentary copy of her films and she had quite a collection. She made a mental note to herself to get rid of them all but felt that having answered the doorbell, she had no choice but to accept the delivery on this occasion.

'OK, come up. Second floor. Turn right out of the lift.'

Nicola went to the door and opened it to meet the delivery man. After a few moments, the lift arrived and he stepped out. He had his head down, appearing to study the brown Jiffy bag in his hand, so she could not see his face. As he arrived at the door, it occurred to her that something was wrong but it was too late.

The man suddenly rushed forward preventing her from closing the door and pushed her so hard that she fell over backwards in the hall of her flat. The man then followed her in and was quickly followed by a second man who must have been waiting in the lift as the bogus delivery man walked down the corridor.

As she looked up at them from the floor terrified, she knew immediately who they were.

'Hello, Susie,' the first man said with a grin. 'Thought you'd seen the last of us, did you?'

The second man, who was the shorter of the two and the one who had prevented her from closing her car door at Huntingdon, stepped over to her and hauled her roughly to her feet.

'Where's the living room?' he snarled, and without waiting for an answer, shoved through the half open door behind her. He then threw her down on to the sofa.

'What do you want?' Nicola managed to shout in the most defiant tone she could muster.

'Nothing like that! Well, not for now anyway!' the man smirked.

'To begin with, we want to show you something,' the larger man replied. He opened the package in his hand and took out what looked like a CD or a DVD. 'I presume you've got a DVD player. I expect you like to watch your own performances. Turn you on, does it, to see yourself on screen? Like to show your friends and family what sort of things you get up to?'

Seeing a DVD player on the other side of the room under the television, he walked over and switched them both on. He inserted the DVD and picked up the remote control.

'Which channel for the DVD?' he demanded.

Nicola didn't reply, whereupon the shorter man leant over and slapped her round her face.

'Twelve,' she sobbed.

The two men sat down on either side of her on the sofa, facing the television. They were both so stocky that she could feel them pressing against her sandwiching her in the middle. She remembered the nightmare that she had had following the incident at Huntingdon and felt sick.

'We're going to watch a short film,' the larger one said and pressed the play button.

Nicola looked at the screen and to her surprise found herself watching Alec being led back triumphantly to the winners' enclosure at a racecourse. Although she had not been to the Cheltenham Festival herself and had not really watched racing before meeting Alec, she realised that this was a recording of one of his past triumphs there.

Alec punched the air as his horse was led into the unsaddling enclosure. Nicola could see the joy on the faces of the cheering crowd thronging around the enclosure. Hats were thrown in the air. She then saw Martin step forward as Alec dismounted. The two men embraced. She could see that Martin had tears in his eyes. The proud owners stood next to them waiting for their turn to congratulate Alec.

'That's loverboy winning the Champion Hurdle three years ago. Quite a hero isn't he?' said the taller of the two men. 'The nation's favourite jockey. The punters' friend. The country's most eligible batchelor. In contrast, this is you...'

The picture suddenly changed. Nicola saw herself on her knees, wearing nothing but high heels and stockings being taken from behind by one man while servicing another in front of her. The cheering of the crowd was replaced by grunts and groans.

Nicola thought she was going to throw up. She tried to look away but the shorter of the two men put one hand behind her head and the other on her jaw and forced her to look back at the screen.

'…a filthy slag who's wormed her way into his life. A whore who's not even fit to lick his riding boots.'

The picture mercifully went blank and the taller man went over and removed the disc.

'What do you think it would do to Alec if he found out what you're really like?' he asked. 'What with losing his best friend and his guvnor, I reckon this could put him in a nuthouse. There's only so much a man can take.' He paused. 'But we wouldn't want to do that to him, would we?'

Nicola looked up at the man through tears. Was there still hope?

'What do you want?' she sobbed. 'Money? Sex?'

The man laughed.

'Well, that would do us but unfortunately our own guvnor has something else in mind.'

'What?'

'Well, it's simple really. You're going to make sure Alec doesn't ride Deep Secret in the Gold Cup.'

Nicola was shocked.

'Are you crazy? No one can stop Alec riding Deep Secret. Only injury or illness….'

Her words petered out.

The man clapped mockingly.

'Perhaps you're not the dumb blond I thought you were. You catch on fast. We could stop Alec riding the horse by simply breaking his legs but that might arouse suspicion so we, or rather you, are going to make him ill.'

'You are crazy.'

The man ignored her comment but reached into his pocket and held up a small pill.

'You're going to give him one of these the night before the race. Don't worry. It won't do him any permanent harm but he won't be in a fit state to ride the following day. It'll seem like he's

219

got a bad dose of food poisoning. He'll be fit as a fiddle again in forty eight hours max.'

'You can't be serious', Nicola said. 'I'm not poisoning him!'

The man stepped forward and put a large hand round Nicola's throat and squeezed. Nicola started choking.

'Oh, we're serious all right! You'll do exactly what we say or your great romance is over. Not only will Alec get a box of your films but the press will be told your identity. And if you tell anyone about this, you and Alec will end up like Jimmy O'Brien.'

With that, the man lifted Nicola off the sofa by the hand he had round her throat and then threw her to the floor. As she lifted her hands to her throat, he then kicked her viciously in the stomach.

The man looked down at her.

'I hope I've made myself clear', he snarled. 'This isn't a matter for debate.'

He then reached down towards her. Nicola cowered away from him but he grasped her clothing and lifted her up effortlessly before flinging her back on to the sofa. The other man sat on the other end of the sofa grinning.

'Well?' the taller man said, 'Have I made myself clear?'

He took a step towards Nicola, causing her to flinch, then he stopped when Nicola managed to stammer 'Yes'.

'Do this for us', he said, 'and you'll never see us again. You'll be free to go on deceiving Hammond and can live happily ever after. Refuse…well that's not worth thinking about. In addition to exposing you, we'd have to stop Hammond another way and I can assure you, it wouldn't be pretty!'

'How do I know this wouldn't be a regular thing?' Nicola asked.

'Don't worry. This is a one off. We've got other ways of stopping horses. Besides, people would get suspicious if Hammond kept being ill. Particularly as we want to do a dry run.'

'What do you mean?'

'We need to know it works. That's why you're going to give one of these pills to Hammond this weekend. We need to see if one pill is enough.'

Nicola opened her mouth to object but no words came out. She could see the man staring at her.

'Very wise,' he said. 'You know we won't take no for an answer.'

He held out a pill to her.

'Take it.'

Nicola did as she was told.

'Put it in his food Sunday evening. We expect to see that Alec has given up his rides on Monday due to illness. If it works, you do the same the evening before the Gold Cup.'

'What if Alec doesn't want me staying with him during the Festival week?' Nicola asked.

'You insist. You'll get round him…or else…'

'Why is it so important he doesn't ride?'

'You don't need to know that. Do this and you're free. But tell anyone at all about this and you and Hammond are dead. Understand?'

Nicola nodded. She was in on doubt that these men would carry out their threats. She realized that they must have been the ones who had killed Jimmy. They had as good as admitted it. Where Jimmy had fitted in she couldn't begin to imagine but she was under no illusions that these men would stop at nothing.

Without another word, the men got up and left.

43

Needless to say, Nicola did not sleep a wink that night. Her neck and stomach were sore but any physical pain was insignificant compared to the anguish she felt. Her past life was now a source of shame to her. She had been revolted at watching the DVD. The threats of violence were nothing compared to the threat of exposure. Although she had always feared exposure, she had really begun to believe that she could start a new life, a life with decent people, with a man she could truly love. She simply could not bear the thought of Alec finding out about her past. However much he loved her, he would surely reject her for what she had been before he met her, indeed what she still was when he met her. Or would he? Maybe if she told him in her own way…Perhaps after his shock and an explanation as to how she ended up in that world, he'd accept her for what she was, not what she had been before? But could he take all that after Jimmy and Martin's deaths? The press would have a field day. Then there were the threats of violence. Could she expose him to that risk?

All these things she turned over in her mind, but in the end decided that she had little choice but to co-operate for the time being although she did not know whether she would be able to bring herself to administer some unknown drug to Alec. Supposing one pill was too much. Supposing it killed him…

Nicola did not go down to see Alec till the weekend. Alec rode a winner on the Saturday and wanted to go out to dinner afterwards. He picked at his food as usual but noticed that Nicola was eating even less than him. She had been fairly quiet since coming down from London after racing.

'Is something the matter?' he asked her. 'You've hardly said two words since you arrived.'

Nicola attempted a smile. 'I'm sorry. I haven't been very good company have I? I think I must have some bug.'

'As long as you don't give it to me!' Alec grinned.

Nicola winced but outwardly smiled.

'There's a lot of that sort of thing going around,' she said.

'I was only joking', Alec replied. 'I never seem to catch anything.'

On Sunday evening, Nicola said that she would make them some soup for supper. While Alec watched television in the living room, Nicola prepared the soup in the kitchen. Her heart was thumping. She took out the pill and changed her mind several times as to whether to use it. Eventually, she crushed it into a powder and with tears in her eyes poured it into Alec's bowl.

The effect was fairly dramatic. Within half an hour, Alec was rushing for the loo and while Nicola quietly sobbed, Alec spent the whole night alternating between the loo and the sink. By morning, he was weak and exhausted. He tried to get up but couldn't. It was clear that he would not be able to get to Fontwell let alone ride if he did get there.

He asked Nicola to phone Melanie to tell her that he was ill.

Melanie did not seem very sympathetic.

'Ill? I doubt Alec's ever missed a day's racing through illness in his life. I suppose I'll have to put Billy Johnson up. The owners will disappointed at not seeing Alec,' she complained.

Nicola felt as if Melanie was blaming her. If only she knew!

Much to Nicola's relief, Alec began to show signs of improvement by lunchtime and despite her feelings of guilt, she could not help wondering whether there was some hope for her. Maybe she could get away with this. Maybe the men would leave her alone if she co-operated. Maybe pigs might fly....

Frank Morris switched on the television in his office and tuned in to the Go Racing channel for the coverage from Fontwell. The presenter who introduced the programme explained that due to illness, Alec Hammond's mounts would be taken by the stable's conditional jockey, Billy Johnson.

Morris smiled.

44

With just two weeks to go to the Cheltenham Festival, excitement was mounting to a degree which Nicola would never have believed possible. Before meeting Alec, she had never read the sports pages let alone the racing pages and the specialist journals. Although the racing press had been speculating about Cheltenham all season, it seemed that every article was now obsessed with what horse was running where at the meeting, who was riding what and what the latest odds were. Of course, the biggest coverage was given to the Gold Cup for which Deep Secret was now the 2 to 1 favourite. Some sections of the press had attributed the contraction in the price to the 'Alec factor'. It seemed that everyone not involved with another runner wanted Alec to break his duck in the race and the general public were backing Deep Secret out of sentiment as much as on form.

Nowhere was the excitement greater than at the Saunders yard. Apart from the favourite for the Gold Cup, the yard had a number of other fancied runners and the stable staff were determined to have the horses ready to run for their lives as a tribute to Martin. Melanie was proving to be a tough and able successor but as she confided to Alec and Bill, a successful Cheltenham was essential for the continuity of the yard. Any winner at the Festival increases a racing yard's profile, particularly in one of the championship races. Although the owners had remained loyal after Martin's

225

death, she wanted to prove to them and the whole racing world that the yard could still turn out the big winners. Then, there was a chance that none of them would take their horses away at the end of the season.

In the meantime, the show had to go on, although the horses running in the last couple of weeks before the Festival were largely the lesser lights, not deemed good enough for the big meeting.

During this period, Alec seemed pre-occupied for much of the time. Nicola could see how much Cheltenham meant to him and in particular the Gold Cup. He had explained to her that although he really wanted to win the race for himself, that was not of paramount importance. Many top jockeys had never won the race. What was of paramount importance was winning the race for Martin.

None of this made Nicola feel any better but she was grateful that Alec's pre-occupation meant that he did not notice her own anxious state of mind. Nicola was also aware that at this time, none of the jockeys wanted to suffer an injury that might put them out of the Festival. However, her feelings of guilt increased when she found herself wondering whether a moderate but temporarily disabling injury to Alec like a broken collar bone might mean that she did not have to 'poison' him again.

With seven days to go, Nicola had still not heard any more from the two thugs who had threatened her at her flat. She was staying with Alec until the Festival was over and had not been going to the races. The thought occurred to her that if the men did not know where she was, they might think that she had changed her mind and carry out their threat. However, she soon found out that the men knew exactly where she was. She was sitting having breakfast while Alec was sorting through his mail.

'There's one for you here!' he said, passing her a letter. 'How does anyone know you're here?'

Nicola looked at the brown envelope and knew exactly whom it was from. The name and address was handwritten but before 'Nicola', the writer had first written 'Sus' and then crossed the letters out.

Nicola felt as if she had been winded but managed to reply 'I gave Sol this address because there was some tax form I needed to fill in.' She glanced across to Alec but to her relief, he had already turned his attention to the Racing Journal.

After a few moments, Nicola got up and took the letter into the bathroom, where she locked herself in and opened it. There was a single sheet of paper and a very small brown envelope with a small object inside. She did not need to open it as she knew that it contained a pill. She unfolded the sheet of paper with her hands shaking and read the words on it:

'Susie,
Sorry about the envelope. Can't get used to Nicola. You know what to do. Do it and you'll never hear from us again. Doublecross us and you'll wish you'd never been born.'

Nicola sank down on to the toilet seat. At that moment, she did wish that she had never been born. It took a good five minutes before she composed herself. She slipped the pill into the pocket of her jeans, tore up the note and flushed it down the toilet and forced herself to smile as she went back to join Alec.

45

Things had not been going well for Pat Duggan either. Jimmy O'Brien's murder had hit him hard. Duggan had never felt much guilt or remorse about stopping racehorses but even though he had never liked O'Brien, he could not help feeling that he was partially responsible for his death. He was also terrified that he might suffer a similar fate and bitterly regretted ever getting involved with Frank Morris.

He had never had many friends but was usually content with his own company. However, since Jimmy's death he had taken to spending his lonely evenings in company with a whisky bottle.

His state of mind and his drinking had begun to affect his riding. Never known for his sparkling personality, he had relied on his ability alone for rides but now he was making mistakes that he would never have made before.

It was not long before he noticed a reduction not only in the number of rides that he was getting but also in the quality. He had slipped down to third in the race for the jockeys' championship and a month before Cheltenham, he had never had such an empty book of rides for the Festival at that stage. Normally, he would have expected to have had rides booked on several fancied runners for each day of the meeting by that time. He had complained to his agent who had just told him to be patient and that there was still time to get some decent rides.

Despite the fact that he had only been back from racing for about half an hour, he had already downed a couple of whiskies when he heard a knock at the door. Who the hell could that be, he wondered, as he opened the door. When he saw who it was, he was tempted to close the door but fear prevented him. The last thing that he wanted to do was to antagonise Frank Morris.

'Hello, Pat,' Morris said cheerfully. 'How's it going? Not so good, I hear.'

Duggan was relieved to see that Morris was alone. Morris would have brought his tame thugs if there was likely to be any violence.

'What do you want?' Duggan asked. 'Why have you come here? Someone might see us together.'

'Glad to hear you can still think straight,' Morris replied. 'Rumour is you're all washed up. If you're worried about us being seen together, you'd better let me in.'

Duggan reluctantly stood aside and Morris walked straight through to the living room and sat down.

Duggan followed him but did not sit down.

'Well, what do you want, then?' he asked.

'Relax, Pat. Sit down. I've got good news for you. Hence the visit.'

Duggan sat down on the edge of a chair and waited.

'Come on, Pat, where are your manners? Aren't you going to offer me a glass of that whisky you've obviously been drinking?'

Duggan got up again, reluctantly poured two glasses and handed one to Morris.

'So what's this good news then?' he asked.

'I only need you to stop one more horse for me and then our arrangement is over.'

'Just one more and no more after that?'

'Yes. It was never going to be a permanent thing and after this last job I won't need your services anymore.'

'What's the catch?'

'No catch. I promise.'

'What's the horse?'

'Deep Secret in the Gold Cup.'

Duggan choked as he was taking a mouthful of whisky.

'You can't be serious!' But as he looked over at Morris, he could see that he was serious.

'Even assuming I could stop the favourite in the Gold Cup, how do you propose that I get the ride in the first place? Deep Secret's Hammond's ride and even if he wasn't available, the stable would never put me up!'

'The Gold Cup's no different from any other race. I don't care what you do, fall off if you like. As for getting the ride, just leave that to me.'

'How could you possibly get me the ride?'

'I told you. Leave that to me. You haven't got a ride in the race yet, have you?'

'No. But I could well be offered one. There's plenty of time. I might be offered one of the Irish runners.'

'Well, refuse. It's not as if any of the horses left are near the head of the market. There are only outsiders left. People will just think you're hoping for something better.'

'But there probably won't be anything better.'

'I don't care what excuse you use. Just refuse. You need to be free on the day. The offer to ride Deep Secret will be last minute.'

'Oh, God, you're not going to do something to Hammond, are you?'

'Hammond will be fine. Trust me.'

'Trust you? You're joking. No, I'm not doing it. It's too risky. The whole idea's madness.'

The change in Morris was immediate.

'Listen to me, you washed up piece of shit, you will do this if you don't want to end up like Jimmy O'Brien. I'm giving you an opportunity here to make a fresh start. One last job and you may even be able to put your career back on track. Plus, as a leaving bonus, I'll give you twenty grand if you make it look convincing.'

Duggan's resistance crumbled due to a combination of fear and greed. Mention of O'Brien's fate alone would probably have been enough but twenty grand in cash was more than the win bonus would have been and maybe this was his last chance to be free of Morris.

'OK. I'll do it. Get me the ride and Deep Secret won't be winning the Gold Cup. And then we're finished!'

Morris reverted to his friendly demeanour.

'I knew you'd see sense,' he said. 'If all goes well, we never need to meet again.'

46

Mary Pickering had been a widow for ten years. She lived in an old rectory about twenty minutes drive from Lambourn. She had been left comfortably off by her husband and her one extravagance in life was her passion for racehorses which she had shared with her husband. After her family and her garden, racing was her main interest. She and her husband had owned many horses jointly before he died and had always had them trained at the Saunders yard.

Mary had continued to have horses trained by Martin after her husband's death and had been one of his most loyal owners and a frequent visitor to the yard. Like everyone else connected to the yard, she had been devastated by Martin's death but had never once considered removing her horses from the yard.

Over the years, she and her husband had had numerous winners but Deep Secret was by far the best horse that she had ever owned. She regretted that her husband had not lived long enough to own a horse that good. Although nothing would have given her greater pleasure than winning the Gold Cup, she wanted to win the race more for the yard than herself. She had known Melanie since she had been a child and knew how much success in the race would mean in maintaining the yard as a major force in jump racing.

Mary had just come back from visiting her daughter and

grandchild and had just finished checking the afternoons racing results on teletext when the doorbell rang. Assuming it was someone from the village, she opened her front door and was surprised to see two large men standing in her porch. Beyond them and through the gate she could see a large black car with another man in the driver's seat.

The older and smarter dressed of the two men took a step forward.

'Mrs. Pickering?' he asked, in a somewhat rough London accent.

'Yes. How can I...' Mary never finished her sentence. The man shoved the door, pushing her back into the hall so that she nearly lost her balance. Both men then entered the house and the bigger of the two men, who was wearing a long black leather coat, slammed the door behind them.

'What do you want? How dare you burst into my house like that?' Mary shouted.

The two men ignored her and started looking into the rooms leading off the hall.

'Is there anyone else in the house?' the first man demanded.

Mary hesitated whereupon the man grabbed her by the hair.

'Listen, lady, we're going to get on a lot better if you cooperate. Do you understand?'

'Yes,' Mary stammered.

The man let go of her.

'Well, I asked you a question. Is there anyone else in the house?'

'No.'

The other man then spoke for the first time.

'The living room's over here, boss.'

The first man then grabbed Mary's arm and pushed her into room indicated.

'Sit down,' he ordered.

Mary did as she was told and sat down in an armchair.

'I don't keep cash in the house,' she said.

'We don't want your money,' the first man replied.

'Well, what do you want?'

'All in good time. But first we've got something to show you.'

The second man knelt down in front of the television and switched it on. He then switched on the DVD player on the shelf below and put in a disc that he took out of his pocket.

'I'm beginning to get used to this,' he said. 'Hope I've got the right disc. I wouldn't want a respectable lady like you watching the last one I played!'

When he was satisfied that everything was working correctly, he stood up and stepped back.

'We'd like you to watch this,' the first man said.

Mary looked at the screen but Frank Morris concentrated on her as he wanted to see her reaction. He was not disappointed.

Mary realised that she was watching some sort of homemade film, possibly a surveillance DVD of some sort. The quality was not particularly good as the DVD was being taken from a moving car in a street which seemed vaguely familiar. The car came to a halt outside a building on the opposite side of the road. There were lots of cars parked on both sides of the road. Some young women were standing about talking in small groups. There was one group of three that the cameraman concentrated on. He zoomed in on one of the women and Mary immediately recognised her daughter. She now knew why the street had seemed familiar. The DVD was being taken outside her granddaughter's school in Surrey where her daughter and son in law lived.

Mary was horrified. What was going on? Why was she being shown this film? Why had these men gone to the trouble of filming her daughter? She realised that she was so tense that she had forgotten to breathe. She let the air out of her lungs and took a deep breath. Where was this leading?

After a couple of minutes, the women all looked towards the building. The camera moved to the entrance of the school and zoomed in on the children who were now streaming out of the building towards their waiting mothers. Eventually, Mary's seven year old granddaughter, Emily, came into view and the camera remained on her as she ran towards the gates.

Her daughter then came into view again as she walked towards the gates to meet Emily. She took Emily's hand and the camera followed them until they reached her daughter's car. As if this was not bad enough, what happened next caused Mary to fight back a panic attack. Just as her daughter had opened the car door, a man stepped into view. A large man wearing a long black leather coat. He walked up to her daughter and spoke to her. The camera zoomed in again. He appeared to be asking directions. He had a smile on his face. After a few moments, he squatted down and appeared to be speaking to Emily. She smiled and the man patted her on the head. He then stood up and turned directly towards the camera and grinned. Mary recognised him as the man who had inserted the disc into her DVD player.

The screen then went blank for a few seconds before flickering into life again.

This time, the cameraman was walking up a staircase. Mary knew exactly where he was. On the landing he turned right and opened a door. He stepped into a room and panned the camera around Emily's bedroom, before lingering on the bed where Emily's teddies were neatly arranged.

The large man in the leather coat removed the disc and put it back into his pocket.

'Well,' Frank Morris said, 'What did you think of our little film?'

'What do you want?' Mary managed to croak.

'Actually, not a great deal. Not when compared to the lives of your daughter and granddaughter. Pretty girl, Emily. It would be a shame if anything happened to her.'

'I'll do anything you want. Just don't harm them.' Mary pleaded.

'Your horse, Deep Secret, is running in the Gold Cup next week.' Morris said, 'There's going to be a late change of jockey.'

'You want me to take the ride away from Alec Hammond? How can I possibly do that? Alec's ridden for me for years. If I do that, people will want to know why. Not just the stable. It would be all over the press!'

'You don't have to take the ride away from Hammond. When I said a 'late change of jockey' I meant a very late change. Hammond keeps the ride until just before the race but he will be 'indisposed' and won't be able to fulfil his engagement.'

Mary gasped.

'You're not going to hurt him, are you?'

'No one need get hurt if you do what you're told. He just won't be turning up and you'll need a replacement and that's where you come in. You tell Melanie Saunders who that replacement will be.'

'Who?'

'Pat Duggan.'

'That's ridiculous! The stable would never put Duggan up!'

'That's your decision. You're the owner. You insist that Duggan rides.'

'But...'

'No buts. As I said, you're the owner. Melanie Saunders will have no option if you insist. She won't want to risk losing your horses if she doesn't do what you tell her. Anyway, you can justify it. This is the Gold Cup. Whatever you may think of Duggan, he's a top class rider and will be by far the best jockey available. Tell her you wouldn't normally use Duggan but for this race, you want his experience.'

'She won't like it.'

'Tough. She'll have to lump it. It's your decision. She will have to do as she's told. As I said, she won't want to lose your horses, particularly Deep Secret! Tell her you'll take the horse away if she refuses. But it won't come to that. She's a professional. She will realise that Duggan's the best option whatever she thinks of him'

'Why do you want Duggan to ride?' But Mary knew the answer before she had completed the sentence. 'You want him to throw the race, don't you?'

'That's not your concern.'

'What if he won't?'

'Like you, Duggan will do as he's told.'

'And if I do what you want?'

'I'm a man of my word. Do what I want and you'll never hear from me again. Your family will be safe. But if you fail me or tell anyone about this conversation, I don't need to spell out the consequences to you. If you're in any doubt as to whether I would carry out my threats, just remember what happened to Jimmy O'Brien.'

Mary blanched visibly.

'We wouldn't want the same sort of thing to happen to Emily, would we? As for the race, well, Deep Secret's still a young horse. There's always next year.'

'You think I give a damn about a horse race when my family's been threatened. I'll do what you want. Just leave my family alone.'

Morris looked at her for a few moments, then nodded, satisfied.

Without another word, he got up and left, followed by the man in the leather coat.

As they drove away, the driver, Chris Higson, asked whether there had been any problems.

'None whatsoever,' Morris replied. 'I've no doubts about her and Duggan but it all depends on Hammond not turning up. So we're relying on that Stone slag to slip him the pill.'

'She's done it once and seen it didn't do him much harm, so why shouldn't she do it again?'

'I just don't like the idea that the whole plan depends on that bitch's cooperation. I want you two to lean on her again just to make sure.'

'When?'

'As close to the day as possible. She'll be at the meeting every day. Hammond will expect her to attend. Find an opportunity to reinforce the message.'

47

As Cheltenham approached, the racing world became more and more excited and nowhere was the excitement as high as at the Saunders yard. It was as if everyone realised that the future of the yard and their jobs depended on the outcome of this one meeting.

The stable, as usual, had a lot of fancied runners, including of course the favourite for the Gold Cup itself. Security was tightened just in case anyone was stupid enough to try to nobble one of the runners. Frank Morris chuckled when he read in the press about the extra precautions being taken by Melanie Saunders.

'The danger lies closer to home, darling,' he smirked. 'I won't be coming through your fences with a syringe full of dope!'

Alec, who normally had such a relaxed attitude to racing, had taken to retreating to his study for hours on end where he watched videos of Deep Secret's latest races and those of the main rivals.

Nicola had made the mistake of commenting that it was only one race and that there would be other years if he did not win. Alec had replied curtly that he was coming to the end of his career and did not have many chances left to win the race and besides, he felt that he had to win it this year for Martin and the stable.

Nicola was also somewhat put out by the amount of time that Alec was spending at the yard and by the fact that even when he got home, Melanie was constantly ringing him about this or that. Alec could see how she felt and assured her that things would return to normal once Cheltenham was over and Melanie was confident enough not to be always seeking his advice.

Nicola, however, had begun to realise that things would never return to normal after the Gold Cup. How could they? How could she continue living with a man whom she had betrayed, having destroyed not only his dream but those of everyone connected with the yard? She knew that she only had two choices, neither of which involved a future with Alec.

Either she refused to cooperate, in which case she had no doubt that the two men would carry out their threats or she cooperated with them, in which case she would have to disappear as she would no longer be able to continue her relationship with Alec in the knowledge of what she had done.

Finally, the first day of the meeting arrived. The weather had been fairly miserable in the week before but had relented and the sun was shining. Nicola had been to some big meetings since she had started seeing Alec but they had not prepared her for what she encountered at Cheltenham. The crowds, the excitement and expectation were like nothing she had previously experienced. Had it not been for her situation she would have revelled in the atmosphere. Never before had she known a crowd to cheer loudly when the tape went up for the first race and the two mile novice hurdlers opened proceedings.

The Saunders stable were delighted with their fourth place in the first with a horse that had started at odds of twelve to one but everyone knew that it was winners which put a stable on the map.

In the second race, they had one of their main chances. Skinflick, the aptly named horse that had been the only the second winner that Nicola had seen Alec ride all those months ago at Sandown, was second favourite for the Arkle Trophy, the championship race for two mile novice chasers.

Nicola was somewhat surprised to be invited to watch the race with Melanie and the horse's owners, Dr and Mrs Robson. The race turned out to be a cracker. Half the field had departed before the final bend when Skinflick and his old rival, Ratcatcher, opened up a gap on the remaining runners and approached the final fence neck and neck. Both jockeys asked for and got enormous leaps out of their mounts and the horses continued locked together up the stiff uphill run in.

Nicola, forgetting her situation in the excitement of the moment, Melanie and the Robsons were screaming encouragement as was the rest of the crowd. In the final fifty yards, Alec gave Skinflick a final blow with his whip and the willing horse seemed to stick out his neck as the post approached.

'Photograph, photograph' was announced over the tannoy immediately but Alec knew that he had won and stood in the saddle punching the air.

Nicola and Melanie threw their arms around each other in celebration and then hugged the Robsons as well before they all hurried down to the winners' enclosure.

There was pandemonium in and around the enclosure. It seemed as if the whole crowd had backed Alec's mount. As Skinflick was led in, there was a mighty roar and Alec raised both arms in triumph.

Nicola held back a bit as Alec dismounted and was hugged, first by Melanie and then by Mrs Robson. As Alec was posing for photos with the horse and being surrounded by journalists, he caught Nicola's eye and gave her a little wave with his free hand. After a while, he took his saddle to weigh in, taking the time to have a few words into Charlotte's microphone.

At that moment, Nicola made her decision. She could not guarantee that he would win the Gold Cup but she was not going to stop him trying. She was not going to deprive Alec and everyone else connected with the horse of the opportunity to win the race whatever it cost her.

48

After that first day, the Hammond/Saunders bandwagon continued to roll. The stable's runners were all running well and another winner was notched up when Alec won the long distance handicap hurdle. Bookmaker reaction to a stable that was obviously in form was to bring Deep Secret down to seven to four for the Gold Cup, apart of course from Frank Morris, who continued to offer the horse at nine to four, thereby attracting a flood of new money. For good measure, Alec also won a race for Robin North and with three winners was heading the race to be leading jockey at the meeting.

By the afternoon before Gold Cup day, Nicola had resigned herself to disappearing after the race, never to return. Perhaps she'd go abroad and maybe stay with Svetlana while the tabloids made their revelations. She decided that she would write to Alec, explaining everything and begging that he should not think too badly of her.

Before the last race, she saw that for once there was no queue for the ladies beneath one of the stands. When she came out, she found her path blocked by two now familiar figures, Marsh and Higson.

'Just checking you're not planning to renege on our deal,' Marsh snarled, as they hemmed her in against a wall. 'You know what will happen if you do, don't you?'

Marsh had expected a timid and affirmative response but was taken by surprise by Nicola's reaction.

'You'll have to wait and see, won't you,' she replied in an aggressive tone. 'Now piss off, you arseholes, and get out of my way.'

With that, she pushed between them and would have disappeared into the crowd if Higson had not grabbed her arm.

'Leave me alone,' she shouted, in a voice loud enough to attract attention from some nearby racegoers.

Higson was unsure what to do but held on to her arm. By this time, several people had had their attention drawn to the incident. A young man stepped forward.

'Is everything OK?' he asked.

Marsh pushed him back.

'It won't be for you if you don't fuck off and mind your own business!'

'Hey, steady on!' came from another onlooker.

'Someone fetch the police!' someone else shouted.

Marsh and Higson looked at each other.

'You'd better let her go,' Marsh said.

Higson released his grip and Nicola hurried away. Some of the onlookers continued to stare at Marsh and Higson. They glared back at them but not wanting to draw any further attention to themselves, they walked away and melted into the crowd.

By then Nicola had long gone.

'What now?' Higson asked when they were some distance away.

'Christ, I don't know.' Marsh replied. 'We'd better report back to Morris. He can decide.'

While the rest of the racegoers were rushing about putting last minute bets on for the last race, they found a spot where they wouldn't be overheard and Marsh used his mobile to ring Morris and tell him what had happened.

As expected, Morris was not pleased.

'Well, is she going to co-operate or not?' he demanded.

'She knows what will happen if she doesn't,' Marsh replied.

'It will be too late by then. Can you be sure she'll do it because I can't take any chances?'

'She seemed different somehow. Not terrified as she was before. She might still do it but I couldn't guarantee it.'

'Well, that's it then. That bitch is history. It'll have to be plan B then. I thought something like this might happen.'

'What the fuck is plan B?'

Morris explained what he wanted done.

Marsh listened for some time without interrupting.

'Jesus Christ, you don't want much, do you?' he said when Morris had finished, surprising Higson, who had never heard anyone talk to Morris in that tone.

'It'll work, believe me', Morris replied. 'And there's an extra ten grand for each of you if we pull it off.'

'OK,' Marsh said, tempted by the bonus. 'You're the boss. You're sure there won't be anyone at this place.'

'No. I checked. It's been empty for months. I'll be there about ten with the gear. I want to see that bitch get what's coming to her.'

When the conversation was over, Marsh told Higson what was going to happen. Like Marsh, he was horrified at first but felt better when he heard about the ten grand. They had only got a bonus of two and a half grand each for topping O'Brien so ten seemed like a fortune.

49

Alec had been awake for a good hour before his alarm went at 6.00am. He jumped out of bed, showered, threw on some clothes and went downstairs to make some coffee. The previous evening he had not felt like celebrating that day's successes as his mind was totally focussed on the Gold Cup. Now, the day had finally arrived and all the waiting was over. He had imagined how the race might pan out in his mind a hundred times with Deep Secret always the winner. He was now determined to make the dream a reality.

He was intending to go over to the stable as soon as he had had a coffee and was just pouring it out when the doorbell rang. His first thought was that it was someone from the stable. Was there a problem with Deep Secret? Was it such that someone had to come over rather than telephone? With these thoughts in his mind, Alec hurried into the hall and opened the front door. He then froze.

Standing in the porch were two men but was caused him to freeze was the fact that one of them was holding a gun which was pointed at his head.

'What's the matter, Alec?' the man holding the gun and the taller of the two asked. 'It's not like you to be lost for words.'

'What do you want?' Alec managed to say.

'Well, to come in for starters.' The man gestured with the gun for Alec to move back.

Alec stepped back and the two men stepped inside and closed the door.

'Where's the slag?' the man with the gun asked.

'Who the hell are you and what do you want?' Alec demanded.

With that, the shorter of the two men punched Alec in the stomach and as Alec bent double, he kneed Alec in the face splitting the skin above his left eye and sending him tumbling on to his back. The man then stood over Alec, grabbed him by the lapel and raised his fist as if to punch him again.

'You were asked a question,' he snarled.

At that moment, Nicola, who had heard the commotion from upstairs, intervened.

'Leave him alone', she shouted from the stairs.

The man standing over Alec immediately ran up the stairs, grabbed Nicola by the arm and dragged her down to the hall.

'What are you doing here?' Nicola shouted at the men. 'I thought we had a deal.'

At that, Alec who was still feeling groggy, stood up.

'Do you know these men?' he asked, bewildered.

The others ignored him.

'And would you have kept your part of the bargain, Suzie?' the man with the gun asked.

'As a matter of fact, I wouldn't have!' Nicola said and spat in his face.

At that, the man lashed out at Nicola but she stepped back and avoided the full force of the blow. She was off balance when the shorter man grabbed her by the hair and forced her down on to her knees.

'Our guvnor was right about you,' he said and with his other hand undid the tie around Nicola's dressing gown. The gown fell open. Nicola was wearing nothing beneath it. 'Well, look at that', the man grinned. 'What a shame we haven't got time for some fun!'

Alec, horrified, and with blood running down his face, took a step forward but stopped when the taller man put the barrel of the gun under his chin.

'Chris, take this slag upstairs and get her dressed. I want to be out of here in five minutes. As for you,' he said, looking at Alec, 'all will be revealed soon so I don't want to hear another word out of either of you. Understood?'

To emphasise his point, he pushed the barrel of the gun further into Alec's neck. Alec managed a small nod.

When Nicola was dressed, she and Alec had their hands tied behind their backs, were gagged and then taken out to a battered Range Rover and told to get down on the floor in the back. They remained in this position for what seemed like an hour or so. When it began to get light, Alec tried to catch Nicola's eye but she seemed unwilling to look at him.

Eventually, the vehicle came to a halt and they were dragged out. They were parked outside what looked to Alec to be some sort of industrial premises but there were no lights on anywhere and no signs of anyone else around. There was a 'To let' sign hanging on the wall.

One of the men pushed open a door and Alec noticed that the lock had previously been broken. They all went inside what appeared to be an empty office. Alec and Nicola were then pushed across the room and through another door into what appeared to be a large storeroom of some sort. There were no windows and the only furniture was two chairs side by side into which Alec and Nicola were pushed. The men then secured them to the chairs with rope.

Satisfied that they could barely move let alone escape, the larger man said, 'Now, we wait' as he and the other man returned to the office and closed the door.

After what seemed an eternity but was probably no more than an hour or so, Alec and Nicola heard the sound of another vehicle arriving and a car door closing.

They then heard talking in the next room and after about five minutes the door opened and the shorter man came in and removed their gags.

'You won't be needing these any longer', he said. As he removed Nicola's gag from behind, he moved his hands down and felt her breasts through the sweatshirt she had on. 'Maybe we should have made you wear something a bit sexier,' he said with a leer. He then left the room and closed the door again.

As soon as he had gone, Alec, having been released from the gag, turned to Nicola.

'What the hell is going on? How do you know these men?' he demanded. 'And why did that thug call you 'Suzie'?'

Nicola did not reply. She could barely look at Alec. Alec could see tears running down her face.

'Nicola, talk to me, what's going on?'

At that moment, the door opened and the two thugs who had kidnapped them entered the room. They then stepped back and looked towards the door. After a moment, a third man entered the room. He was a large man, though not as large as the thug with the gun, and more smartly dressed in an overcoat and brown brogues. Alec could see that the other two deferred to him as they remained in the background as he walked over to Alec and Nicola.

Alec had no idea who he was but could not fail to notice the effect he had on Nicola. The colour drained from her face, her eyes were wide open with shock and it appeared to Alec that she was trying hard to avoid some sort of panic attack as she was breathing deeply and almost gasping for air.

There was a moment of silence before the man spoke.

'So how's my little girl then? Daddy always knew you'd turn out to be a slut. After all, you were already one as a child.'

Alec looked at Nicola. She didn't reply but she let out some sort of moan which Alec assumed was as a result of shock or even fear.

'I've followed your career with interest', the man continued. 'Of course, a lot of your expertise is down to me, isn't it? And how do you repay me? By refusing to do one little thing for me which would have enabled me to avoid ending up in a similar position to the one you're in now and you to continue living your life of deceit with loverboy here.'

Nicola said nothing. She just continued to stare at the man in horror. He then stepped forward and grabbed her by the chin.

'What's the matter? Cat got your tongue?'

'Fuck off!' Nicola managed to spit at him. She hadn't seen her stepfather since running away from home. The sight of him now made all the childhood memories that she had spent so many years trying to forget come flooding back. The assurances that she was 'Daddy's little girl', the caressing, the pornography that he showed her, the indecent assaults and then the rapes. And worst of all, the threats of what would happen if she told anyone and his insistence that it was all her fault and that she was evil.

'What's this all about?' Alec demanded, as Morris and Nicola stared at each other with mutual hatred.

Morris turned to Alec.

'I'm sorry you had to get involved with this, Hammond. It was never meant to end up like this but you can blame 'Nicola'', he said, emphasising the word 'Nicola'. 'You should have been more careful in your choice of women in more ways than one. All she had to do was to stop you riding Deep Secret and we could all have lived happily ever after.'

'What are you talking about? Why don't you want me to ride Deep Secret and how could Nicola have stopped me?'

'If Deep Secret loses, I make a fortune. If he wins...well, let's just say I'd be in a bit of trouble.'

'But if I don't ride him, someone else will and he'd probably be just as likely to win. And anyway, how could Nicola have stopped me?'

'That 'someone else' is going to make sure he doesn't win and your 'Nicola' could have stopped you riding by slipping you the same pill which made you ill last time.'

Alec looked across at Nicola but she would not catch his eye.

'Is this true?' he asked. 'Did you poison me that time I was ill with some sort of drug?'

'They made me do it. But I wouldn't have done it for the Gold Cup, I promise. I could see how much it means to you,' Nicola replied, a desperate edge to her voice..

'And that's why we're here. This treacherous little cow can't be trusted by anyone, not by me and not by you either, Hammond. But I'm going to leave you to find out just what sort of woman you've been involved with. What is it they say? A picture tells a thousand words or something like that?'

At that, the smaller of the two thugs left the room and returned a few moments later with a portable television and DVD player combined into one unit. He then fetched a chair from the office next door and set up the television on the chair which was placed directly in front of Alec and Nicola. He then plugged the television in to a socket on the wall and switched it on. The other thug produced a DVD from his leather coat and handed it to his colleague who inserted it into the recorder and masking Alec and Nicola's view, satisfied himself that there was a clear picture.

He then rewound it to the beginning and stepped back.

The other thug grinned and looked at Nicola.

'I'm getting quite good with these DVDs,' he said. 'I've prepared a selection of your finest hours.'

'You were warned what would happen if you doublecrossed us,' Morris said and with that he left the room. The other two followed him but as the smaller man was leaving, he pointed the remote control at the television and pushed the 'play' button.

Outside in the office, Morris took out two packages in brown envelopes and tossed one each at Marsh and Higson.

'Ok, you know what to do then?'

'Yeah,' Marsh replied. 'We'll leave them to watch the DVD and talk for a while and then we'll do it.'

'Don't forget to torch the place before you go. I don't want any evidence left which leads back to us.'

'What about the woman?' Higson asked with a smirk.

'What about her?'

'What if we tell her we'll let her go if she's nice to us?'

'Do what you like as long as they both end up dead and this place ends up as ashes. I suggest you both make yourselves scarce for a couple of weeks afterwards.'

'We thought we might take a trip to Spain.'

'Good idea.'

'Do you mind if we go and get something to eat while they're watching the video?'

'Ok. I don't suppose they're going anywhere.'

With that the three of them left the building and Morris headed back to London while the other two went off to look for a café.

50

Alec did not know what to expect and was surprised to find himself watching a scene from a hardcore blue movie. A woman was on her knees wearing nothing but black stockings and high heeled shoes being taken from behind by a muscle bound white man with an impressive array of tattoos. In front of the woman stood a black man on whom the woman was performing oral sex. For a time the camera concentrated on the action at the rear of the woman in graphic close up but after about thirty seconds it panned around until the woman's face was in view.

Alec gasped with shock. He felt the blood drain from his face and sweat breaking out on his scalp. He wanted to look away from the obscene images but was transfixed by them. The action continued for several minutes with the three participants changing positions until the scene came to an end in the traditional fashion for such films with both men standing over the woman as the action reached its climax in more ways than one.

With that, Alec leant forward as far as he could and vomited.

However, there was to be no respite. The video quickly changed to an equally lurid scene with Nicola playing the lead role and after that to another and another and another with a constant soundtrack of moans and groans.

Eventually, Alec managed to tear his eyes away from the screen. He looked at Nicola who had been sobbing continually.

'How could you? I really thought you were something special.' he said. 'Is this what this is all about? They were blackmailing you to stop me riding Deep Secret?'

'I'm so sorry, Alec. Please let me explain.'

'Explain? What is there to explain? You're some sort of porn star and they were using you to stop me riding!'

'No, I don't mean that. I mean how I ended up in that situation...'

'What does it matter?'

'Please, Alec, we haven't got much time and I need you to understand.'

'What do you mean we haven't got much time?'

'Well, you don't think they're going to let us go after this do you? After all, they've already killed Jimmy.'

'They killed Jimmy? Why? How do you know?'

'I guess he found something out but they as good as admitted it to me when they first approached me.'

'When was this?'

'I'll tell you. But let me tell you in my own way. From the start.'

Alec sighed.

'All right,' he replied somewhat reluctantly.

So Nicola told him the whole story, about her childhood, about Morris and the abuse, about running away to London, about drifting into the world of porn, about meeting Alec, about how she had fallen in love with him and everything that had happened since.

By the time she had finished, the DVD, which to Alec had provided a sickening backdrop to the first part of her story, had also ended. For a time, there was silence and the only movement came from the flickering but blank screen. Eventually, Nicola broke the silence.

'Well, say something, Alec, even if it's only to slag me off!'

'You want me to say I understand, do you? That your behaviour, your deceit and everything is understandable?'

'Maybe. I don't expect you to forgive me, certainly not for the deceit. But as Morris said, I couldn't go through with it. That's why we're in this mess now. I was going to watch you ride in the Gold Cup and then I was going to disappear for ever.'

'Why? You'd poisoned me once. Why not do it again?'

'Because I couldn't live with myself if I'd been responsible for stopping you winning the race. Because I love you...' Nicola sobbed.

'Funny way of showing it!'

'What else could I have done? Come to you and said I'd lied to you about my past and that in fact I was a porn movie star and that it was going to be broadcast to all the newspapers because I was unwilling to poison you? You can't imagine the torment I've been through in the last few weeks!'

For the first time, Alec looked across at Nicola. He could see the anguish in her face and wondered if he was being too hard on her. What did he know about being abused as a child and running away to London? He'd had a comfortable middle class upbringing in a loving family and what she had been describing was something he might have read about in a newspaper, a different world which existed far away from his own.

'OK,' he said, 'Let's not argue now. How the hell are we going to get out of this situation?'

'There's only one thing I can think of,' Nicola replied, 'but you're not going to like it.'

'What do you mean?'

'Maybe I could offer them a trade. Our lives for sex.'

Alec looked at her. He was tempted to make a cutting remark but thought better of it.

'It wouldn't work. As you said, they can't let us go now. They'd still kill us.'

'I know but if they untie me, maybe…'

'What? You'll manage to overpower them? Two thugs like that!'

'Maybe I could escape and get help or something.'

'Even if you did manage to escape, we appear to be miles from any help and I'd still be here tied up!'

'Well, if they chased after me and I managed to give them the slip, there would be no point in them coming back here to kill you. They'd probably make a run for it.'

'The whole idea is ridiculous!'

'Have you got a better idea?'

'Maybe we could try to buy them off. Offer them a large amount of money for our freedom or something?'

'What, and promise not to say anything to the police? I don't think they're that stupid!'

At that moment, they heard a car pull up outside.

'What's it going to be then?' Nicola asked.

'All right, do what you have to do and when they are least expecting it, run like hell! Let's hope they don't lock the outside door!'

51

Higson pulled up outside the building and switched off the engine. Neither man left the car immediately and they just sat there in silence for a moment. Marsh reached inside the glove compartment and took out a hip flask. He took a long swig and passed it to Higson.

'Dutch courage!' he said.

'What's the matter? Nervous?' Higson replied, but he too took a long swig.

'Don't know whether I'm nervous or excited. Never had sex with someone before and then topped them! Come to think of it, I've never topped a woman before.'

'Me neither. What if Suzie doesn't fall for our offer and play ball?'

'Makes no difference. Just means we'll have to slap her about a bit first!'

'Yeah. Maybe that would be more fun anyway!'

They took another drink and got out of the car.

Alec and Nicola heard the two men enter the building and moments later they came through the door to the storeroom.

'Enjoy the film?' Marsh asked.

Neither Alec nor Nicola replied. They could see that he was holding the gun in his right hand.

Marsh then walked over to Alec and raised the gun. He put the barrel against Alec's forehead and cocked the gun with his thumb. Alec screwed up his eyes and tried to flinch away but the cold steel followed him.

'No!' Nicola screamed. 'Leave him alone. Please don't kill him.'

'Why shouldn't I?' Marsh replied.

'You don't have to kill us,' Nicola said. 'We can come to some sort of arrangement surely.'

'What sort of arrangement?' Marsh asked.

Higson had moved behind Alec and Nicola and was grinning from ear to ear. This was going to be easier than they had anticipated.

'Well, perhaps if I was nice to you, you might just leave us here tied up. No one would find us for days.'

'What do you think, Chris?'

'Sounds good to me,' Higson replied. 'But she'd have to be very nice indeed!'

'OK,' Marsh said, 'It seems a shame to kill such a famous pair. But remember, Suzie, the lives of you and superjock here depend on you giving the performance of your life!'

With that, Higson stepped forward and untied Nicola. She got up unsteadily and Marsh levelled the gun at her and indicated that she should go through to the next room.

52

There was a battered old sofa in the office next door and Marsh and Higson both sat down on it. Nicola stood in front of them and was disappointed to see that Marsh appeared to have no intention of putting the gun away.

'Well, what are you waiting for?' he asked. 'And you'd better make this good!'

Fighting back the revulsion that she felt, Nicola told herself to imagine that she was back on a set and that this was just a scene in a film. She tried to switch her mind off just as she had done all those years ago when Morris had come to her bedroom while her mother lay asleep in the next room.

Slowly and as seductively as she could manage given the way in which she was dressed, she started to take her clothes off. First she kicked off her trainers. Then she took off her sweatshirt and tossed it at the two men on the sofa.

'That's more like it!' Higson grinned.

Nicola then slowly pushed down her jeans and stepped out of them, leaving her in just her bra and knickers. She then turned her back on the two men and removed her bra, tossing it back over her shoulder. Then with her back still turned, she bent down and removed her knickers, thrusting her now bare bottom towards the men. She then turned round, giving them their first full frontal view. Both men were staring at her and she could see the lust in their eyes as well as the bulges in their trousers.

'Come on boys, am I the only one going to strip off then?' she said, with a mischievous grin on her face.

She walked over to the men and leant over them, placing a hand on each of their knees and running it slowly up their thighs.

Higson reached up and took hold of one of her breasts while Marsh leant over and put his left hand between her thighs, forcing a finger inside her. Nicola fought to keep the disgust off her face and a smile on it. She sat between them just as it had been in the nightmare she had had about these men and undid their trousers while they pawed her. To her relief, she saw that Marsh had put the gun down on the floor beside him while he concentrated on other things.

Higson then lifted his bottom off the seat and pushed his trousers and pants down hurriedly. Nicola feigned a squeal of delight and reached out for him. Higson moaned with pleasure and while she gave her attention to him, she was conscious of Marsh pushing down his trousers as well.

Suddenly, Nicola felt a surge of hope. She knew she had control of the situation now. Like so many men she had known, these two were prepared to let their groins take over from their brains.

She slid off the sofa and turned towards them on her knees.

'I can't reach you both', she purred, 'just move a bit closer together.'

The men shuffled towards each other, enabling Nicola to service Marsh with her mouth while at the same time caressing Higson with her left hand. She continued in this vein for about a minute with both men groaning with pleasure.

Then, suddenly, she clenched her teeth together as hard as she could around Marsh's erect penis, so hard in fact that she could taste the blood running into her mouth. At the same time, she also squeezed Higson's testicles with her hand as hard as she could.

Both men let out a huge roar of pain. Nicola backed away just in time to avoid Marsh's flailing fist. She threw herself to her right and grabbed for the gun beside the sofa on the floor. She managed to grasp it and rolled away from the sofa.

Both men were still howling in pain but Marsh sensed what she was doing. He stood up but was doubled up in pain and had his trousers caught around his ankles. He managed to lurch across the floor towards her but it was too late.

Nicola had managed to get to her feet. She saw Marsh staggering towards her. She raised the gun and fired twice. The noise was deafening. Marsh collapsed to the floor and lay motionless with a look of surprise still on his face as his sightless eyes stared at the ceiling.

By this time, Higson had stood up too but he made no progress across the floor at all. He looked at Nicola in horror as she turned the gun on him and fired two more shots. He fell back on to the sofa with blood pumping out of two holes in his chest and eventually lay still.

53

For a moment, Nicola just stood there, paralysed with shock and unable to breathe. Her ears were ringing and it felt as if the gunshots were still reverberating around the room. After a few seconds, she dropped the gun and resisting the urge to vomit pulled on her clothes hurriedly, taking care to avoid looking at the two dead men in front of her.

In the next room, Alec had heard nothing until the four gunshots. He had resigned himself to the fact that Nicola would not succeed in what seemed to him to be a completely hopeless plan. When he heard the shots, which seemed to him to be deafening even through a closed door, he could not understand why so many shots had been fired after such a short time. Even so, when the door eventually opened, he expected to see the leering faces of the two men who were surely coming to kill him.

Instead, he was shocked to see Nicola alone, looking as white as a sheet.

'What's happened?' he asked.

Nicola did not reply but knelt down and started to undo the ropes securing him to the chair. He could see that her hands were shaking and she was having difficulty with the knots.

'Nicola, speak to me! What's happened?'

Eventually, Nicola managed to free his hands and Alec undid the rope around his feet.

He stood up unsteadily. Nicola was just standing there as if in a trance. As if in answer to the question he was about to repeat yet again she glanced towards the open door.

Alec walked to the door but stopped when he reached the doorway.

'My God!' he whispered, more to himself than to Nicola, as he took in the scene comprising the two men, both with their trousers round their ankles and heavily bloodstained chests. Now it was Alec's turn to enter a state of shock. Nicola, however, seemed to shake off her own sense of shock and felt a new sense of purpose when she went back into the room. She was surprised that she felt no guilt or regret at having just killed two men and was certain that if she had not done so, they would have killed her and Alec.

Nicola walked over to Higson who was lying on the sofa and started going through his pockets.

'What the hell are you doing?' Alec asked.

'Looking for these.' Nicola replied, holding up a set of car keys and a mobile phone.

'Yes, yes, you're right,' Alec said. 'We must phone the police.'

'Yes, but not yet!'

'Not yet? Why not now?'

'What's the time?'

'Who cares about the time! Just phone the police!'

Nicola took hold of Alec's wrist and looked at his watch.

'It's nearly one o'clock', she said. 'What time's the Gold Cup?'

Alec looked at her in bewilderment.

'The Gold Cup, Alec. What time does it start?' Nicola demanded.

'Er, 3.45. Why do you want to know?'

'Because you've got a race to ride in!'

Alec looked at Nicola in astonishment.

'You can't be serious! I can't ride now, not after all we've been through. We have to phone the police.'

'Leave all that to me. You've got to get to the course as quickly as possible!'

'Don't be ridiculous. I can't. Even if I got to the course, I'd be in no fit state to ride!'

To Alec's astonishment, Nicola then slapped him round the face.

'Sorry, but you've got to pull yourself together,' she shouted.

Alec just stood there staring at her. Not long ago, she had seemed a broken woman. Now there seemed to be a steely determination about her.

'Think about it, Alec', she continued, 'If you don't ride Deep Secret, then they will have won. Some bent jockey will stop him winning and my stepfather will win a fortune.'

'But surely the police…'

'The police can do their job eventually but in the meantime we've got to stop his plan. Think about it, Alec. What evidence is there connecting him to any of this anyway? We owe it to everyone, the stable, the owner…and Jimmy to stop him!'

'But we don't even know where we are and whether I can get to the course in time.'

'Well, we'll have to do our best won't we?'

With that, Nicola pushed Alec towards the door.

54

Outside, she rushed over to the Range Rover and got in the driver's side.

'Come on, Alec, get in.'

Alec climbed into the passenger seat and Nicola thrust the mobile phone into his hands.

'I'll drive. You phone Melanie and tell her you're on your way.'

'But I haven't got my riding gear.'

'Well borrow some then!'

'It's not as easy as that…'

'Just do as I tell you for once!'

With that, Nicola started the car and with the wheels spinning headed towards what appeared to be the entrance to the industrial complex. At the entrance, she stopped briefly, saw that it appeared to be more built up towards the left and turned that way.

Alec punched in Melanie's number and was relieved to hear it ringing. Melanie answered after only two rings.

'Melanie?'

Alec could hear noise in the background.

'Who is this?' Melanie replied.

Alec realised that she would not have recognised the number.

'It's Alec!'

'Alec? Where the bloody hell are you? You never came to the yard should have been here two hours ago!'

'I'm sorry. It's difficult to explain. I'm not sure where I am.'

'Is this one of your jokes?'

'Just listen. I've been kidnapped but managed to escape. I'm on my way now.'

'Christ! Are you drunk or something?'

'No. Just trust me. I'm going to try to get there in time to ride Deep Secret but I'm not sure when…'

At that moment, Nicola cut in.

'Reading,' she said. 'I've just seen a sign. We're ten miles from Reading.'

'Melanie, I'm not going to get there for sometime. You'll have to put up Billy in the Triumph.'

By this time, Melanie had detected the urgency in Alec's voice.

'Are you OK?'

'Just about but…'

Alec was interrupted by a mechanical voice telling him that he had one minute of talk time left.

'Shit. This is a pay as you go phone and I'm running out of time. Melanie, whatever you do, if I'm delayed, don't put up any other jockey on Deep Secret…'

'I'll have to if you don't get here!'

'No!' Alec screamed. 'They're trying to…' At that moment, he was cut off.

Nicola drove on for a few minutes until she saw a sign to the M4, whereupon she stopped the car.

'Why have you stopped?' Alec asked.

'I'm getting out here,' Melanie replied. 'You can find your own way to the course from here.'

'But why?'

'As I said before, you've got to get to the course. I'll sort out the rest. Don't worry. Just leave everything to me. I will contact the police. You just ride that horse to victory!'

Before Alec could say anything more, she opened the car door and got out.

She looked back at Alec and he could see that she had tears in her eyes.

'I'm so sorry, Alec,' she said, and before he could respond she shut the door and ran down the road.

For a moment, Alec thought of running after her but he then switched seats and headed towards the M4.

55

Once Alec had reached the M4, he was able to put his foot down and make good time. He by-passed Swindon and headed towards Cheltenham on the A419. However, just as he was beginning to think that he was going to make it in time, he heard a siren behind him and looked in his mirror to see a police car rapidly approaching with its blue light flashing.

Alec slowed down and pulled in a little, hoping that the police car was en route to some emergency. The police car overtook him but immediately slowed down and made it clear to Alec that he was being required to stop.

Alec stopped the Range Rover and wound down the driver's window. Both policemen got out of their vehicle and while one proceeded over towards Alec, the other started looking around the Range Rover. As the policeman approached, Alec looked at his own reflection in the driver's mirror. He had an open wound above his eye where he had been assaulted back at his house all those hours ago and dried blood all down his face and he still had vomit all over his clothing from when he had been forced to watch the DVD back at the industrial estate. He was also driving a car which did not belong to him. The situation did not look promising, particularly as he was in such a hurry.

'Good afternoon, sir,' the policeman began. 'Are you aware of what speed you were doing?'

'Er, no, officer,' Alec replied.

'You were doing nearly 90 in a 60 limit area.' At that, the policeman looked in the window and took a closer look at Alec.

'Are you all right, sir?' he asked.

'Yes, yes, I'm fine.' Alec replied, hoping he would be issued with a ticket and would soon be on his way.

'Is this your car?'

'Er, no, I'm borrowing it.'

'I see. Do you have your driving licence on you or some form of identification?'

'No…look I can explain. I have to get to Cheltenham racecourse as soon as possible.'

'I see. Hoping to have a bet are we?'

'No,' Alec replied with increasing urgency, 'I'm riding the favourite in the Gold Cup!'

The policeman looked at the vomit down Alec's front.

'Very funny, sir. Have you been drinking?'

'No, I haven't!'

At that the other policeman joined them.

'The car's registered to the Alhambra Snooker Club in Fulham,' he said.

'Are you associated with that club?' the first policeman asked Alec.

'No, but I can explain!'

'So you said before. Would you mind stepping out of the car?'

Alec got out of the car and the two policemen looked him up and down.

'Wait a minute,' the second and older of the two said, 'Aren't you Alec Hammond?'

'What, Alec Hammond, the jockey?' the first asked.

'Yes, I didn't recognise him like that until he got out of the car.'

'He's just told me that he's riding the favourite in the Gold Cup.'

'He is! He's supposed to be riding Deep Secret. I've had a bet on the horse. You're cutting it a bit fine, aren't you?'

'Please,' Alec said, 'just let me explain!'

'Go on.' The first policeman said. 'And it had better be good!'

So Alec gave them a shortened version of what had happened including the kidnap that morning, their dramatic escape and Alec's mad dash to the course to thwart the plan to stop Deep Secret winning.

The policemen were clearly stunned and Alec wondered if they believed him. He doubted that he would have in their situation.

'And you can't give us the precise location of where you were held and where you say these bodies are, nor the whereabouts of the woman who you say fired the gun?'

'No. But it's all true, I promise!'

'Wait here.' The older policeman said. They then went and talked together for a couple of minutes before returning.

'This is obviously a matter for CID,' the older one said. 'We're going to call this in. In the meantime, we know who you are and that you are indeed due to ride in the Gold Cup. You're a national celebrity so it's not as if you're going to disappear. We suggest you follow us. After the race, you can make a statement to CID who will no doubt be waiting for you!'

The policemen returned to their car and put on their siren again.

Alec followed close behind them as they drove at speed towards Cheltenham. He imagined that the policeman in the passenger seat was relaying the story that he had told them back to their station and he prayed that the officers' initiative would not be countermanded by a superior officer ordering that they stop and arrest him. Fortunately, they continued driving and it was not long before they had made up the time lost due to Alec being stopped. It occurred to him that to other roadusers, it must have seemed strange that a police car with its siren blaring and blue light flashing was being hotly pursued by a battered old Range Rover.

56

By the time they arrived at the course, Alec knew that Melanie only had minutes before she had to declare another jockey to ride Deep Secret in his absence. Helpfully, when the police car arrived at the course, it pulled over to allow Alec to overtake it, presumably Alec thought because the policemen realised that he was more familiar with where to go.

Alec shot past them and the police car followed but instead of heading to the jockeys' car park, Alec took the Range Rover as close as he as could to the nearest entrance to the course, slammed on his brakes and sprinted over to the entrance, throwing a wave of thanks in the direction of the police car which had stopped although its occupants made no attempt to follow him.

Fortunately, the gateman was someone that Alec had come across before and recognised him.

'Alec, what on earth's happened? You look terrible!'

'Can't explain now, Bert. Just let me through. Please!'

The bewildered gateman did as he was asked and Alec ran as fast as he could towards the weighing room, pushing through the dense crowd and creating quite a stir.

He eventually reached the weighing room and spotted Melanie and Deep Secret's owner, Mary Pickering, deep in conversation and from the looks on their faces, it was not a pleasant conversation. Alec ran up to them, out of breath.

'Thank god you've arrived!' Melanie said. 'Another couple of minutes and I would have had to declare another jockey! Are you OK? You look awful!'

But before Alec could reply, Mary Pickering intervened.

'I'm sorry, Melanie, but Alec's too late. I still want Duggan to ride.'

'Duggan?' Alec almost shouted.

'Yes. Mary was just telling me that in your absence she wanted Pat Duggan to ride Deep Secret. I can't say I was too happy. Mary, Alec's here now. He's declared to ride and if he says he's fit enough, that's fine by me.'

'I don't care, Melanie,' Mary replied. 'I'm the owner, and I'm telling you to go and declare Duggan.'

'Look, I don't know what this is about, Mary, but Alec rides and that's that!'

By this time, Mary was looking increasingly distressed. Tears formed in her eyes and she looked as if she was about to collapse. Alec was not feeling too good himself if truth be told but he put out his arm to steady her.

'But you don't understand…if Duggan doesn't ride…'

'What?' Melanie asked. 'Why does Duggan have to ride?'

'I think I can answer that,' Alec said. 'They got to you too, didn't they, Mary?'

By this time, tears were flowing down Mary's face.

'Alec, please, you've got to let Duggan ride…they threatened my granddaughter. If I don't arrange for Duggan to ride they'll kill her!'

'Mary, you've no need to worry anymore. I've just managed to get away from them. Two are dead and Nicola is arranging for the police to arrest her stepfather.'

Both women looked at Alec in astonishment.

'Nicola was being blackmailed by her stepfather, a bent bookie, to stop me riding Deep Secret by poisoning me so Duggan could

273

ride and ensure he didn't win. She refused and they kidnapped us this morning but we escaped. It's a long story.'

'And you're sure this man can no longer get at my daughter and granddaughter?' Mary asked.

'Nicola's stepfather doesn't know we've escaped. He left after ordering his men to kill us. He won't know we've escaped until he sees I'm still riding the horse. By then, Nicola will have arranged for him to be arrested.'

Mary thought for a moment.

'OK. I'll trust you, Alec. Go and ride the horse and make sure you win!'

Alec hurried off into the weighing room and one of the first people he saw was his valet. He explained that he needed some kit that would fit, including a saddle. He then went into the jockeys' changing area where he received some strange looks, not just because of his appearance but because news had spread around the course that he had gone missing. One or two of the other jockeys asked if he was OK but he ignored them and walked straight up to a man who was looking extremely agitated at Alec's arrival.

Alec did not hesitate and put all his pent up aggression into the punch and Duggan fell to the floor where he lay groaning. One or two of the other jockeys pulled Alec away from him.

'What the hell are you doing, Alec?' one asked.

'This bastard and his friends are responsible for Jimmy's murder!' Alec replied.

There was a stunned silence.

Duggan got to his feet and hurried out of the weighing room.

'Shall we go after him, Alec?' one of the other jockeys asked.

'No. The police will deal with him,' Alec replied. 'I need to concentrate on the race now.'

The other jockeys could see that Alec was in no mood to

continue the conversation and left him alone. There was always tension before a big race like the Gold Cup but on this occasion the tension was greater than usual.

56

By the time Alec had changed into his borrowed kit and got out to the parade ring, the events of the day had finally begun to catch up with him. He felt terribly tired, his head was swollen and throbbing and he had serious doubts as to whether he was in a fit state to ride. There was little conversation between him, Melanie and Mary as the horses were led around the outside of the parade ring. Mary was still worrying about her family as by now, anyone watching on the television would know that Alec was still riding Deep Secret. Melanie was still shocked at what Alec had revealed but knew better than to question him further at this time. There was also no need for her to give Alec any riding instructions about a horse that he had ridden in all its races.

When the time came for Alec to be given a leg up into the saddle, he was relieved as he had felt on the point of collapse. He was grateful just for the opportunity to sit down on the big horse's back.

The horses were led out on to the course and paraded in front of the stands. Alec could hear the cheers as Deep Secret went past and it was obvious where a sizable proportion of the crowd had put their money.

It was as the parade ended that disaster struck. Just as Alec turned Deep Secret to canter down to the start, he felt a wave of nausea, lost his concentration and fell off, leaving the horse to follow the other horses down the course without a rider.

Alec staggered to his feet, took off his helmet, bent double and retched a couple of times. A steward ran up to him and asked him if he was all right. Alec nodded and said that he would be in a moment and then shook his head to try to clear it.

Up in the stands, Melanie and Mary could see Deep Secret cantering down the course riderless and like most people who had not seen Alec fall off were informed by the racecourse commentator that Alec Hammond appeared to have been taken ill.

'Oh, no,' Mary sighed, 'We'll have to withdraw him!'

'Let's just wait a moment,' Melanie replied.

To her relief, the racecourse commentator then announced that Alec was putting his helmet back on but that there would be a short delay while Deep Secret was caught and re-united with his jockey.

Fortunately, Deep Secret did not take much catching and an embarrassed Alec soon found himself being given a leg up into the saddle for the second time. It was all Alec could do to stay in the saddle as the horse cantered down to join the other runners. In most other races, one or two jockeys might have taken the mickey out of Alec or complained that he had kept them waiting but they were all concentrating on circling their horses and doing the best they could to keep them relaxed during the delay.

Alec could not even raise the energy to take Deep Secret to have a look at the first fence as was customary before any race and when the starter called them out on to the track he relied on the horse to take them both out and line up with the others.

As it was, he got into the wrong position with Deep Secret's head over the starting tape.

'No, no, no, Hammond!' the starter shouted from his rostrum. 'Get that horse's head off the tape! I'm not starting you like that!'

Alec had to take a turn as did a number of other jockeys, who by this time were getting impatient.

'Jesus! Get a grip, Alec!' one shouted.

Eventually, the horses lined up again and this time the starter seemed satisfied.

Alec looked at the course ahead of him and began to wonder if he'd make it to the first fence let alone get over it.

But it was too late to do anything about it now.

'They're under starters order!' the racecourse commentator announced.

The starter let go of the tape, there was a huge roar from the crowd and sixteen thoroughbred steeplechasers thundered towards the first fence.

57

How he and Deep Secret got over the first fence, Alec will never know. With his head spinning, Alec had no choice but to rely on the big horse beneath him. Deep Secret jumped the fence with Alec hanging on as best he could but instead of their usual position up with the pace, they were outjumped and passed by all the other runners and approached the second fence as the backmarker by a couple of lengths.

Up in the stands, there was a murmur from the crowd as the racecourse commentator said that Deep Secret appeared to be losing ground. Melanie gripped her binoculars. 'Come on Alec, what the hell are you doing?' she said to herself.

Deep Secret sensed that something was wrong. He took off a stride too early at the second fence, nearly unseating Alec, but managed to sail over the fence with plenty to spare. It seemed to Alec that they were in the air for ages, sufficient for a replay of the day's events in his mind, and when they eventually landed, he experienced a sudden sensation of clarity. The escape, the dash to the course, it would all be for nothing if he did not pull himself together. He took a firm grip of the reins and used his legs to tell Deep Secret that he was back in charge.

For a couple of fences, Alec kept Deep Secret in last place but gradually closed the gap on the rest of the field. There were two frontrunners in the field battling it out for the lead and the horses were already well strung out.

By the end of the first circuit, the punishing pace was already proving too much for some of the runners and Alec moved smoothly through the field until there were about six horses ahead of him including the two runners, whom he and Melanie had identified as their main rivals.

Alec maintained his position and as the field passed the stands for the final circuit, he could see that one of the frontrunners was beginning to struggle and he soon dropped back out of contention. The other frontrunner still had a lead of a couple of lengths but halfway down the back straight, he was off the bridle and Alec could see that it was only a matter of time before he too dropped back. The other runners closed in on him with no one ready as yet to take up the running. But after they had turned out of the back straight, they had no choice as the tired horse in front fell at the third last.

It was that point that Alec made up his mind to go. He gave Deep Secret a squeeze and let out some rein. The big horse surged into the lead and the suddenly the crowd could see the pattern of the race change. Deep Secret's main two rivals covered his move and the three horses soon put a gap of some ten lengths between themselves and the rest of the field toiling behind them.

Deep Secret jumped the second last half a length up on his two rivals. Alec had the rail for the final bend and stole a look to his right. 'OK, let's see what you're made of,' he thought. The response was immediate. Within a few seconds, Deep Secret had gone five or six lengths clear.

Up in the stands, there was a huge roar. Melanie was still gripping her binoculars for all they were worth but this time in anticipation not concern.

Alec realised that he only had to jump the last to win. The other two horses had had no answer to Deep Secret's sudden acceleration. Did he try to play it safe? The horse answered the question for him. He was in full flight with his ears pricked. To try to ease him down now and fiddle the fence could end in disaster. They sailed over the last bringing a huge collective cheer from the crowd who then cheered Deep Secret all the way up the hill to the finishing post. Alec was oblivious to the noise. He lifted his goggles halfway up the run in so the tears could run down his face. The crowd assumed that they were tears of joy. Only Alec knew differently. He may have won the race but as the horse galloped its way into racing history, Alec's thoughts were not about glory and what he had won but what he had lost, Jimmy, Martin, and Nicola too, because he sensed that when Nicola had got out of the car, that was the last that he would ever see of her.

58

In a betting shop, just off the Fulham Road, the attractive blonde started to make her way back through the cheering crowd of punters as soon as she had seen that Deep Secret had jumped the final fence and was heading for an easy victory.

The betting shop had been packed out with punters gathering to watch the Gold Cup when she had entered the shop. Everyone had turned and stared as the immaculately made up woman dressed in red high heels, red leather mini skirt and low cut white top had come in. The noise levels dropped and the crowd had parted to allow her through to the front from where she could watch the race on the large TV screen. Nobody dared approach her as she had a fixed and determined expression which remained unaltered throughout the race.

After leaving the shop, the woman crossed the road, oblivious to the stares that she attracted from both men and women, and entered a doorway sandwiched between a kebab shop and a downmarket electrical store. A tarnished brass plate outside the door read 'Frank Morris, Turf Accountant, First Floor'.

On the first floor of the building, another blonde sat on reception filing her nails and idly wondering what delights the evening would hold in store for her. Nineteen years old, she was fairly content with her life. She knew that she was not that bright but she would have chosen looks over brains any day. Men fell over themselves to take her out and she was sure that one day she would snare some wealthy guy to take her away from her dead end job. Maybe a footballer or one of those city traders, she was thinking, just as another blonde woman appeared at the top of the stairs and shattered all her illusions as to how attractive she was. The woman walking towards her was simply different class and made the receptionist feel like a cheap little slapper in comparison. She stopped filing her nails and looked at the other woman with unrestrained hostility.

'I've come to see Frank Morris,' Nicola said.

'You got an appointment?' the blonde sneered. 'Cos you ain't seein' him if you 'aven't as he don't want to be disturbed .'

Nicola smiled sweetly at the receptionist.

'I don't need an appointment. I'm his daughter.'

There was a moment's silence before the receptionist reluctantly relented.

'Second door down on the left,' she replied, pointing to a corridor with her nail file.

Nicola entered the room without knocking. It stank of whisky and sweat. Across the room was a battered and untidy desk. Morris was sitting behind the desk staring bleakly at a television screen on the wall to his right. Nicola glanced at the screen and could see Alec and Deep Secret being led into the unsaddling enclosure to ecstatic cheers from the crowd even though the volume was turned right down. She quickly turned away as tears began to well in her eyes.

At first, Morris did not appear to have noticed that anyone had entered the room but maybe it was her perfume that caused him to turn round.

'You?' he croaked.

'Hello, Frank', Nicola replied. 'Enjoy the race?'

Morris hauled himself to his feet and gripped the desk to steady himself.

'You bitch!' he snarled. 'How the hell did you manage to escape?'

'Your boys were a pushover. And they won't be doing any of your dirty work again!'

'I may be finished but you made a big mistake coming here dressed like a tart to gloat.'

Morris then stepped around the desk and lurched towards Nicola. He then stopped suddenly when Nicola produced the gun from her bag and pointed it at him.

'Go on then, pull the trigger', he shouted. 'You may as well, because if you don't someone else soon will!'

Nicola's heart was thumping. She knew that the revolver only had two bullets left after the events back at the premises where she and Alec had been held.

'You haven't got the guts have you?' Morris continued and he started to move towards her again.

Nicola had read somewhere that people rarely survived being shot in the stomach and that such wounds were also very painful. She lowered the weapon and pulled the trigger. The noise was deafening and seemed even louder than back at the industrial unit.

Morris staggered back against the desk and clutched his stomach. Nicola could see the blood flowing through his fingers. He slid to the floor until his upper back was propped up by the desk. He stared up at her, a look of astonishment on his face. She in turn looked down at him and held his stare until blood poured out of his mouth and the light went out of his eyes.

At that moment the door was flung open and Morris's bookkeeper, Lennie Cohen, stood there with a look of shock on his face. Nicola raised the gun and pointed it at Cohen's head. One shot left. She then put the gun to the side of her head and pulled the trigger.

59

Back at the course, there was pandemonium. Alec was lead back to the winners' enclosure to ecstatic cheers from the crowd. He tried to push the day's previous events out of his mind and managed to raise a smile in acknowledgement of the cheers. He also gave a somewhat subdued interview from the saddle to Charlotte as she trotted beside the horse on the way back to the enclosure.

When he finally entered the enclosure, a huge roar erupted and a number of hats were thrown in the air. Of course, none of the crowd knew anything of the drama which had preceded this victory and would not know about it until the news broke in the following days.

Alec again managed to smile and raised his hand to acknowledge the cheers. As he dismounted and unsaddled Deep Secret, he could see that despite her joy at winning race, Mary still looked rather strained. As they all posed for photos, Alec whispered to her to stop worrying as it was all over, despite his ignorance of what was going on at that precise moment in Fulham.

No sooner had Alec weighed in than he received a message that Detective Chief Inspector Fuller would like to see him. Alec found Fuller, Detective Sergeant Green and a senior officer from the Gloucestershire Police waiting outside the weighing room. He gave them a slightly expanded version of what he had told the two policemen who had escorted him to the course and agreed to go with them to make a full statement after the trophies for the Gold Cup had been presented.

After the ceremony, Alec told Melanie that he would have to give up his rides in the remaining races and accompanied the policemen back to Cheltenham Police Headquarters.

Meanwhile, back in London, the police also found themselves with an unusual chain of events to investigate.

It took a lot for the receptionist's attention to be diverted from her nails, but the first shot, which resounded through the building, certainly did the trick. Terrified, she watched as Lennie Cohen rushed across the corridor from his office to Morris' office. He then seemed to stand transfixed in the doorway and after a short pause, a second shot boomed out. Then, after hesitating a few seconds, Cohen entered Morris' office. After he had been in there a couple of minutes, the receptionist decided that whatever was going on, it was time to dial 999.

No sooner had she put the phone down than Cohen rushed out of the office, clutching a bag and ran past her towards the stairs.

'I've called the police!' the receptionist shouted as he passed her without even giving her a glance.

'Good for you!' Cohen replied as ran down the stairs and disappeared.

The receptionist looked back towards Morris' office and considered whether she should take a look now that there was silence. However, she soon decided against such a course and followed Cohen down the stairs to await the police outside.

When the police arrived, their first thought was that some sort of armed robbery had taken place, confronted as they were by the bodies of Morris and his 'daughter' and the fact that the door of the wall safe in the office was hanging open and the safe empty.

However, with some difficulty they finally satisfied themselves of the sequence of events from the near hysterical receptionist and realised that they were dealing with a murder and suicide followed by what may have been a theft afterwards by the disappearing bookkeeper.

Back at Cheltenham Police HQ, Alec gave the police as much detail as he could about the day's events. The priority for the police was to locate the premises where Alec and Nicola had been held and where according to Alec, the bodies of their kidnappers lay. Since it appeared that they had been held not far from Reading, Sergeant Green left the room to arrange a search of the area. He and Fuller seemed confident that on the basis of Alec's information, it would not take too long to locate deserted industrial premises of the type described by Alec.

Although Alec was able to give a detailed description of what had happened that day, he was less clear about the preceding events, relying on what Nicola had told him and what he had picked up from their kidnappers.

No sooner had Green returned to the room from organising a search of the area to locate the premises than he was sent out again, this time to trace a bookmaker by the name of Frank Morris.

Fuller was particularly interested in the link between the kidnap and Jimmy O'Brien's murder.

'Nicola specifically told you that they had admitted killing Mr O'Brien?'

'Not just Nicola. They also referred to what had happened to Jimmy when they were threatening Mary Pickering, the horse's owner!'

Fuller thought for a while.

'Hopefully that will be confirmed as soon as other officers have gone to see Mrs. Pickering. Things are beginning to make sense now! You tell us that Pat Duggan was the bent jockey who was supposed to stop Deep Secret from winning. The only event which could conceivably be considered unusual that occurred prior to Mr O'Brien leaving the racecourse was the phone call which he took on Duggan's mobile and which caused an argument between the two of them.'

'But you investigated that and concluded that it was irrelevant?'

'I didn't know Duggan was bent then! We know something happened which caused Mr O'Brien to want to speak you as a matter of urgency and which was of sufficient importance to get him killed before he could do so! I reckon Mr O'Brien heard something on Duggan's mobile which incriminated Duggan or others. That's why Duggan got so annoyed and why Mr O'Brien was so agitated about it. Duggan then reported the incident to someone, probably this Morris, and that's what got him killed so quickly!'

At that moment, Sergeant Green put his head around the door. 'Can we have a quick word outside, guv?' he asked.

Fuller left the room and the questioning was resumed by the officer from Gloucestershire CID.

Fuller was gone for about twenty minutes and when he returned, he was looking grim faced.

'I'm afraid I've got some bad news, Alec,' he said. 'It didn't take us long to trace Frank Morris, a private bookmaker with a bit of a dodgy reputation. But when we asked our London colleagues to pick him up, we were told that they are already at his premises investigating a double shooting there. There's no easy way to tell you this, Alec, but I'm afraid Nicola's dead. It looks like she killed Morris then turned the gun on herself. I'm so sorry.'

60

The policemen sent to arrest Pat Duggan got no reply when they rang his doorbell despite his car being parked outside his house. One of the officers bent down and looked through his letterbox. What he saw caused him to step back shocked. His colleague had a look too and saw what appeared to be two feet dangling down some distance from the door. The two of them then kicked in the front door to be confronted with Duggan's body swinging from a rope which had been tied to the banisters on the landing. There was no suicide note, just an empty bottle of whisky on the kitchen table.

It did not take the police long to locate the industrial premises where Alec and Nicola had been held captive and of course, the bodies of Marsh and Higson just as Alec had described.

A couple of hours later, Lennie Cohen was arrested as he attempted to board a ferry at Dover carrying a bag containing nearly £50000 in cash. As the only surviving member of the Morris team, Fuller and Green as well as the Gloucestershire and the London police were all anxious to question him.

To begin with, he simply said that after Morris had been killed, he knew that he was out of a job and had seized the opportunity to empty the safe before Morris's creditors got hold of the money.

The money had been taken from clients betting on the Cheltenham Festival who preferred to deal in cash most of which had been wagered on Deep Secret. He categorically denied knowing anything else about Morris's affairs and claimed that he simply did his books.

However, he soon changed his tune when he realised that he was being questioned as a suspect in the murder of Jimmy O'Brien, the kidnap and attempted murders of Alec and Nicola and the blackmail of Mary Pickering.

He readily confessed to being a party to race fixing through the services of Pat Duggan but vehemently denied any involvement in violence and Morris's scheme to prevent Deep Secret from winning. He maintained that he knew that Morris was up to something so far as Deep Secret was concerned due the huge amount of money that Morris had taken at ridiculous odds but had had no idea what.

In an attempt to persuade the police that he was being co-operative, he revealed that like any good bent book keeper, he had kept a record of every race that Duggan had thrown for Morris and the amount of profit that Morris had made from those races.

The police realised that there was no evidence linking Cohen to the more serious charges, so he was charged with conspiracy to defraud and eventually remanded in custody as he had already shown an inclination to flee the country.

On the following morning, the Gold Cup made the headlines on both the back and front pages of the daily papers. Of course, by then, the press only had a few of the details and nothing like the full story but Alec's dramatic arrival at the course, bloodied and vomit stained, his assault on Duggan, and Duggan being found hanged later in the day led to some lurid speculation on the part of the tabloids, none of which was anywhere near the truth. At that stage, the press had not made the connection between the events at Cheltenham and the shootings in London, let alone the race fixing, Jimmy O'Brien's murder, Nicola's background and all the other matters which gradually made their way into the public domain over the next few days.

Not surprisingly, the story ran and ran as each new revelation emerged. Several of the tabloids devoted pages to the story and had reporters working full time on dredging up new pieces of information. One of the more disreputable papers gave their readers a list of Susie Stone's films and even featured scenes from the films with the explicit bits blanked out. The paper even posed the question as to how Alec, the nation's favourite jockey and pin up to thousands, could have got himself involved with such a woman. Another even managed to trace Goran, who had first introduced Nicola to modelling, and obtained an 'exclusive' from him on such matters as Nicola's bedroom skills. Even the specialist racing journals seemed more interested in the story than the rather mundane horseracing which took place in the period after the Cheltenham Festival.

61

Alec was oblivious to the press coverage although he could imagine what was happening.

After the police had taken him home, he had closed all the curtains of his house, unplugged the phone and tried to go to sleep. He eventually slept fitfully for about an hour before waking to noise outside his house. He checked the time and saw that it was just after 5 o'clock in the morning.

Without putting on a light, he went into a front room and looked though a gap in the curtains. He saw that the quiet country road outside was full of vehicles. There were lots of people standing around outside his gate wrapped up warm against the cold. As the day progressed and more details of what had happened leaked out, more and more reporters gathered outside. Some people were setting up cameras. There were even television cameras. Not just the national press but even the international press had arrived and there they remained camped for several days.

Alec had no intention of speaking to the press and hoped that they would go away if they thought that he was staying somewhere else. When it got light, he left the curtains drawn and made sure that he remained in the back of the house for fear of any movement being detected outside. Even then, he had to be very careful as people started to arrive to tend to the horses that he kept in his yard at the back of his house.

At about 7 o'clock, the doorbell rang. He ignored it.

He did not dare put on the television, not that he had any desire to anyway, or even his computer in case someone managed to get round the back and saw flickering through the curtains.

He realised that he had very little food in the house but food was of little concern to him and he just sat in an armchair hoping and praying that the whole world would go away and leave him alone.

On the following day, after another bad night's sleep, he was horrified to hear a key in the lock of the front door at about 8 o'clock in the morning. Surely, they couldn't have got hold of a key?

The door to the living room slowly opened and Alec felt a wave of relief.

Vera Wilson had acted as housekeeper/cleaning woman for Alec ever since he had moved into the house. Three times a week she came as regular as clockwork not just to clean the house but also to do Alec's washing and ironing and anything else that needed doing. A large, red faced woman in her fifties, she was not the sort to put up with any nonsense and had dealt firmly with the journalist who had had the cheek to ask if he could have a look round when she had arrived that morning on her bicycle.

'Alec!' she exclaimed, when she entered the living room, surprised not only to find him there but also at his dishevelled state.

'Shhh!' Alec cut her short. 'I don't want them to know I'm here!' he whispered.

Vera closed the door behind her.

'It's OK,' she said. 'They can't hear us! They must be over fifty yards away! God, you look awful! How long have you been holed up here?'

'Since the night before last. I'm hoping they'll just go away if they think I'm staying somewhere else.'

'They're also outside the stables. Melanie has had to employ security people to stop them getting in. She's ordered the staff not to have anything to do with them. She says anyone who talks to the press will be sacked! Have you seen the papers?'

'No. And I don't want to!'

'Probably just as well. The papers are full of the story although how of it is true and how much is speculation no one knows.'

Vera could see that Alec wasn't really in the mood for talking but insisted on making him some soup.

'What do you want me to do about the curtains?' she asked.

'What do you mean?'

'Well, if I don't open them now it's daylight, aren't they going to wonder why?'

'Oh. I see what you mean.'

Alec thought about for a minute.

'Pull them back now and I'll keep well out of sight but when you leave, draw them again and if you get the chance, tell them that you don't want people creeping up to the house and taking pictures through the windows.'

The plan worked. When Vera left some three hours later, she was surrounded by journalists, bombarding her with questions.

'You're wasting your time. He's not here and I have no idea where he is. And I'm not having you sneaking up to the house to take pictures through the windows! Now get out of my way!'

And with that she pushed her bicycle through the throng of reporters crowding in on her and rode off towards the village as quickly as she could.

The plan worked or perhaps it would be more accurate to say that the plan half worked because it was not until later that the mob finally decided to call it a day, packing up their equipment and leaving.

62

Alec had hoped that he would feel better when they left but he didn't. He realised that as soon as his whereabouts were known, they would be back. He only had a temporary reprieve.

On the following morning, Alec again heard the key in the door but when the living room door opened, he was shocked to see not Vera but Melanie come in.

'Hi,' she said with an embarrassed smile, 'Vera came to see me earlier. She was worried about you. I persuaded her to lend me the key as I'd heard the press had left. So don't be angry with her. It was my fault!'

Alec glowered at her.

'What do you want? She presumably also told you that I'm not in the mood for visitors,' he managed.

What do I want, Melanie thought. What I've always wanted from almost the first moment you came to the stable all those years ago! You! She thought back to the crush she'd had on him as a child, his rejection of her when she had made a pass at him as a sixteen year old, how she had then flaunted her boyfriends in front of him out of spite, her self-imposed exile in the years that followed because she couldn't bear to be in his presence if she couldn't have him and that moment when she walked back into the stable after her father's death, saw him in the kitchen and realised that nothing had changed. Now, here he was, depressed and vulnerable and all she wanted to do was to put her arms around him.

'I just wanted to see how you are,' she said.

'Well, now you've seen, I just want to be left alone!'

Alec looked terrible. He was gaunt, dishevelled and unshaven, with a barely healed cut over his eye. The room was a mess despite Vera having tidied up only two days earlier. Melanie had never seen Alec like this before. He had always been one of life's winners, happy, confident and carefree. She desperately wanted to help him.

'You can't hide away for ever! You have to face people sooner or later! Everyone understands what you've been through. Why don't you come and stay at the stables for a while? We all miss you and I won't let the press in through the gates. It will do you good to get back to some work.'

'I'm not sure I want to go back to the stables. To be honest, I'm thinking of retiring and just disappearing somewhere.'

'You can't mean that! We...I need you!'

'You don't need me anymore. You're quite capable of running the stables with Bill's help.'

Tears formed in Melanie's eyes.

'You don't understand. When I came back after Dad's death and said I was taking over the stable, I was only doing it because I thought you would be there to help me. Bill's been great but I can't do it without you!'

'I'm going away for a while.'

'Where?'

'I can't stay holed up here so I'm going to stay with friends over in Ireland. They live in a remote area and it will give me time to think.'

'I think you'll find this is big news in Ireland too!'

'I realize that but I'll take my chance. I'll go by ferry rather than fly.'

'Ok. But promise me you'll keep in touch?'

'I'll see...'

63

A week passed with no contact from Alec. The press had finally moved on to other things although there had been much speculation as to where Alec was, Melanie assumed that he had managed to get over to Ireland without anyone recognizing him.

She managed to keep the stable going but had the constant worry as to how she would be able to cope if Alec never came back.

One afternoon, she sat in the office on her computer, trying to concentrate on which horses she would be sending to the Grand National meeting at Aintree in a fortnight's time.

She sensed rather than heard someone come into the office behind her. Her fingers froze on the keyboard. Her heart started racing and she held her breath. Was her mind playing tricks with her? Was she imagining this because she wanted it so much?

There seemed like a long pause but she had not been mistaken. She felt two hands on her shoulders. A firm, yet gentle touch which seemed to pass right through her body. She bit her lip to stop herself bursting into tears and then she heard the familiar voice.

'What do you want me to ride at Aintree, then?'

Lightning Source UK Ltd.
Milton Keynes UK
UKOW022140051211

183245UK00004B/5/P